D0013845

A Fish

Trapped Inside

the Wind

Christien Gholson grew up in a navy family, living in Belgium, Italy, and numerous places across the North American continent. He has been a union organiser, janitor, farmhand, bookseller, teacher, cartoonist, itinerant poet-musician and freelance editor. He attended Naropa University, the first Buddhist-inspired university in the Western Hemisphere, and the creative writing programme at the University of California at Davis, and is the author of *On the Side of the Crow* (Hanging Loose Press, 2006). He lives in Swansea, Wales.

DISCARD

A Fish Trapped Inside the Wind

Christien Gholson

PARTHIAN

Parthian
The Old Surgery
Napier Street
Cardigan
SA43 1ED

www.parthianbooks.com

First published in 2011
© Christien Gholson 2011
All Rights Reserved

ISBN 978-1-906998-90-5

Editor: Lucy Llewellyn

Cover illustration by Chris Iliff
Cover design by www.theundercard.co.uk
Typesetting by Lucy Llewellyn
Printed and bound by Gomer Press, Llandysul

Published with the financial support of the Welsh Books Council.

British Library Cataloguing in Publication Data – A cataloguing
record for this book is available from the British Library.

This book is sold subject to the condition that it shall not by way
of trade or otherwise be circulated without the publisher's prior
consent in any form of binding or cover other than that in which
it is published.

For
Mamá & Papá

And for my sisters

Freya
&
Kirsti-Bronwyn

who were there...

I walked around as you do, investigating
the endless star,
and in my net, during the night, I woke up naked,
the only thing caught, a fish trapped inside the wind.

'Enigmas'
Pablo Neruda

Things are not what they seem. Nor are they otherwise...
Lankavantara Sutra

Contents

Contents

April 8th, 1987
Saint Woelfred's Festival Day in Villon,
a Belgian town on the French border

1

And the Fish Is a Fish of...

Philippe Souzain leaned over a dead cod, poked it with a stick. The still eye reflected columns of grey smoke from the cement factory behind him. He raised his head, made a count of all the dead fish lying scattered across Madame Foulette's pasture, then looked into the face of Madame Foulette's cow. The cow kept chewing.

'Get away from my cow!'

Philippe turned toward Madame Foulette's back door. The old woman stood in the mist-covered grass just outside her back door, waving a broom. She looked like a potato. The boy laughed and waved – '*Bonjour, Grosse Patate!*' – picked the fish up by the tail and slid beneath the lowest wire of the pasture fence, dragging the carcass behind him. He dumped the cod into the handlebar basket of his bicycle and pedalled down a narrow road between the cement factory and a vast, rectangular quarry. Conveyor belts carrying limestone up out of the quarry lake creaked through a tunnel beneath the road, into the factory.

The boy stopped at the guardrail above the belts and felt his pockets for something to throw over the side, onto the shuddering piles of wet limestone. He did this every time he rode past. Marbles, rocks, empty cans, and once, the head of a doll he found alongside the canal. Short black hair, huge black eyes. The head had miraculously settled onto the limestone upright, staring back at him – fierce, defiant – as it took its last journey towards the mysterious grey-dusted interior of the factory.

Philippe thought of dropping the cod, but looked over the side and saw a magpie passing beneath him, sitting on the shaking belt, picking at the eye of a dead whiting. He scooped some pebbles from the road's shoulder and flung them at the magpie. The gravel fell short. The bird paid no attention.

He crossed the road, leaned his forehead against the chain link fence, and looked down into the quarry. Leftover fog hung over the water. No matter how many times he looked down into it, the sight of such immense space always made him giddy, as if the lake was sending a current up through his thighs, into his chest, tugging him gently towards the edge.

The boy's Uncle Casimir once told him you could fit fourteen towns the size of Villon into the quarry. Casimir had done the maths.

Philippe mounted his bike again, pedalled past the factory gate and coasted down a short hill, through the last remnants of an ancient stone wall that once encircled the town. Some said the wall was built by the Romans. Casimir said that was absurd, the wall was definitely from the Christian age. If it had been built by the Romans, he told the boy, it would still be standing. But the boy wasn't interested in the history of walls.

2

He rolled past the alternating patterns of cracked plaster, stone, and brick of the terraced houses on rue d'Arcy – windows shuttered, everyone still asleep – into the Grand Place.

Four streets and three alleys emptied out into the cobbled circle at the centre of town, like spokes fitted into the hub of a wheel. Casimir once told the boy that all circles contained a certain amount of magic, leftover from pre-Christian times. But it was something you could only feel late at night. Philippe had slipped out of his house in the middle of the night several times over the past few months, wandered around the Place, waiting for something magical to happen. Nothing ever did. Once, pigeons scattered from the belfry of the church. Another time, Marie Ledoux – Poisson's wife – appeared from the dark alley next to the brasserie, alone, with no coat, holding herself. She looked right through him, then disappeared up rue Demesne. It was strange, but not magic. The boy thought he should tell Casimir that if he was looking for *real* magic, all he had to do was go down to the east end of Foulette's field on Saturday morning and watch Guy Foulette perform. That man could make anything disappear.

The sound of Philippe's rusted wheels bounced over the cobbles, echoed between the wooden doors of the church and the aluminium shutter covering the large window of the brasserie. The boy steered the bike towards rue Lefebvre, dodging Poisson, who suddenly lurched into view, probably drunk.

Poisson screamed his wife's name across the Place, but Philippe had already turned the corner down rue des Ecoles, and heard nothing but the sound of his own tyres.

II

And the Fish Is
a Fish of Distraction...

1 The Illusionist

Guy Foulette watched his mother walk across the kitchen and drop a mackerel the length of her forearm onto the table. 'Philippe Souzain put dead fish in the pasture,' she said. 'I'm going to call the *gendarmes*.'

Guy leaned forward, ran the tips of his fingers across the flank of the dead fish. It hadn't been dead long. No canal fish, this one. Too big. Guy frowned, stood up, and limped to the kitchen window. The pasture was scattered with them. The cow stood at the far end of the pasture, near the cement factory road, tail flicking, oblivious.

Beyond the pasture, four tall factory smokestacks belched white smoke and dust into the grey sky. A lone seagull circled the stacks, probably following the Sunday morning cement barge picking up a load of bags at the factory dock. Guy lifted his hand to his face, inhaled. Seaweed and death. The smell of Chiqui's breath those last days in the hospital...

Guy looked past his fingers at the spire of Villon's church, a stone antenna rising above the town roofs beyond the factory. 'How could a boy the size of Philippe carry all those fish into the field?' Guy said, turning to his mother.

Madame Foulette reached for the phone, hanging on the wall next to the fridge. 'I'm going to call the *gendarmes*,' she said again and began dialling.

'You suspect the boy simply because he's Doctor Souzain's son,' Guy said.

His mother cradled the phone between her shoulder and cheek, listened to it ring. He took a step towards her and a fierce pain shot up through his leg. He sucked in a deep breath through his nose, then, to mask the sudden inhalation of pain from his mother, huffed the breath out into a little laugh.

How typical. He was going to perform one of Chiqui's hardest tricks, alone, in front of hundreds in the Grand Place in a matter of hours, and his foot was acting up.

'Are you laughing at me?'

Guy hobbled over to his mother, took the phone from her hand, placed it back in its cradle. 'I think the fish are a sign from God,' he said, smiling.

'Why do you make fun of my beliefs, and in my own house?' the old woman said.

'Sorry,' Guy said, then added, 'but Jesus *did* multiply the fishes, didn't he?'

'Stop!'

Madame Foulette lifted the phone off the hook and Guy gently took it from her again. The dial tone buzzed between them. 'We don't know anything yet,' he said.

'That's why I'm going to call the *gendarmes*,' the old woman said, opening her arms in a pleading gesture, talking to some unknown, invisible witness in the corner of the room. 'It's their job to find these things out.'

'No, it's their job to *look like* they are finding things out, not to actually find things out. They'll just make you fill out forms. Then they'll tell us what we already know.'

'And that is?'

'That there are fish in the pasture.' Guy placed the phone back in its cradle again. 'Calling the *gendarmes* only adds to the confusion.'

'That boy Philippe needs discipline,' Madame Foulette said, and once again lifted the phone off the hook.

Discipline? The boy had nothing but discipline, Guy thought. The boy was always coming and going from the library. Studying, studying. Poor Philippe Souzain was going to become a doctor, just like his father, grandfather and great grandfather before him. No one was leaving anything to chance for that boy.

Guy shrugged. 'Have it your way.' He limped slowly back to the kitchen window. A crow landed on a fish carcass out in the field, hacked twice at the white underbelly, then pulled something long and glistening from the body. Intestine.

'No one is answering,' Madame Foulette said. 'How can the police not answer the phone?'

Guy turned to his mother. 'They've got to deal with both the kermesse *and* the rally today and there are only four of them.'

Guy suspected the police still had no idea how many people might show up for the rally. Contexture – the eco-anarchist dance troupe performing at the rally – always

6

brought the crowds, the cameras. Ever since their naked dance and arrest in front of the Vatican.

It was Liesl who had roped him into performing with the troupe. She'd told the leader and founder, Stephanie Mertz, about his skills during a long distance telephone interview. A wily move. Liesl knew someone like Stephanie wouldn't pass up using someone in her performance who had (he could hear Liesl's breathless, enthusiastic tone) 'performed with a Buddhist magician at a live sex club in Amsterdam'.

He'd rejected the idea at first. There was no time to practise with the group, and, more importantly, he'd never performed such an elaborate illusion in front of an audience without Chiqui.

Guy's mother put the phone back on its hook. 'How can they not have someone at the station to take calls? I was never allowed to choose whether or not I could serve someone when they came to my register at the Delhaize.' She frowned, pointed over his shoulder, out of the window.

Guy turned. The crow had lifted off the fish carcass and was flying low, over the cow, towards the cement factory road, intestine dangling from its beak like a snake.

'That's not a good sign,' Madame Foulette said.

Guy turned back to his mother. 'Things are symbols for themselves,' he said.

'There you go again, with that talk you learned in Amsterdam,' she said, then suddenly frowned and winced, holding her side. Guy took a step towards her and she lifted an open hand up to indicate she didn't need any help. 'It's just my digestion,' she said, shuffling to the kitchen table.

Making a sucking sound through the space between her large front teeth, she settled into a chair. In the last few months she'd started making more and more of those sounds. Almost the same sound he made whenever pain shot up his leg. Only she didn't mask it with laughter. Last week he'd seen her out in the pasture limping almost as badly as he did on his worst days. When he asked her what was wrong, she told him she had a stone in her boot.

Why didn't she tell him what was going on? Fear that something more serious was happening? He would have to call his sister Tamarine soon.

'You must learn how to die,' Chiqui had endlessly told him, 'to let it all go. That's the key, *petit*.'

Madame Foulette stared intently at her own hands resting in her lap, as if she'd just discovered them. What a pair we are, Guy thought. Both of us wincing, shuffling, limping. Years ago, when he was a boy – lying in his bed, across the room from his sleeping sister, staring out of the window at the factory stacks – imagining what his life would be like as an adult, he never would have imagined this. He smiled. Who would have thought he'd be the one staying here, taking care of his mother in her old age, and Tamarine would be in Madrid, translating tourist brochures?

Guy leaned over the mackerel. 'This monster must have come from the North Sea,' he said. 'There's nothing like that around here.'

His mother lifted a hand from her lap, touched the fish on the snout. Guy edged around the table, put a hand on his mother's shoulder.

'It'll be days before we get rid of the smell in here,' she said.

'Why did you bring it in?'

'Evidence.'

Guy lifted his hand from his mother's shoulder and

produced a twenty centime piece from behind her ear. He smiled to himself, then dropped the tiny coin into his pocket.

The old woman waved a hand next to her ear, irritated, as if she was brushing away a fly. 'What are you doing with my ear?'

'There was a strand of hair out of place,' Guy said. 'I moved it.'

Madame Foulette looked up at Guy, frowning. 'What are you talking about? All my hair is out of place.' She smoothed her grey hair back from her forehead with the palms of both hands, eyes closed.

'Now your hair will smell like fish,' Guy said.

'Evidence,' Madame Foulette said.

Guy shook his head, turned, went to the phone.

'Who are you calling?' his mother asked.

Guy didn't answer, started to dial.

'You're calling the German. Soon you'll be off to Germany...'

'She's not –' he started, then gave up. The phone rang at the other end of the line. He reached up to the photo of his dead father, produced a twenty centime piece from his father's mouth.

2 The Stranger

Liesl Grafft parted the curtains of the hotel window, looked across the street at the Mons train station. A few people stood around under black umbrellas, beneath a ceiling of sagging black electric tram wires, waiting for a bus. There was the usual orange haze around the streetlights. The pavement was wet, but she could see no drops falling across the light. She opened the window, put out her hand. Her skin became instantly damp. Rain so fine it looked like fog.

'Fish?' she said into the phone. 'What would be the meaning of fish?'

'I don't know,' Guy said on the other end.

'Do you think it might be the factory? Because you're involved with the rally?'

'Why would the factory put fish in the pasture?' Guy said. 'They haven't even acknowledged there's even going to *be* a rally.'

'Well, maybe it's finally come to their attention. You know the saying by Gandhi?'

'He only had one?'

Liesl rolled her eyes, sighed. 'First they ignore you, then they ridicule you, then they fight you, then you win.'

'It doesn't make any sense,' Guy said.

'Gandhi?'

'No, that the factory would scatter fish everywhere.'

'I'll get a bus as soon as I can.'

'I'll wait for you at the canal bridge,' Guy said and hung up before she could tell him which bus she planned to take. She started to dial his number, then put the phone down.

He's a magician, he can figure it out.

She stared at the halos around the streetlights. Through the mist she could make out the silhouette of the slag heap behind the station, a few scraggly trees rooted precariously at the top. When she had first arrived at the train station two months ago she thought it was an odd geological formation, jutting up at the edge of the train yard. That night, lying in her tent at the municipal campground, listening to the freezing rain drizzle

10

against the roof of her tent, she suddenly realised what the strange formation was: 'Slag heaps,' she heard Raoul's voice say, 'they're all over the countryside. The ground turned inside out.'

Liesl looked at her reflection in the mirror above the hotel sink. She'd grown thin, very thin, since she'd first arrived. She normally had a round face, like her father, but now her cheekbones were prominent, like her mother. The small, almond shaped blue eyes in combination with the sharp cheekbones gave her the feeling that she was looking at one of her lost Russian relatives, emerging through her skin, out of the past.

She pulled her red sweater off the armoire door, swam through it, then looked in the mirror again and ran her hand through the tangles in her shoulder-length black hair. The brown hair roots were almost an inch long now.

Why would the factory dump fish all over Foulette's field? She stepped back from the sink, sat on the edge of the bed, pulled on her jeans, then fished through her backpack at the end of the bed, found her little box of earrings. Which earrings would be a good talisman for the rally? Amber? Haematite? She held up a pair of turquoise stones dangling from tiny silver braids. Her mother had bought them for her in Santa Fe, New Mexico. She thought of the Indians she'd seen sitting on their blankets, selling turquoise and silver jewellery, in the central plaza in Santa Fe, and the drunk men and women in tuxedoes and evening gowns walking past. All the women in evening gowns were wearing turquoise.

She put the turquoise earrings back in the box, lifted up a gold hoop with a small speckled white and purple coquina shell slipped onto it. She'd found it in her pocket two weeks ago and had asked Guy if he'd put it there – sleight-of-hand quick –

when she wasn't looking. He'd shaken his head like he always did, feigned a frown. 'Why would I do that?'

'Because I always find things in my pocket after being with you,' she'd answered. A tiny braid made from a cow's tail hair. Small pebbles. Dried flower petals. Once, a bleached mouse skull.

She stood up, zipped up her jeans, stuffed her hands into her front pockets to smooth them out, and felt something dry and crumbled in the right pocket. She pulled some of it out. Leaves and stems. Dried parsley.

She'd been standing behind him, watching while he milked Valotte. He'd bent one of the udders up, squirted a jet of milk in the direction of the cat, sitting in the doorway of the cowshed. The cat followed the beginning of the white arc with her eyes, then lifted herself up onto her back legs and opened her mouth, catching some of the milk on her tongue. The rest sprayed her face, the floor around her. The cat dropped down on all fours, began licking the milk before it sank through the straw into the dirt below. Liesl burst out laughing and Guy let fly a short jet of milk at her open mouth. It hit her cheek. Still laughing, she held out her hands to stop any more from hitting her in the face, but Guy arced the next jet high up, over her hands, so that it rained down on her head.

She screamed, held her hands up to the top of her head. Guy sprayed a line of milk down the centre of her body, from her neck to her waist, and she stumbled forward, eyes closed, and knocked him off the stool. Her head bumped against the side of the cow and the cow shifted its hind legs, making a soft snorting noise through its huge rubbery nostrils. He wrapped his arms around her and rolled her away from the cow, across the straw, to the shed wall. When they rolled to a stop, he found her mouth. The raw milk, still warm, was all over her face, straw in her hair. She had unbuttoned his shirt, opened it, and he had opened hers, his face above hers, taking in a deep breath of the milk on her skin.

They never quite got their jeans off.

When Liesl started to button up her stained shirt, Guy zipped up and told her to wait for him to come back before she finished her buttoning. He ran out of the cowshed into the just sprouting garden and came back with a tiny sprig of parsley. He broke it apart, sprinkled it across her belly, between her breasts.

'What's this?' she said.

'Parsley.'

She shook her head and laughed. 'I *know* it's parsley. I mean why?'

'Because there are no flowers.'

He took one of the sprigs and brushed a line from a point between her breasts to the zip of her jeans, then circled each nipple and held the sprig up to her mouth for her to eat.

She chewed the sprig slowly and swallowed. 'Can I button my shirt now? It's cold.'

When they were both standing, facing each other, she realised 'Oh my God, your mother could have come out here while –'

Guy shook his head. 'My mother never comes out here.' Then he smiled his magician's half-smile. 'Well, almost never.'

'She doesn't like me,' Liesl said.

'She doesn't like change,' Guy answered.

Liesl stood up, looked in the mirror again. Last day in Villon. Then, back to her father's apartment in Paris to compile her notes, write the story. She slipped the gold hoop into her left ear, flicked the tiny shell with her middle finger, and watched it swing back and forth.

'Hocusem Pocusem,' she said to the mirror.

She gathered her damp clothes and papers off the bed, stuffed them into her backpack. Beneath the papers she found the book of Rimbaud poems Raoul had given her before she left Paris. The pages were still damp from so many days and nights sitting in her tent at the municipal campground. One of Raoul's letters fell out of the book, onto the bed. She picked it up. The postmark was from Cyprus.

Her first time in the Villon brasserie, Dehanschutter – the old coffin maker, sitting at his usual post at the end of the bar – had asked her if she was a friend of 'that idiot Raoul'.

'How did you know?' she'd answered.

'Ah,' the old man waved a tiny Turkish cigarette in the air, 'you have the same feel he had. The questions are different, but the feel is the same. He was on and on about Rimbaud. You're on and on about the factory renting the empty quarries out for toxic waste, but it's the same feel.' He took a deep drag of the cigarette, saying, as he blew out the smoke: 'That Raoul was a homo, if there ever was a homo.' Then he pointed a long, nicotine stained finger at Liesl: 'Although, I must say on his behalf that his French was much better than yours, Mademoiselle Allemande.'

'I'm not German.'

'Your friend and Casimir were bosom buddies for a while. Casimir will talk to anyone. It's an excuse for him to listen to himself.' The thin old man raised the hand holding his cigarette and flapped his fingers against his thumb, imitating a mouth. Ashes from the cigarette flicked onto the bar floor. 'Casimir's father was Doctor Ducasse and the father before that was Doctor Ducasse. Doctors all the way back to Christ. But he couldn't make it as a doctor. That's why he talks so much. Trying to show everyone he's as smart. He teaches *géométrie* at a *lycée* in Mons.' The old man pointed at the line of stuffed birds on a shelf above the bar mirror. 'He's the one responsible for those abominations.'

Ducks, geese, crows. Glass eyes stared down at the patrons.

Liesl slid the letter back into the book, stared at the sad portrait of the adolescent Rimbaud on the cover. Over the past two months she had begun to use the book as a kind of oracle, flipping through the pages before going to sleep, reading random paragraphs.

Will the rain ever stop? Can the factory be stopped? What is love? Who am I?

And Guy? She opened the book, closed her eyes. What was she going to do about Guy? It wasn't as if Paris was that far away. When she'd asked him if he would come down to Paris with her after the rally, he'd just smiled his familiar half-smile. 'C'mon, you could perform on the streets,' she'd said. 'You could teach me to be your assistant. We could easily make a living...'

Did he understand what she was trying to say to him?

She dropped her index finger onto the page, opened her eyes and looked down:

Qu'on me loue enfin ce tombeau, blanchi a la chaux avec les lignes du ciment en relief – tres loins sous terre.
(When they finally rent me this tomb, lime-washed, cement-cracks brought into relief – deep beneath the earth.)

Not exactly what she'd been looking for. Well, oracles are cryptic. And tricky. As her mother always said: 'Make sure you understand the question.'

She had no idea which question had been answered.

Hocusem Pocusem.

3 The Player

The knocking wouldn't stop. Casimir opened his eyes and moaned. Marie Ledoux, lying next to him, shot up into a sitting position.

Casimir stared at the two empty wine bottles standing vigil next to the headless owl on the fireplace mantel, at Marie's brown smock hanging from the bedside lampshade. His head pounded. He closed his eyes.

The knocking continued. Marie shook Casimir's shoulder. He pretended sleep. She leaned into his ear and hissed, 'What if it's Poisson?'

'It's not Poisson, Marie,' Casimir said, eyes open again, wondering why sleep was always denied the wicked. 'If I know Poisson, he's still stretched out on your kitchen floor where you left him last night.' He placed both palms on either side of his balding head and pressed, trying to squeeze the pain out. The remedy worked for a brief moment, then the pain came back worse than before. He needed water.

'Where is the owl's head?' Casimir asked Marie.

'You tossed it over there somewhere.' Marie pointed at the shelf of stuffed birds in front of the bedroom window. The owl's head lay between the feet of a tiny emerald North American hummingbird and his masterpiece – a huge white pelican, wings outstretched, with bright blue marble eyes.

'You were showing me the poems. Don't you remember?'

Casimir stared at the headless owl. He remembered leaping out of bed, padding to the fireplace naked, taking the owl off the mantel.

'I showed you the poems?' Casimir asked.

'The ones your father gave you,' Marie said.

Casimir scanned the room. 'Where are my cigarettes?'

'I don't know,' Marie said. She followed his gaze around the room. 'I threw them to you last night when you were showing me where the poems were hidden. Don't you remember?'

He remembered Marie clapping, laughing, her mouth wide open. He hadn't seen that since her husband Poisson had broken her two front teeth six months ago. How had he got her to laugh? He was juggling the pack of cigarettes and the headless owl and – what else? The packet of poems?

Christ.

'Are you going to answer the door?' Marie said, pretending to rub her nose, so that her hand covered her mouth as she spoke. Casimir could only see her huge black eyes.

Sorrow, the devil's aphrodisiac.

He dropped his gaze to the few sharp ribs beneath the shadow of her tiny breasts, then jumped out of bed and went to the owl, looked inside.

Nothing.

He placed both hands flat on the mantel and stared at the ashes in the fireplace. *Oh God.* He hung his head, closed his eyes. *Come on, Casimir, think!* He remembered standing there, twisting the owl head twice around, lifting it off the body like the lid of a jar. Then? He drew a blank.

No, some of it was coming back. He'd told Marie the story,

repeating what his father had told him: 'For almost one hundred years these papers have been in the family.' His father, the good doctor, had then pulled the packet of papers out of the body of the owl like a rabbit out of a hat and held them in front of Casimir's eyes. 'These papers, Casimir, they are gold. A kind of insurance. I am entrusting them to you.'

'You have insurance papers hidden in an owl?' Casimir had said to his father, sarcastic as ever.

'*Non! Non!* These are the original poems of a famous poet!' his father had shouted.

'Poems?'

'By Arthur Rimbaud.' His father's voice dropped almost to a whisper, eyeing the plastic-wrapped paper.

The idiot, Casimir thought, he didn't even know who Rimbaud was. He was just reciting what Grandfather had told him. 1870: Rimbaud had walked through Villon, on his way to Brussels – a boy of fifteen, running away from home, no money, filthy from the road – and was taken in for a few days by Casimir's great grandmother Clothilde. 'He wrote these poems while staying with her, right here in this house,' Casimir's father said.

But the good doctor never let him touch the packet while he was alive. He was waiting until Casimir had matured enough to realise the true importance of the family investment. 'I don't want you to gamble these things away while you're drunk,' he said to Casimir. 'Like a good wine, they become more valuable with age. They have been kept and protected in this family as a final safeguard against... how shall we say... a turn in fortune?' The old man was delicately referring to Casimir's recent failure in school. Casimir responded with a surly grin. 'Remember, these papers are not for personal gain,' his father continued, ignoring his son's expression. 'I want you to think of them as a safety net for your mother and sister. I am counting on you to be a responsible guardian of that net. Do you understand?'

But his mother was long dead and his sister Adele was married to the good doctor Souzain. He could do with them as he pleased. They were *his* insurance now.

'What did I do with the poems?' Casimir said to Marie.

Marie pulled the packet of poems from under her pillow. 'They're right here. You said I should sleep on them, that it would...'

Casimir spun around, stared at the small pack of yellowing papers in Marie's hands. 'You are beautiful!' He leapt onto the bed, grabbed the packet out of her hands. 'Thank God!'

'Are you going to answer the door?'

Casimir remembered something else and laughed. 'Did I chase you around the room last night, swatting at your skinny little ass with these poems?'

4 The Seer

Marie stood on the first floor landing in one of Casimir's flannel robes. She softly bit down on the tip of her tongue with the stumps of her broken front teeth, watching Casimir's back as he opened the front door. 'I found it in Foulette's field,' she heard Philippe say. 'They're everywhere.' Casimir opened the door wide and Marie saw Philippe, standing on the front step, holding a fish by the tail. Casimir pointed down the white and black marble hallway, past the stairs, towards the back of the house. 'Put it in the kitchen.' The boy stopped at the bottom of the stairs, looked up at Marie. The stench of the fish hit her immediately, wrapped its odour around her.

The smell of late winter. The beach at Ostend. The first time her mother had taken her there, to show her where her father worked. They had sat wrapped in a blanket, staring out to sea. 'Out there,' her mother had said, 'beyond those ships. He works on a huge derrick, pumping oil.' Marie had imagined her father standing over the waves with a large bicycle pump. Later, when her mother had fallen asleep, she had wandered down the empty beach and found a pile of whiting, wrapped in a net. All the fish were dead, except one. The lone living fish gulped and writhed among the others.

She had no knife, nothing sharp, so she knelt next to the net and tried to pry it open with her fingers, but only succeeded in cutting her hands. She rushed up into the dunes, looking for a rock – to put the thing out of its misery – and found one no larger than her fist. When she returned to the pile, she stood over the fish, rock in hand, immobile, until it finally stopped moving.

When she sat back down on the blanket, her mother opened her eyes, sniffed the air, then wrinkled her nose. 'What is that smell?' She leaned towards Marie, breathing deeply. 'My God, you're filthy, Marie. Where have you been?'

'They left him to die,' Marie said.

'Who left what to die?'

Marie never knew how to explain. Where do you start? *The last fish alive was imitating the moon beneath a net of seaweed, silver gills opening and opening, calling the tide back from the black ships on the horizon, and far beyond the ships stood her father with a pump, pumping the sea, pulling out the last fish who could imitate the moon, and that last fish would someday turn into a man, looking at her through blue eyes, the way a man looks at a bride...*

She grabbed her mother's hand, took her to the pile. Her mother stood over the dead fish, frowning from the stench, shaking her head. 'Don't ever touch something like that again!'

Marie put a hand to her mouth and stared down at Philippe. The boy turned and looked at his uncle for a clue.

'It's alright Philippe,' Casimir said softly, 'it's just Marie Ledoux.' Philippe nodded and ran off to the back of the house.

Casimir met Marie at the bottom of the stairs and tried to give her a kiss, but she pushed him away.

'Why did you let him in?' she said. 'He'll tell everyone.'

'No, he won't. He's my nephew. If I ask him not to tell, he won't tell.'

Marie's feet were cold. All this cold marble. Why would someone want marble beneath their feet each morning? She spoke through her fingers. 'I don't know what Poisson would do if he found out.'

Casimir took her hand from her mouth, led her towards the kitchen. 'No one's going to tell.'

Philippe sat at the kitchen table, the fish stretched out in front of him. Casimir winced at the smell. 'Put it in the sink!' Just as Philippe was about to dump the fish in the sink Casimir held out his hands, palms facing the boy, and yelled, 'No! No! It's too much! Get it out of here! Take it out back!' Philippe laughed, looked at Marie and winked, then hustled the fish out of the back door, through the pantry, into the backyard.

'He winked at me,' Marie said to Casimir.

'Oh, he means nothing,' Casimir said and sat down at the table, rubbing his eyes with the heels of his palms. 'He winked at you because I winked at him.'

Philippe came back into the room, brushed past Marie, and washed his hands at the sink. He looks like his father, Marie thought, washing his hands after seeing a patient. The boy turned and looked at Casimir, smiling that innocent all-knowing smile that some boys get when they think they've discovered something no one else knows. Emile, her son, had that smile early in the morning when he crawled into her bed half-asleep, whispering to himself. Poisson, too, when he used to play football. After scoring a goal he would turn and scan the sidelines, looking for her.

'They're all over town, in the fields, everywhere!' the boy announced.

Marie saw Philippe as a man, the doctor he would become: *short black hair, black glasses, walking the white corridors of a hospital in Zaire. So soon, so soon, he will turn his emaciated face to that white wall, drenched in sweat, smiling on his deathbed, eyes lit with delirium, remembering the fish, the fish everywhere, all over Villon.*

Marie closed her eyes.

'Who's all over town?' Casimir asked the boy.

'The fish. They fell out of the sky. Look out back!'

5 The Lover

... and the world smells of fish... and the world was born from a fish...

Father Leo moved his lips, dressing by the light of a small reading lamp in his cold room. In the middle of the night he had risen, chilled, inside a dream of fish swimming circles around the spire of a great cathedral. He remembered crossing the room to

22

PARTHIAN

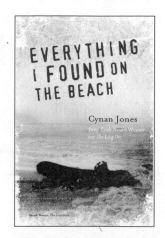

www.parthianbooks.com

eyed babbling about Marie and Chiqui and Guy and Liesl and Father Leo, and, most importantly, during the final stages, helped me clarify the themes and ideas in the novel with her keen poets' eye, her many philosophical questions, and her lyrical suggestions.

That said – any faults in the book can be attributed solely to my *self* (that elusive, slippery fish...).

the window, to see if it was open, and discovering fish swimming through fog. They nibbled the moss on the gravestones, then slid – happy and blind – against the stained glass windows of the church. He'd dropped to his knees and prayed.

... and that fish is Christ... and Christ is love, the first fish...

He made his way down the stairs, through the tiny kitchen, out into the alley between the stone refectory and the church, lips still moving, pausing for a minute in front of the old wood door that opened into the ambulatory to look at the scattered dead fish in the graveyard.

... and the first fish breathed over the surface of the waters...

He opened the door, crept along behind the chancel to a small door that led up a narrow stone spiral staircase to the belfry. When he reached the top, he opened a tiny porthole-sized window that looked down onto the town. There were fish all over the Grand Place.

He imagined the men's faces, rigid, hair slicked back with a quick comb, lost in their own thoughts while he offered Mass; and the attentive, penitent faces of the old women, haunted by cement dust, always scrubbing their doorsteps, eyes staring straight ahead, half-listening. What would he say to them? The entire town would show, no doubt. They always did on Saint Woelfred's day. Although the Church no longer recognised Saint Woelfred, the people of Villon continued to pay their respects: believers, non-believers, the pious and atheists, cynics and martyrs, Social Democrats, Liberals, Socialists, Greens. They all showed up, if only for the kermesse in the Grand Place that followed.

Even that magician son of Madame Foulette usually showed up with his mother. To mock. Once, two years ago, just after the boy had returned from Amsterdam, sitting in the rear pew, he'd released a bat into the church. Produced from his bare hands. No one saw it but Father Leo. Had it been a real bat? Something dark had flown up into the high rafters and disappeared.

... and Saint Woelfred is a fish... and I am a fish...

Madame Ducasse, the old doctor's wife – Casimir and Adele's mother – kept telling him about the falling fish. He'd nodded and nodded, barely listening, giving her last rites, concentrating hard on the prayers that would send the smoke of her soul closer to God. He knew she deserved the same effort he gave to any other person in Villon, but it was so hard to shake his prejudice against the rich. He had fought it all his life, asked for divine help in vanquishing it from his mind, but he'd looked down at that old woman and felt the familiar pity and scorn rise inside him.

Even now, he could still feel it. That same thought: God knows the rich need our prayers more than others.

Ornate wooden boxes had lined the mahogany shelf next to the old woman's fireplace. No books in the room, just boxes of all sizes and shapes. They looked Italian. He'd seen similar boxes on his only trip to Rome. The delicately carved grape leaves twining up the corners, the painted decorations on curved lids: an aqua-green knight doing battle with a fiery dragon; a comet bursting from a deep blue night with pearl-bright stars; still lifes of oranges, apples, halved melons; a yellow crescent moon swaddled inside the face of a smiling orange sun. He'd wondered

24

what all those boxes contained. Jewellery? Or maybe the boxes weren't meant to hold anything, being ornaments themselves. And then there was the horror of Casimir's stuffed birds on the windowsill. Where had Casimir been that day?

The souls of the rich are weighted down so heavily by all the things they own.

Adele had nervously held her mother's hand while her husband, Doctor Souzain, had tended the fire. The old woman had grabbed Father Leo's arm with her other hand. She had been trying to tell him – what? He'd leaned down to hear her.

... and Madame Ducasse is a fish... and her daughter Adele is a fish... and so it follows that Adele's husband, Dr Souzain, is a fish...

Father Leo pulled his head back in through the circular window. Madame Ducasse must have seen this, these fish, as she was slipping into the place between worlds, where past and future are revealed, where he imagined the guiding angel's torch burns through all veils.

What was he going to say at Mass?

He descended the stairs, padded softly across the back of the church, closed the door quietly behind him, and made his way back up to his bedroom. He stared out of the window, into the churchyard. Marie would be coming soon, to ring the bells. Every Sunday morning, for the last six months, she passed through the cemetery, and always – without fail – glanced up at his window, accusing.

Those black eyes. What did she see?

... and God is hiding somewhere inside the open mouth of the first fish...

6 The Wanderer

February 22nd, 1987
Marseilles

Dear Liesl-the-anti-biologiste,
I'm sorry I did not meet you at the station, to give you a proper
send-off on your Villon adventure. The day before I had an
encounter with one of those illustrious, industrious young
national guardsmen that haunt every street corner in Paris these
days à cause du *terroristes. (Bombs! Bombs in everyone's*
pocket! Did I ever tell you what my father did while we were
living in Villon? He worked in Nuclear Operations at SHAPE –
Supreme Headquarters Allied Powers Europe – planning World
War III. He worked in an office deep beneath the earth, encased
in lead – to keep out the spies with X-ray vision.)
They stopped me near the hotel, took my passport to one of
their little vans for further examination, and left one of their
Hitler Youth to guard me, wearing his automatic weapon on his
sleeve. Being a nervous sort, I started to pace. I began pacing
further and further away from the poor boy and eventually he
started fidgeting with his rifle. I, of course, enjoyed the pain I
was causing him (because how dare they stop me and make me
wait?) and so, when I reached the outermost perimeter of good
judgement (and my pacing), instead of turning and shuffling
back to him like a good dog, I kept going, heading towards the
van where they'd taken my passport. 'Arrete!' the boy called
behind me. I kept walking. He called again (so loud it made the
pigeons scatter). I finally stopped, turned. The kid had raised the
rifle, was looking down the barrel at me. I think I heard the
safety catch release (a click that sounded around the world) and I

26

realised right then that it was possible he could gun me down. I could see it in his eyes. Duty. Fear. Anger at the fear.

I froze.

The other guard eventually brought back my passport and they let me go. I was shaking the rest of the day, into the night.

What is the point of words when you're looking down a barrel? The press of a trigger and it's all over. Poetry? All night I kept thinking of Rimbaud. Not his poems any more, but his silence. Why had he reached the end of the line at – what? – twenty-one? Why had he taken to wandering the world for the rest of his life without ever writing anything even resembling a poem again?

I leave for Greece tomorrow. Then, on to Cyprus, where he worked as a construction foreman. After that, I head to Egypt and, hopefully, Aden, the port city in Yemen, where he worked for some coffee exporter. I am determined to follow Rimbaud's trail through the Middle East, all the way to Harar in Ethiopia.

No more words. There is an answer inside Rimbaud's silence. Do not be angry with me.

Raoul

III

And the Fish Is a Fish of Distraction-Called-Desire...

1 The Illusionist

Guy stood in the kitchen doorway, watched his mother put the kettle back on the stove after pouring hot water into a cup.

'What is the hat for?'

'Kermesse,' Guy said. 'I'm meeting Liesl at the canal bridge and I won't be back before kermesse starts.'

'Shouldn't you have a mask instead?' Madame Foulette said. 'Or has kermesse changed to being about hats?'

Guy tapped his top hat, pushing the brim down to his ears. 'The hat *is* my mask.'

Madame Foulette shook her head and waved a hand in the air, dismissing him. He closed the door behind him, walked across the pasture towards the cement factory road.

The smell of the sea was strong out in the field. He bent down, examined a few fish lying in his path, gently touching

28

the fins, running the tips of his fingers along the scales of each tail. At the fence that separated the field from the road, he kneeled in the wet grass in front of a dead cod, touched the edge of the gill. Cut, he jerked his hand back, and instinctively stuck the bleeding finger into his mouth. It tasted like nori – Japanese seaweed – mingled with the iron trace of blood.

Some time at the end of his first year in Amsterdam, Chiqui had taken him out to a Japanese restaurant. Raw fish and rice wrapped in seaweed. Nastiness. He still didn't like it. But he had been desperate to change, erase who he'd been before, so he'd washed it down with a lot of sake and ended up throwing up in the alley next to the restaurant. Chiqui had stood behind him, hand on his back, laughing.

Guy stood up, finger still in his mouth, and stared down the road, towards the factory. Fish were scattered along the shoulder all the way down to the factory gate.

He climbed the fence, jumped into the ditch next to the road, landing on his good foot. A cement truck passed and he quickly turned away from the spray flying off the massive tyres, both hands on his top hat. The truck turned in at the factory gate, stopped next to the small guard-box-sized office where some clerk – usually Ernst Pizou or his brother Luke – checked the trucks through.

Back when he had worked at the factory, whenever he had asked Ernst or Luke how it was going, they had always made it a point to look hassled, overworked. 'Paperwork, paperwork.' He suspected they used that line to shelter themselves from the accusation that their job involved nothing more than dozing off or watching TV and waiting for the next truck. He had always wanted to tell them: 'I don't give a fuck if you watch TV all day. At least someone is getting away with a life – of sorts – in this place.' But they wouldn't have understood. No one understood. For them, it was about increased wages, job security. Guy wanted nothing more than to be free of the whole slaving wheel. He didn't want his time owned by anyone else, no matter what they paid him.

Liesl said that that was probably the reason for the accident. His unconscious was trying to get him out of an abhorrent situation in the only way it knew how.

Motives – slippery as fish.

He still wasn't sure why he was performing today. A political act? An act of love? An act *for* love?

Guy walked into the middle of the road, stood in the silence created in the wake of the truck noise. Plumes of smoke rose up from the four factory stacks. To his right, wet weeds sloped gently down to the concrete apron that ran alongside the canal. The black canal water rose and fell so slowly that it looked still to the naked eye. An occasional raindrop hit the surface and ripples spread out in perfect circles. Black ribbons on black water.

He walked down the middle of the road, in the opposite direction to the factory, towards the canal bridge. He'd thought it was all behind him – love's desperation, confusion; the haunted feeling of joy and loss at the same time.

All illusion.

Monica touched the side of his face in the dark of his tent in the Bruges campground. Australians were partying in the campsite next to them. An incomprehensible cacophony of voices so loud it seemed to come from inside the tent, inside his head. Flashlight and lantern light raked across the canvas, illuminating Monica's dark silhouette for brief seconds, her eyes sometimes closed, sometimes open, staring down at him, through him, hair falling across her breasts, arms stretched in front of her, palms flat on his chest; the outline of her head, body, absorbing the sour smell of the mould growing in the corners of the tent, transforming it into the thick sea-salt perfume of her sweat that mingled with suntan lotion and the marsh-mist of days and days of sex without a shower (so that when they took off their clothes each night in the tent, the smell of the last time they were together would ripple from their skin like heat off a sun-drenched seaside road).

He'd seen Monica in a crowd gathered around Chiqui's street show. She had just slipped a wallet out of a woman's bag and lifted her eyes to his. Instead of quickly disappearing into the crowd with her prize, she'd approached him, grinning. He'd grinned back. And they'd stood side by side, watched the show together. At that moment Chiqui was gently lifting a canvas sunhat off a middle-aged American tourist's bald head. The American had laughed with the rest of the crowd, but was obviously uncomfortable being the centre of attention, or embarrassed by the sudden exposure of his baldness (he kept running a nervous hand across the crown of his head, smoothing down the few strands of grey hair left).

Chiqui quickly produced three eggs and cracked them – one by one – into the hat, then stirred the contents with her black wand. She blew a kiss at the hapless American, her thick, sensuous lipstick glistening red in the sun. The American smiled, sheepishly looked at his wife and laughed, then looked back at Chiqui. Everyone was mesmerised. Chiqui suddenly lifted the hat up, flipped it over onto her shining blonde hair. No egg matter drained down over her face. She walked over to the bald man, stuck the hat back on his head. Applause.

She lifted a long index finger to her lips.

When the crowd quietened down she turned slowly and lifted the hat back off the American's head, turned it over, stuck her hand in it, felt around – eyes to the sky, very dramatic – and produced three yellow chicks so small that all three fitted in the palm of her hand. More applause. She tossed the hat back to the American, strode to her blanket of magic paraphernalia and put the chicks in a little golden cage. Then she hooked a finger around a ring at the top of the cage, lifted it, and held it out to her side.

Guy couldn't take his eyes off her. So strange: blonde hair, high cheekbones, a long forehead, thin nose, red lips, a tight, sequinned red dress and a red and orange chiffon scarf wrapped around her waist as a belt. There was something amiss, but he couldn't put his finger on it. It was as if all the parts were beautiful, but didn't quite cohere into a unified whole.

Chiqui slipped her finger out of the ring and the cage hung suspended in mid-air. As if on cue, everyone in the crowd gasped. The pickpocket pressed up against him – ever so lightly – as Chiqui walked around the cage, waved her wand above it, beneath it, then undid the scarf from around her waist – slowly, almost as if she was doing a striptease – and let it wave in the breeze for a minute.

Everything flashed in the sun. Chiqui's mouth, her dress, the scarf.

Chiqui covered the cage with the scarf, then, in one swift movement, pulled it off. The cage with the chicks was gone.

Applause.

It was only later that night, lying in the tent after making love with Monica, that he realised the magician had never made the cage reappear. Monica was curled up, facing away from him.

'That woman magician never made the chicks reappear,' Guy said.

She rolled over, propped herself up on one elbow. 'You're kidding,' she said.

'I just think that's odd –'

Monica dropped her head onto the rolled up pair of sweat pants that served as her pillow and began to laugh.

'What? Why are you laughing? Did she make the cage appear again?'

Monica lifted one eye from the cloth and blinked. 'You don't know, do you?' She buried her head in the sweat pants again and laughed.

'What's so funny?'

Suddenly he knew. Had the American known? Had everyone in the crowd? He felt like the village idiot.

'You are so funny,' Monica said, cupping his face in her hands, kissing him all over – cheek, forehead, eyelids, mouth.

One afternoon, he came back to the tent to find his transistor radio missing. He was sure one of the Australians had done it. Like a fool, he mentioned it to the old woman at the tiny front office. She called the police.

The van pulled up in front of his tent and the *gendarmes* grilled him for forty-five minutes, asking where he came from, where he was going. 'This isn't about me,' he finally told them. Then they grilled Monica. She couldn't find her passport. They made her fill out several forms, telling her to report to the *gendarmerie* the next morning for further questions.

She disappeared that night. Went off to the bathroom with her pack to take a shower and never came back.

She had said she was from Amsterdam, so he rode his bicycle north into Holland, heartsick, to try and find her. An act of futility. But as long as he was pedalling north – doing something – he felt there was hope. It was only when he reached the edge of the city two days later that he realised how foolish the whole adventure had been. How was he going to find her in such a large place? What did he really know about her?

That she was a thief.

Was he so pathetic? Like a dog on a chain for any woman who would give him the time of day? It was no wonder the American, Caryn, had treated him the way she did.

He sold his bicycle for pocket change, wandered the streets. One afternoon, two weeks after he'd arrived in the city, greasy and thin, he walked through a crowd gathered around a street performer (how he'd begun to love the way the tourists would part for him and his limp – like the Red Sea for Moses), scanning the faces for someone who would make the mistake of looking him in the eye (the first step to successfully begging change), when he found, on reaching the front edge of the crowd, the performer they were all watching was the same magician he'd seen in Bruges.

'Hocusem Pocusem Platz!' she sang. The golden cage with the three chicks disappeared from beneath her chiffon scarf.

When the show ended and she was busy counting up all the bills and coins in her top hat, Guy approached her. She slowly raised her eyes from the hat, looked him over. 'Can I help you?' she said in English.

Guy smiled. He responded in his best English. 'I have… question.'

She held the hat to her chest and waited, looking straight into his eyes. Up close, Guy could see the tall, thin man – around thirty-five, maybe forty – behind the make-up.

'I am seeing you in Bruges,' Guy said. 'Same…' He

pantomimed pulling something out of a hat. 'What I ask – where are...' He couldn't find the word. He flapped his arms and peeped like a chick.

Chiqui laughed. 'Isn't it strange no one ever asks? You are French?'

'Belge.'

Chiqui raised her pencilled-in eyebrows, then nodded, put her hand into the pile of bills in the top hat, rummaged around and pulled out one of the little yellow chicks, eyes bulging, peeping loudly. Then she reached behind Guy's left ear and produced a second chick. She handed both to Guy. Guy looked down into his cupped hands – little claws tickling his palms – then back at the magician and said 'You have... three?'

Chiqui nodded, reached into the top hat again, rummaged around, and pulled out a crumpled bill. She looked at it as if she was surprised the chick wasn't there. Then she smiled, nodded – as if she'd arrived at the right solution (so dramatic!) – and crushed the bill into her fist. When she opened her hand again, there was the third chick, peeping like crazy.

Guy laughed. 'Can you teach?'

Chiqui gathered the chicks from Guy and dropped all three in the hat, then looked down at him – she was almost a head taller than he was, standing at six foot three in her high heels – and smiled. 'Are you sure, my smelly little friend?' she said in French. 'It's not an easy thing to do. It requires that you walk through the mirror.'

'What do you mean?'

'The illusion will be broken,' she said and showed him the interior of the top hat. It was empty. No bills, no birds. 'Do you really want to lose that?'

Guy was confused. 'Lose what?'

Chiqui laughed. 'The illusion, my little vagabond, the illusion.'

Guy shook his head. '*Non,*' he said, then stopped, frowned. 'Wait. I mean yes. I want to know how it's done.'

Chiqui laughed again. 'Okay, I'll think about it. But first, you seem to be in need of a bath. Come home with me, we'll get you cleaned up, and then I can look you over and see if you have any talent.' She winked.

Oh, so it's going to be like that?

Guy helped Chiqui carry her props home. As they moved through the summer crowds the tourists in their big shorts and sandals kept pointing their cameras at Chiqui, clicking away. Chiqui ignored them, asked Guy questions: where was he from? What was life like in Villon? Why did he limp? How had he become stranded in Amsterdam?

The magician raised her eyebrows again when he told her about Monica. 'Ah, so you think I'm some kind of sign that will help point the way to your little girlfriend?'

Guy shook his head. 'I don't think I will find her.' He looked down the narrow street they were walking. The crowds had thinned. The street seemed familiar to him, but he had walked so many streets over the last two weeks, they had all started to blend. Doorstep, railing, brick, doorstep, railing, brick.

'I don't think I want to find her any more,' he said.

Chiqui stopped, looked down at Guy. 'If I hear you correctly, it seems you are looking for a purpose?' She tapped the end of his nose with the cold tip of a lacquered red fingernail, then briefly touched her finger to his .lips. Guy instinctively pulled back. Chiqui smiled, continued walking down the street, the clop, clop of her high heels on the pavement echoing around them.

Guy stood still, sized Chiqui up. Taller, but thinner. Guy

certainly couldn't outrun anyone, but he had more muscle than she did, so if they ended up in a struggle... well, he'd take that risk for a bath.

Guy took off his clothes, stepped into the lilac-scented bath water Chiqui had run. As he settled in his own smell rose to the surface of the water. Bus diesel, soot, piss, garbage-reek, all floated off his skin. He was in the process of unplugging the drain, with the intention of running a new, clean tub of water, when Chiqui opened the door (hadn't he locked it behind him?) and waltzed into the bathroom with two towels in one hand, a cigarette in the other. She had replaced the red dress with a loose red blouse and billowing red and black silk pants. The blonde hair had been replaced by a white turban, the make-up all but gone. She placed the towels on a counter next to the sink and looked down at Guy, taking a deep drag from the cigarette. Guy raised his knees up to his chin, wrapped his arms around his shins.

The last of the water drained from the bathtub, leaving a brown ring. Chiqui pointed at the ring. 'If you refill the tub, you'll have to use the cold. I'm next and, sad to say, there's barely enough hot water to feed even one person in this place.' She scooped Guy's clothes off the floor, wrinkled her nose. 'And these, my friend, must disappear...'

When he was finished rinsing himself off with cold water, he stood up, shivering, and quickly rubbed himself down with one of the towels Chiqui had left next to the sink. He looked at himself in the mirror. A bit thinner than when he'd left home, but pretty much the same. He opened the bathroom door. The sound of something crackling in a frying pan and the smell of onions drifted down the short hallway from the kitchen.

It had been so long since he'd had a decent meal. Clutching his towel tightly to his waist he padded back to the front room where he'd left his backpack, looking for some clothes that didn't stink. The magician had laid a pair of loose black cotton trousers and a white T-shirt on top of the pack. Guy held them up. The trousers were a little long, but what the hell. He shrugged, looked furtively over his shoulder in the direction of the kitchen as he dropped the towel to the floor, and quickly slipped the trousers on.

Guy stared across the canal bridge at a gravel road that continued on through several grass fields before ending at another small limestone quarry. A cloud of yellow dust rose over the road from the tyres of another huge truck churning dirt and pebbles, heading towards the canal. He slid down the weed bank, towards the cement apron of the canal, and limped beneath the bridge.

A large fin broke the surface of the canal, then disappeared.

'You never told me what happened to the cage.'

'Ah, we come around to the cage again.'

'And the chicks.'

Chiqui flipped the hissing vegetables in the wok one more time, turned off the burner, opened the cabinet next to the stove, and pulled out two bowls. From a pot on another burner she spooned out steaming white rice, scooped the stir-fried vegetables on top of the rice, then plonked a bowl down in front of Guy. Sitting opposite him, she handed him a set of chopsticks, then lifted her own bowl up to her mouth, pushing the mixture of rice and vegetables into her mouth with the sticks.

He stared at the food in the bowl, so hungry. He'd never used chopsticks before. Then he looked back at Chiqui, greedily shovelling away, and suddenly he saw it: the game. He folded his hands on the table in front of him and waited for her to finish eating. She looked over the rim of her bowl at him, frowned, put down the bowl.

'You're not hungry?'

Guy said nothing.

She pointed at his chopsticks with her own. 'You don't know how to use them?' She lifted the hand holding the sticks, to show him how to position them.

'You never answered my question,' he said.

'Which one?' Chiqui laid her chopsticks on the table next to her bowl, settled her eyes on him.

'What happened to the cage?'

'Good, good, you're beginning to understand.' She picked the chopsticks up in her right hand, pointed them at herself. 'We go through our lives not really looking at anything with any clarity. We spend most of our time listening to nothing but the noise in our skulls.' She pointed the sticks at Guy. 'Most of us are focused primarily on the distractions, so we can't see what is right there in front of us. We mistake the distraction for reality.'

Chiqui raised the bowl to her lips again, scooped the remaining vegetables and rice into her mouth. She put down the bowl, chewing and talking at the same time, gesturing with the chopsticks. 'All magic is the art of distraction, yes? When I plunge my hand into a hat...' Chiqui dipped her free fingers into the bowl '... and pull out a rabbit, you are focusing on my hand, what I'm saying, or any number of things.' She pulled a coin out of the bowl, showed it to him, closed her hand quickly into a fist and opened it to reveal a piece of broccoli. The broccoli slid off her palm, fell back into the bowl. She opened her mouth and stared at the bowl, eyes wide with surprise – imitating her audience – then pointed the chopsticks at Guy.

'The more you learn about the mechanics of illusion, the more you understand the nature of reality. Do you see?'

Guy smiled. 'You still haven't told me what happened to the cage and the chicks.'

Chiqui laughed. 'You are quick, my little Belge!' She put the chopsticks down. 'Would you like some water? Wine? I rarely drink anything with my meals. It's bad for the digestion.'

'The cage? The chicks?'

'That will be revealed in due time, my inquisitive friend. What you have learned today is far more important.'

'So you will teach me some tricks?'

'As long as you remain attentive.'

The cement truck rumbled over the bridge above Guy, turned onto the factory road. He stepped out from beneath the bridge, looked down the length of the canal at the factory. Cement, that wonderful illusion of solidity. Smoke poured from the factory stacks, raining dust over the town, the surrounding fields, the canal, back into the quarries.

Another fin cut the surface of the water, trailing a V of turbulence behind it. He walked along the canal a few metres, searched the water for more fish. A few raindrops dotted the surface. He looked up into the sky, closed his eyes and breathed in through his nose. Cement dust, damp soil. The slight odour of cow.

Liesl in the cowshed.

There was an ache in his chest where he could feel empty

space push out, begin to grow. Liesl in the shed. Liesl in the tent. Liesl in the brasserie. Liesl in the church. Liesl on the wind. How absurd, he missed her and she wasn't even gone yet.

More illusion.

A brown and white cat stepped carefully through the high grass on the other side of the canal. The fin appeared again and the cat stopped, turned quickly in the direction of the movement. Guy pulled a twenty centime piece out of his jacket pocket, stared at it. He closed his fist, opened it. The coin was gone. He closed his fist and opened it again. The piece reappeared. Guy flipped the coin into the air over the canal and the coin became a small rose petal fluttering softly down onto the water.

Guy looked across the canal at the cat, now staring at the floating petal.

'You were probably quick enough to have seen the secret,' he said to the cat. 'But who will *you* tell?'

The cat looked at him – blinking slowly, pretending boredom – then sat back on its haunches and began licking one of its paws. Guy put his hands in his pockets, his left hand fingering the twenty centime piece, and walked back up the embankment to the cement factory road.

2 The Stranger

Liesl stood in front of the train station, waiting for the bus to Villon. She stared across the street, back at the hotel where she'd spent the night. Seven storeys of white curtains, all closed. Except one. On the fifth floor, at the last window, where the hotel brick met the darker coloured brick of the

41

apartment building next to it, a man stood naked to the waist. Maybe he was completely naked. It was hard to tell from such a distance.

Why does he assume he's invisible?

On a bridge overlooking the Seine, Raoul had told her about a period during his childhood when he would steal out of the house at night, stand in the trees beside a nearby road, and pull down his pants. He said it made the world more vivid. She'd laughed, but he'd been serious.

A small boat was ploughing through the black water below, heading towards them. The people on deck were playing with flashlights, scanning the stone banks and arches under the bridges, and Raoul had suddenly unbuckled his belt, pulled his pants down below his balls and leaned forward, elbows against the stone wall of the bridge.

What was the point, she'd thought. The boaters below couldn't see anything but his head and shoulders.

As the boat chugged closer, Liesl pulled off her sweater and undershirt and waved at the boat below. Yoo-hoo! The people on the boat – mostly teens – raised their flashlights up, caught a glimpse of her bare breasts right before they scooted under the bridge. Claps and cheers bounced off the wet stone of the arch beneath them. The chug of the boat dissolved, the heavy wake sloshing against the banks. Raoul shook his head. 'You're not supposed to draw attention to yourself,' he said, pulling his trousers up. 'It wasn't about shocking people, or trying to get people to look at my dick. It was about...' He searched for the word, as if he had never articulated the feeling before that moment. '... a change in consciousness.'

Without Raoul, she would never have heard about the rally, never met Guy. Liesl wondered if Raoul had finally made it to

Yemen. She hadn't received a letter from him since he'd left Cairo.

She met Raoul in the middle of an argument with her father in the Deux Anges café in Paris. Her father was telling her about a lecture he had just attended on bioremediation: the development of genetically engineered organisms used to consume and transform toxic waste into something more benign. Halfway through his explanation, she had started shaking her head like she always did.

'Why are you shaking your head like that?' he'd said, frowning. 'Here's a perfect example of how science can –'

She had cut him off: 'No, it's just another false promise that science is making. Science keeps promising to fix the problems science started but –'

'Just because you had a bad experience at university –'

That's when Raoul had leaned over to their table and said, 'I think she's right Pops, the answer seems to be to just stop making the fucking waste.'

Her father had stared at Raoul for a couple of seconds, then smiled (his eyes so angry), and said, 'We are having a private conversation, do you mind?'

Liesl had suggested they let Raoul in on the conversation and her father had thrown up his hands and stood up, motioning for Raoul to take his place, telling her that she would obviously have a better time talking with a complete stranger about how wonderful it will be when everybody goes back to live in caves, and then stormed off home.

'Sorry about that,' Raoul said, taking her father's chair.

'He'll get over it.'

Raoul asked her who the old guy was. When she told him, he looked down the avenue in the direction her father had taken and said, 'Not often you come across a father and daughter talking bioremediation.'

She explained that her father was a biologist who worked for the World Health Organisation. And she was, well, a failed biologist. She had quit near the end of her first year of postgrad study, disgusted. Ever since then they'd been involved in an endless argument. 'I think the argument is less about science than it is about my not being able to get my shit together,' she said. 'I've been drifting from job to job for two years now. Recently, I've started to write. Essays on this very subject – the false promise that science will cure all our ills. But I don't dare tell him, he'll just roll his eyes, think it's more dabbling without any real design.'

Raoul, a sometime poet, a full-time Rimbaud scholar, had quit university too, to go tramping in the footsteps of the famous French poet, searching for some lost poems a collector had hinted might exist somewhere in Southern Belgium.

'What got me listening to you and your father,' he told her, 'was the whole bioremediation thing. My little journey in search of the poems led me – oddly enough – right back to a town I'd lived in when I was a kid. A Belgian town on the French border, called Villon. They've got a cement factory there that's going to lease empty quarries as waste dumps. Contexture is going to be performing at a rally in April protesting against the whole thing. The factory has been talking about bioremediation as a panacea against the dumps. You want to write, go up there and write about that. Contexture's always good copy.'

When she told her father about the plan, he sighed. She knew what he was thinking: 'Just like your mother, flitting from this to that…' But he gave her enough money to last her

44

at least one month. Living in the municipal campground, she had stretched it to two.

The naked man stepped away from the fifth floor window, back into the darkness of the hotel room. Liesl looked around at the people waiting at the bus stop. Everyone had an umbrella but her. What was the point? This constant misting was like living inside the idea of rain. It came from all angles at once. Her eyelashes were wet; her face, damp. Her red sweater twinkled with tiny drops, clinging to the fine hairs of wool. When she blinked, beads of water holding tight to the ends of her eyelashes fell down her cheeks. Everyone stared straight ahead, through the hotel across the street. All except a woman with a green plastic kerchief over her head, small eyes set above chubby red cheeks. She was staring at Liesl. As soon as Liesl glanced at her, she looked away, down at her black rubber boots.

Liesl recognised her. One of the countless women in Villon always scrubbing their doorsteps, locked inside their tiny world of cooking, shopping, gossip, going to church to confess their breadcrumb sins; hard-hearted and bitter from the monotony, but still able to wrap a grandchild in the folds of their immense aprons. Liesl had seen it enough. The women stood inside their front doors, staring at her (thinking she was one of the rally's organisers – no matter what she said), arms crossed over their chests, faces of stone, blocking the way into their warm, narrow houses.

Sometimes a child would slip through the crack between old woman and doorframe, and the woman would reach out and touch the child's hair with a gnarled index finger. A touch so light the child felt nothing.

How she'd wanted to be invited in, if only to get out of the constant rain.

Marie Ledoux was the only one in the entire town who'd invited her in. Having been in a different school every year for the first ten years of her life Liesl understood that the first one to make friends with the stranger is always a stranger herself: the kid without friends.

Marie was a small, thin, sparrow of a woman. Very apologetic about everything. The coffee is too weak, sorry; the house is so cold, sorry; I don't know anything about the *cimenterie*, sorry. But there was a fierceness in that sparrow-woman's black eyes that was beautiful. Was it anger? Hatred? Sorrow? A combination of all three? Liesl imagined the sparrow-woman suddenly exploding – rising up and striking her husband down – then slipping away into the night. Only to be discovered years later in a convent. Or she imagined Marie going off to live in some stone hut at the edge of a remote field. Like Saint Woelfred, who, some time in the seventh century – after being visited by the Virgin Mary in a dream – disappeared into the wilderness to live the remainder of her days in constant prayer. Word soon spread of a holy woman, a healer, in the surrounding countryside, and peasants began flocking to her door.

During her interview with Marie, her husband, Poisson, had walked through the front door, hair tousled, drunk. He'd eyed Liesl up and down, scratching his crotch, and asked her what business she had with his wife.

'I'm asking her a few questions about the factory,' Liesl had answered.

Poisson had laughed. 'My wife knows nothing of the factory.' Marie seemed to shrink into herself. Then a boy had appeared from the back room, hair tousled in the same way as Poisson's. Poisson put his big hand on the boy's head.

46

'Then maybe *you* can answer some of these questions,' Liesl said to the drunkard.

Poisson ran his free hand through his greasy black hair, smoothing it down over his bald spot. 'The factory is not worth knowing,' he said, 'and Marie is not worth knowing. No one in Villon is worth knowing. Why are you *really* here?'

It was the suspicious mind of a drunk who thinks everyone is trying to take away his wife – the only one in the house bringing in enough money to support his habit. Angry, Liesl had looked straight into Poisson's dark blue, bloodshot eyes and had seen the confusion of a child.

What had she expected to see?

She had then closed her notebook, stood up. 'Maybe we can continue this some other time,' she'd said to Marie. Marie had cast a sorrowful sidelong glance at Poisson, but he was busy picking up the child and hadn't seen.

The woman with the green kerchief held a net bag of apples and oranges in one hand, a black umbrella in the other. Liesl imagined this woman kneeling in front of a candle she'd just lit, watching the smoke rise up to the vault of the church and disappear through the ceiling. What did these women see when they closed their eyes to pray? Smoke sailing through the space between stars, folding gently into a pair of angel wings, the angel guiding their prayer up to a chorus of saints and martyrs?

She'd tried to talk to Guy's mother about it, but the old woman rarely said more than yes or no to her. Did the old woman think she was mocking her faith the way Guy was always doing? How could she be making fun of these women? Scrubbing down doorsteps with their sharp brooms, trying to keep cement clean of cement dust? There was a strange beauty to their devotion. She told Madame Foulette that she had not been brought up with any religion in particular (she failed to mention that her mother currently owned a tiny New Age bookstore in Philadelphia and belonged to a wicca coven), but that sometimes, when she was sitting in a cathedral, she felt a kind of grace run through her. Then, like an idiot, she told the old woman of the three days she spent in a stone hut in the Cevennes, at the edge of a small town in Languedoc, reading the New Testament for the first time. While she told the old woman the story, Guy sat across from her at the kitchen table, grinning his magician's half-smile, letting her ramble on and on...

She reached the town at twilight, right when it began to snow. The village dogs circled, sniffed her and ran ahead, all in a pack, through the narrow winding streets of the village, leading her to the square. In the square, all the windows were shuttered against the cold. She sat down on the front steps of what looked like the grocery store (simply because there was an old metal advertising sign for Côte d'Or chocolate in the window of the house) and waited for someone to walk by. Each snowflake sounded like a tamped candle flame as they dissolved into the cobbles around her. Just as she was beginning to think the town was enchanted, that everyone had been turned into dogs, two girls – both about eight years old – passed by, talking, completely ignoring her. She asked them if the house she was sitting in front of was a grocery store, and if it was, when did it open? They stopped and answered as if she had been sitting there all their lives. The store opens around seven in the evening for a couple of hours, they told her. Liesl then asked if they knew a place where she could get warm. They shrugged. You can stay in Madame Givrac's shed, they said, she rents it to the shepherds. They showed her Madame

Givrac's house and wandered off. The town dogs followed the girls, sniffing, scattering, regrouping.

A woman about sixty years old, white hair wrapped in a tight bun behind her head, large black-framed glasses, opened the door. Liesl rented the stone hut for the outrageous sum of fifteen francs a night. There was an iron cot and a gas stove inside. Nothing else. Snow fell all night long. Liesl caught a cold and stayed huddled in her sleeping bag on the cot for two days, venturing out only once to buy groceries. The dogs followed her to the store. The grocery lady, whose store was in her front room, got her rice and beans and bottled water without ever looking her in the eye. The surrounding hills and trails were dotted with memorials to the fallen dead of the French Resistance who'd been ambushed, betrayed and murdered in the Second World War, and, slightly feverish, Liesl wondered if the woman thought she was German.

Liesl woke the first morning, freezing cold, and peered through a chink in the stone wall above the bed at a long alley covered in snow. Snow and stone. She was surrounded by snow and stone, so cold. There had been no sun for days before the snowfall and, at that moment, she couldn't imagine the sun would ever shine again. Her fever continued into the second morning and she began to believe that the alley outside the stone hut wound on forever through endless cold mountains.

She'd been given a small green New Testament by an American Christian missionary at the market in Aix-en-Provence. The missionary woman had accosted her right after she'd bought seven francs worth of asparagus, and her boyfriend at the time – Billy Cannasi – was bitching at her for spending so much money, asking her how they were going to eat all that asparagus before it went bad, and –

jesusfuckingchrist – at this rate of spending he'd be back in Toronto inside two months, a wage slave once again, and – holyfuckshit – why had she handed the vendor the money without questioning the price?

In the middle of Billy's harangue the missionary had stepped out of the crowd and asked her if she had accepted Jesus as her saviour. The statement had cleared her mind. Later that night, after they'd made a pot of asparagus soup in their hotel room, she'd turned to Billy and said, 'This isn't working.'

She began reading through the little green book that second day in the hut. Halfway through the Gospel According to Matthew it started to snow again. She slept fitfully between each book. Between the gospels of Matthew and Mark she dreamed the Virgin Mary was in the hut, swaying back and forth above the bed, wearing bluish-black robes that resembled the New Mexican sky at dusk. Between the gospels of Mark and Luke she dreamed a group of men put on a play in a corner of the hut. It was dark – night – and she could barely see what was being performed. She didn't recognise the language they spoke, but she guessed from the tone that accusations were being thrown back and forth. She finished the Gospel of John at twilight and stared up at the wood rafters above the bed for a good half hour, grief-stricken for the poor man nailed to the cross. Then she cried. She cried for hours. It snowed and she cried. It was the same feeling she had had as a child when she was sick, feverish, and knew there was nothing her mother could do for her pain, and her mother would sing to her.

The snow passed, her fever broke. The third morning she shouldered her pack, feeling as open and cleansed as the clear sky. Crows circled over Madame Givrac's house. No sign of Madame Givrac. Dogs followed her out of the village, circling her, sniffing everything. When she passed the gate through which she'd come, they turned and loped back towards the village wall, circling each other, forgetting her instantly.

At the end of Liesl's story, Madame Foulette had simply looked over at Guy and asked him something about the cow.

Liesl wiped her wet eyelashes with the back of her hand.

'Today's the day for the big rally, eh?'

A familiar voice. Liesl turned around. It was one of the cement factory workers who hung around the Villon brasserie after work. She could never remember his name. He was the constant companion of another worker, the talkative one: Marc Didier. Marc, who spent all his time trying to seduce her with his innuendos, his winking eye, his cigarette leer, and his why-don't-we-do-it-and-get-it-over-with-because-life-is-short-and-after-the-rally-you'll-never-be-back-here-again *savoir faire*. This one was tall, thin, a huge Adam's apple protruding from his throat, and quiet. He wore a grey raincoat, brown slacks, polished black shoes. Globes of rain clung to his slicked back hair.

'I don't think I've ever seen you without your work clothes,' Liesl said. The bus for Saint Ghislain pulled up. Two women, standing next to the woman with the green plastic kerchief, got on. 'Are you going to the rally?'

The tall man shook his head. 'I must go to Binche. To pick up a car from my cousin.'

Liesl nodded down at his shoes. 'You need shiny shoes for that?'

The man blushed, looked down at his shoes. 'His wife has a sister...'

'I see.'

He nodded awkwardly and turned toward the station. After

a few steps he turned back. 'Did you know there are fish all over Villon?'

'Guy said there were fish in his mother's field,' Liesl said. 'They're all over Villon?'

The man once again nodded awkwardly, then raised a long, thin hand and turned towards the station again. He hesitated a second, turned back once more.

'I am curious. Are the fish part of your rally?'

'First off, it's not *my* rally,' Liesl said. 'I'm just writing about it. And second, why would the people against the dumps scatter fish all over Villon?'

'I thought maybe... to show what would happen if waste is shipped to the quarries? Theatre. I heard there would be dancers.'

'Killing fish for the rally would be murder. Exactly what the rally is trying to prevent, don't you think? Maybe it's the factory playing tricks.'

The tall man frowned, obviously puzzled, then waved again and went into the station. Liesl turned back to the growing bus crowd: grey raincoats, black raincoats.

Daudet. The man's name was Daudet.

3 The Player

Casimir watched Philippe run to the gnarled grapevine trunk along the garden wall that divided his yard from the Brunuels'. Old branches and new leaves twisted around several rusted wires that had been nailed into the brick. Philippe reached up into the lower branches, stuck an index finger into the mouth of a dead cod. The fish looked as if it were still swimming the grapevine, leaves around it shining wet from the lifting fog.

'Get your finger out of the mouth of that fish!' Casimir shouted at the boy, pressing his thumb between his eyes to staunch the pain in his head.

Philippe pulled his hand back and giggled, then ran along the winding gravel path that wove a figure eight around two small circles of wet grass. A plum tree stood in the middle of each circle. The trees hadn't been pruned in years so their branches stretched over the gravel walk that surrounded the grass, providing unwanted shade to the plants in the rectangular gardens along each wall. Culinary herbs, rhubarb, myrtle. God knew what else. The roses – what was left of them – had gone ragged and long-armed because he never pruned them either.

The boy leapt up, knocked a fish from the lowest crotch of the plum tree nearest Casimir. Plum leaves fell onto the wet grass.

'Watch out for the tree!'

Philippe held the fish by the tail, at arm's length, and held his nose. 'Maybe we should have fish for breakfast.'

'Put that fish down!'

Fish in the grass, fish at the foot of the tangled rose branches, fish crushing the rhubarb, fish smell in his head. The boy dropped the fish, wiped his hand on his trousers, and ran to the back of the garden, under the cherry trees.

'Watch out for the nettles!'

Who would do such a thing? One of his students in *cinquième* came to mind. Simon Patroche. Casimir immediately dismissed it. How could that boy carry so many fish – and so large – into a locked garden? Too small and frail. His rebellion was all in his tongue, his wit. Day after day the boy would raise his hand while Casimir was explaining – droning, really (he knew he was boring, but who cared, it was expected of him) – some Euclidean proof, drawing different coloured lines on the board, all the other children copying everything into their little gridded notebooks. The swift ones, the slow ones, the bright ones, the fools, all copying, their faces slack, devoid of passion and enthusiasm; copying, copying, their minds gone off to some other place – a beer, a bed, a pair of breasts. He knew it was their only defence. He'd done the same thing as a boy. Everyone copying the same thing off the blackboard that students had copied down thirty years before. An endless round of pain. (My God, some of the teachers in the *lycée* were the same ones who'd taught him!) Everyone copying except Simon. Simon sat attentive, ready and willing to be right there in that room on a Friday afternoon, hand raised, waiting to be called on so he could perform his next trick.

He probably had no life outside of school.

The previous Friday – like every day for the past year – Casimir had turned around from the board and sighed. There was Simon, wide-eyed, smiling, hand raised. 'Yes?' Simon stood up the way he always did whenever he was called on. '*Monsieur*, I want to show you a card trick I learned from a film I saw on TV last night.' It was never a question about geometry. It was about diverting attention away from the lesson. The other students smiled, some giggled, their eyes suddenly animate, flickering briefly with life. Casimir sat down at his desk and opened his grade book – the way he always did after Simon had stated the nature of his performance. 'Proceed.' The boy produced a pack of cards from his leather satchel and began shuffling them on his desk, talking the audience through the boring, preparatory introduction.

54

He was a natural comedian.

'It was a western called *Trinity Is My Name*,' Simon said. 'An old film from the seventies. Do you remember it, *monsieur*?'

Casimir shook his head and the boy continued: 'There was a part where Trinity is in this bar playing cards. You need to know he's the fastest gun in the West. The speed he can draw his gun from his holster is incredible, monstrous! Almost too fast for the human eye. Don't you think that's monstrous, *monsieur*?'

Casimir never responded. It was all part of the game they played with each other.

'But the people in the bar don't know that he's this fast gun. They think he's an idiot. He sort of acts like an idiot, always smiling and nodding. So all the people think he's an idiot with cards, too. They play for a while and he loses for a while. Then, it's his turn to shuffle and he shuffles the cards the way he spins his guns. It was amazing.'

Simon spread the pack out in an arc on his desk, pulled a card out of each end of the arc and used them to flip the entire spread – like dominoes – face up, face down, back and forth.

'Is that your trick?' Casmir said.

'*Oh non, monsieur*. I'm just warming up. You see, at one point Trinity lifted the pack...' Simon scooped the pack together with both hands, shuffled a few more times, then held the pack in his right hand, the bottom of the pack against the heel of his palm, the top of the cards held by the curl of his fingers. He held his left hand out, about half a metre away from the facing deck, '... and he shot cards across the space between his hands.'

Everyone waited. Simon took a deep breath, looked at Casimir, smiling – always that smile – and said, 'I practised this all night.'

He bent the deck – slowly, slowly – into a bow between his thumb and middle three fingers, until they shot, one after the other, out of his hand and sailed across space to the other waiting hand. Zing, zing. The cards hit the open palm of his left hand and flew every which way, all over the room. It sounded like pigeons landing on a roof: the whirr of wings, scratch of claws. The cards spun and fluttered in the air, fell slowly to the floor. Then, silence. The cards were everywhere. Ariel, the girl sitting next to Simon, stared down into the pile of cards in her lap, disgusted.

'It seemed easier on television, *monsieur*,' Simon said.

Casimir shook his head like he always did and said, 'Simon?'

'*Oui, monsieur?*' The expectant grin.

'*Zéro.*'

Then, still in character, Casimir put his pen to the grade book and drew a little circle in the line of zeroes next to Simon's name. Some of the students laughed. Casimir had laughed at the beginning of the year. But now the zeroes were real.

He'd called the boy into his office after class at the beginning of the spring term, told him he would end up doing something he didn't like for the rest of his life, simply because he didn't take school seriously. 'Look at me,' he'd said to the boy. 'I ended up teaching geometry instead of becoming a doctor. All because I messed around in school – the way you're doing.' The boy had listened with his usual silly grin, then he'd smirked and said, 'That's too bad, *monsieur*,' and left.

Philippe was searching through the brambles and nettles beyond the cherry trees. There was an untended patch of lily-of-the-valley back there, growing in the farthest corner of the yard, having spilled over from the Brunuel yard next door, through a space in the wall that had started out as a crack in Casimir's youth, and over the years, with the help of curious children's hands, grown larger and larger. The Brunuel children were the latest vandals. Sometimes, when he was up in the attic, he'd look down into the yard and see them slip through, crawl around, rise up on their fat little toes to pick the cherries that hadn't been stolen by the magpies. The last time he'd been back there – last year? – the fragrance had been overwhelming.

'Try not to step all over the flowers!' Casimir yelled at Philippe.

Why did he bother? He touched three fingers to his right temple and winced. His temple felt bruised.

Philippe started to make a pile of fish under the plum trees, dragging the long heavy grey carcasses by the tails through the grass, dumping them one on top of the other. The pain behind Casimir's right eye spread to the back of his skull, down the muscles of his neck. It made his hearing strangely acute. He could hear individual fish scales rubbing together each time Philippe dropped a fish onto the pile, the sound of a bird in Brunuel's garden shaking water off its wings, and behind him, the groaning slats of the kitchen window blinds – rust and paint-flaked wood grinding together – ah God – as Marie pulled the rope inside the kitchen, raising them. Casimir pressed the heel of his right palm to his right ear.

Maybe he was having a stroke. No, he was too young to be having a stroke.

Someone opened the back door of the Brunuel house. Georges Brunuel? Georges had gone to school with Casimir, was two grades his junior. He now worked in the main office at the factory. He was a big man, with a barrel chest and pork belly, whose father had worked a forklift at the factory. But the new generation got to put on a clean suit every morning, didn't they? Brunuel hated Casimir because Casimir had inherited this house, and lived in it all alone, far from a world of fat wives and daughters.

When the Brunuel family first bought the house Casimir had suffered Georges's constant cracks with a smile.

'Ah, Casimir, how is the house treating you? Do you think it's big enough?'

And: 'What do I have to do to get such a house? Teach school?'

And: 'Imagine what could be mine if I hadn't screwed around in school.'

All this right to his face.

Why wasn't Brunuel content? He had more money than Casimir. All Casimir had was this stupid house. And, as Brunuel continually pointed out, he couldn't live in all of the rooms at the same time.

Brunuel's kind would never be content. They always wanted something more. Another car. Another title. More money. Like an American. Bigger, better, faster. Try for beauty, get another fat child.

Six months after they'd moved in, he'd been working up in the attic, when he'd looked down into the Brunuel yard and had seen the eldest girl – Elise – shout something back into the house, then storm into garden. She held herself for a while, staring into space, flabby arms over large breasts, large legs stuffed tight into black jeans, toes spread apart in the cool dirt. He had taught her geometry years before, remembered her as a gregarious girl, always accompanied by a boy, or a herd of boys, her great laugh booming in the halls. He'd always wondered what the attraction was.

Was that when he got the idea?

One Saturday afternoon a few months later, he'd come home from the brasserie pleasantly drunk, and there she was, sitting on his front steps. She smiled and waved and he sat beside her. Hers wasn't an unpleasant face. Made more pleasant by the way she laughed. (Though her new haircut made her look a little ridiculous – a rock star haircut – spiked on top, down to the shoulders in the back. She had nice ears, though; small for such a broad face.)

He asked her what she had been doing since she left school. She told him she had been working at Delhaize, then touched him on the wrist and asked him how school was going. He shrugged. The same. 'I think you were one of the better teachers in that school,' she said, her fingers still resting on his wrist. 'All the others, such boredom.' He laughed. He knew it wasn't true, but it was good to hear. Now he understood the attraction. What she lacked in looks, she made up with her ability to flatter.

That was when he got the idea.

When they parted, he told her to come by for a drink some time. One week later, she was at his front door, holding the hand of her youngest sister, Solfege (pudgy little Solfege, her lips always red and sticky from sucking on red sour balls). Elise stepped into the house as if she were stepping through a mirror, into a different world. Her feet were so small, naked and clean, under the straps of her black shoes. She took a few dainty steps – so dainty for such a big girl – on the cool marble, leading her chubby little sister into the house.

He took them on a tour of the house. Down the marble hallway, up the stairs, to the first floor landing, into what used to be the maid's room when he was a child. It was a kind of waiting room, he told them, opening the door onto a world of stuffed birds; stones of all shapes and sizes; a few doll heads he'd found on the side of the road; jars of exotic lizards, garden snakes, cow's eyes, even a goat foetus with two heads, floating in formaldehyde; papier mâché masks picked up from carnivals all over Europe; bolts of fabric; shards of broken tile; hourglasses, pocket watches, spectacles missing one lens, ocean smoothed glass, vacuum tubes from the radio his grandparents had listened to, copper wire, silver wire, rings, keys – the million and one things of civilisation.

'This is where I keep everything I collect,' he told them. 'Then I assemble them into little cabinets of wonder.'

Solfege picked up one of the doll heads, turned it over in her stained hands. The older girl instantly grabbed the doll head away from the little one, used the bottom of her shirt to rub it clean, apologising profusely. Although he was disgusted by the little girl's sticky hands, he dismissed the whole thing with a wave. 'No problem, no problem.' Then he reached out, touched one of Elise's dangling earrings – some kind of green stone hanging in the middle of a silver triangle.

'Oh, these are nice,' he lied, 'they would work in one of my cabinets.' He curled his fingers around the stone, the back of his middle finger brushing against the side of her neck. And she leaned, ever so slightly – did he imagine it? – into the pressure of his finger.

'Would you like to see some of my cabinets?'

The cabinets he was currently working on he kept in his parents' old bedroom. The two girls stared into the cabinet he called 'Dusk'. On the top shelf, a tiny, stuffed sparrow perched above a jagged shard of glass. On the second shelf copper wire snaked around vials of sand – pink, black, green, white – from beaches all over the world, around a jar containing the floating body of a Tulorian tree frog sprouting a dorsal fin, around the stone from a twelfth-century Ukrainian crypt. The bottom shelf contained only one thing: the clay death mask of a Congolese baby, from 1894. At some point, one of the previous owners had actually fastened straps to it. He planned on surrounding the mask with oriental type fabric he'd found in Brussels: cranes winging through a deep blue background, swirled with lines of gold, silver.

'Cabinets of Wonder came about when Europeans began exploring the New World,' he told the girls as they walked, hand in hand, from cabinet to cabinet. 'The explorers brought back all kinds of strange specimens, things no one had ever seen before. People began assembling them in little cabinets. At first, they just wanted to see the strange new creatures of the New World, of Africa, India, but as time passed, and Europeans got used to the idea of a larger world out there, their appetite changed. They needed to see things that were more and more, how shall I say it – radical? – in order to feel satisfied. They started using strange things found in the burgeoning science of medicine, from our own world: huge gallstones, vases made of the inflated *tunica albuginea* of the testis, two-headed cats, all manner of deformities preserved...'

He knew they weren't listening. No one ever listened. Raoul – that strange Rimbaud scholar – was the only one who'd ever listened to him talk about the cabinets. And even Raoul hadn't understood.

'Yes, yes!' Raoul had cried, turning the death mask of the Congolese baby over and over in his hands, smiling, orange hair hanging over his eyes, 'this fucking civilisation, digging up everything, turning it into a fucking commodity, separating it from any meaningful context!'

Raoul had thought the cabinets were a form of protest. But Raoul was an idiot. It was more interesting than that. They were a form of glorification. Praise. A modern prayer to the million useless things. He looked over at Elise. She had no idea what they were all about. And that was as it should be. They were supposed to appeal not just to the mind, but to the eye.

'You know so much about all this,' Elise said.

He took them up the fourth flight of stairs, to the attic, where he stored his finished creations. It was cold, musty. The roof served as ceiling, slanting down at a thirty degree angle, like a circus tent, until it reached the floor. Solfege wandered through the maze of boxes, touching the edges of this box, that box, running her fingers along the edge of a dusty blanket. She stopped in front of one blanketed cabinet, pinched the hem with her sticky fingers and gingerly began to lift it to peek underneath.

'Solfege!' Casimir shouted, startling the girl. She immediately dropped the blanket and hurried over to Elise, burying her head in her older sister's belly.

'I'm sorry I shouted,' Casimir said, more to Elise than Solfege.

'It's okay,' Elise said, 'She's always getting into places where a little girl shouldn't.' She led Solfege back to the window, and they stood there together, side by side, looking down into their own backyard.

'Nice view,' Elise said. She looked over her shoulder at Casimir. 'Do you spy on us from up here?'

Philippe was pulling a fish through what remained of the rosebushes. Thorns caught on the fish's scales and the spindly rose branches dragged along the ground, almost to the breaking point, before they ripped free and bounced back into the air, dew flying everywhere.

It gave Casimir a grim satisfaction to see the roses treated this way, having spent too many hours as a child forced to wipe cement dust off the leaves and petals.

Philippe dragged the fish under the plum tree. What was it? Cod? Flounder? No, flounder are flat, two-dimensional fish, with both eyes on the same side of the head.

Philippe began dragging more fish from the area around the rosebushes back to the plum tree, making another pile. Casimir looked up into the sky. Even though the morning was overcast, the light made him squint. The fish smell coated the inside of his nose, his lips.

Elise was at his door again. She wanted to take another look at his cabinets. He offered her wine. Up in the attic she asked to see the cabinet that was forbidden Solfege. Her exact words: 'Forbidden Solfege.'

'The way you shouted at the poor girl,' she said, 'made me think there was something you didn't want her to see.'

'I'm not sure if you're old enough either.' No, that was wrong, don't remind her of the age difference.

The big girl took a step towards him. The smell of her soap filled the small space between them. He felt excited. And terribly silly.

He lifted the blanket dramatically and they both stared at a pair of manikin breasts protruding from the back wall of the cabinet, black Egyptian eyes drawn in where there should have been nipples. Half of a plastic hip and thigh rose from the cabinet floor like a small mountain landscape. In the crevice where there should have been a hint of pubic hair, there were feathers. Small blue feathers, white down. The entire inside was lined with crushed black velvet. A red bulb hung suspended from the ceiling of the cabinet, dangling between the breasts and the hip.

'It looks so sombre now,' Casimir whispered, 'but when you turn the red light on, it changes the mood completely. Sadly, there is no plug up here.'

Elise ran her hand along the inside of the cabinet, then placed an index finger on one of the nipple-eyes.

'It's an abstract,' Casimir explained. 'In honour of… a woman.'

'What was her name?'

'Judy.'

He didn't tell her he'd placed Judy's lace underwear – all the ones she'd left behind – beneath the velvet. He wondered what Raoul would have thought of this particular piece. He'd have thought Casimir was protesting against pornography, no doubt. Casimir could hear Raoul's loud voice – for such a skinny boy – shouting: 'Yes! Yes! The commodification of the flesh! The body cut up into pieces, served on velvet…' How could Raoul know the desire that went into gluing those feathers onto the smooth surface of the manikin? Soft, so soft, almost too small to be handled by human hands.

Elise held Casimir's hand, and they stood there, in front of the cabinet in silence for a minute, then he leaned over, kissed her cheek. She turned, pressed her lips to his. Within seconds she was groping his zip. He was surprised at first, then relieved. Ah, good, she is too young for long, lingering foreplay. She pulled his pants down to mid-thigh and grabbed him, her mouth still on his, tongue squirming around in his mouth like a worm.

He lowered her onto the dusty floor, slipped her pants off, and there she was – white legs in the air, open. She made a small mewping sound when he slid into her, began playing with her left nipple, pinching it over and over, as he moved back and forth inside her. Repulsed by the way she played with herself, he stared up at the manikin breasts inside the velvet cabinet. Soon enough, she began to thrash and moan and writhe and pound her fists on the attic floor (Was she coming? She must be coming), and he let go, feeling suddenly naked and vulnerable, imagining that someone was standing at the attic door, watching the whole thing, staring into the crack of his hairy ass.

Good God, if there is a hell...

He saw Georges Brunuel get into his car the next morning. After spending such a raucous night with the man's daughter, he thought he'd be able to take anything the insipid boor said to him. But Georges looked worried, preoccupied, no time for his usual jibes. As Georges backed into the street, he looked up from behind the steering wheel, saw Casimir, and lifted his hand in a friendly wave.

Marie stared at Casimir from behind the kitchen window. Those black sorrowful eyes. 'But who would do such a thing?' he said to his own image, superimposed on the glass over the image of Marie.

4 The Lover

... and the floor is the backside of a great fish... riding the skin of the world, which is a fish swimming through space...

Father Leo sat on the edge of his bed, unrolled yesterday's socks off his feet, planted his bare soles on the cold wood floor. Damp, the floor always felt damp. He lifted his feet off the floor and sat cross-legged on the bed, knees tucked under his robe, like a Buddhist monk. He placed his palms together and bowed slightly.

On his one trip to Rome he'd met a Buddhist. A French citizen who lived in Reims, originally from Vietnam. When he was young Father Leo had been curious about Asian religions. He'd chatted with the Asian man for a few minutes after the train had pulled out of the station in Aix-en-Provence. Idle chatter. When the man mentioned he was Buddhist, Father Leo had leaned forward and said – point blank – 'What is it that you believe?' The man had smiled and looked out of the window. Did the man not understand him? Father Leo was about to pick up his newspaper and read when the man turned back to him and said, 'I don't ascribe to what you call a belief. My religion is more about trying to pay attention.' The little man looked out of the window again, at the rows of grapevines crisscrossing each other as the train shot past a huge vineyard, then said 'It occupies all my time' and laughed. A high, soft laugh.

'But what of the monks who set themselves on fire?' Father Leo asked, still leaning forward, forearms on his thighs, hands dangling between his knees. 'Didn't they believe in something? Can you really do that without some kind of belief... in something?'

The man placed his hands on his knees, leaned slightly forward also. Suddenly Father Leo felt huge and ungainly, his own knees as big as melons. He sat back in order to give the little man more room.

'I can't speak for those monks,' the Buddhist said, 'only myself. Are you a monk?'

Father Leo told the man he was a priest. When the man only smiled and nodded he felt obligated to tell him the difference between a priest and a monk.

'How did you become a priest?' the man asked when he finished his explanation. His smile was so genuine – or seemed so genuine – that Father Leo found himself telling how when he was a boy, his father took him to the glass factory where he worked.

'That month the factory was contracted to make these small glass crosses,' he said. 'I remember standing beside a conveyor belt, the glass crosses rolling by. The glass torso and legs of Christ curved so gently into the glass of the cross that they were almost indistinguishable. My father was the one operating the machine that made these wonderful, sparkling things.

'Now I'm sure if I saw them in a store today I would think them cheap, like a toy. But back then, I thought them magnificent.'

'Yes,' the man responded, nodding, 'images from childhood can be very powerful.'

'I tell you this as a way of explaining that I see myself – my becoming a priest – as someone standing between those glass crosses, the kingdom of heaven, and my father working that strange cross-making machine. The glass crosses were beautiful, but the machine was terrible. Terrifying, really. It was a cylindrical affair with many needle-like components, inserting molten glass into moulds, hissing from hydraulic air pressure, twisting this way and that, spitting crosses out of its mouth onto the belt.

'The glass was pretty, alluring, reflecting the fluorescent factory light. But to have that sort of beauty, someone like my father had to work that monstrous machine.'

'Aha. I see.' The Buddhist relaxed back into the black vinyl train seat, folding his hands in his lap.

'This was a puzzle I struggled with for many years. I think

I became a priest in order to find an answer to that puzzle.'

The man looked down at his folded hands, nodding, but said, 'I am sorry, I am lost. What was the puzzle?'

'You see, my job as I see it – a calling, if you will – is to be of service to those who are living the words of Christ and to be available to those who are not. For so many years the church has told the people to accept their lot, do their duty, and their reward will be the Kingdom of Heaven.'

The little man nodded. 'This is the glass cross?'

'Yes, exactly. The beauty. But at the same time the church has ignored the fact that there are so many people who are suffering to make that beautiful vision possible. Their lives are not beautiful.'

'Your father, for example.'

'Yes, exactly.'

The Buddhist asked him if his father was a religious man.

Father Leo shrugged. 'He was a strict man. A man of discipline. He would stand at the bottom of the stairs on Sunday morning and whistle once to wake me so I would be on time to serve Mass. He attended Mass every Sunday, but I never thought of him as a religious man. Yet, when I told him I wanted to become a priest, he cried. Other than at my grandmother's funeral, it was the only time I ever saw him cry.'

'There are many ways to be religious,' the Buddhist said.

'Yes, many,' Father Leo said and looked out of the window. He had lost his train of thought when the Buddhist had asked about his father. He fished around in his mind for what he had been saying, but came up blank. Glass crosses, his father... suffering.

'The lives of my parishioners are very similar to the life my father led,' the priest said.

'They are poor?' the man asked.

'No, not poor,' Father Leo answered. 'I mean, not starving. Labourers. My father wasn't poor. Not Third World poor. We always had food, clothes. I mean that their working lives have been reduced to a kind of dull repetition. I am a priest in a town that houses one of the largest cement factories in Europe. It used to be the largest one in the world. In the nineteen twenties, I believe. Most of the people in town work in the factory all their lives. I have only recently begun to question the whole structure.'

'The economic structure?' the Buddhist asked. He sounded surprised.

Father Leo had never said this to anyone else. He wasn't sure if he could find the right words. And he was almost sure he could not find the right words to explain it to a Buddhist.

'I'm not talking about revolution,' he said and laughed. The other man continued to smile, but didn't laugh. 'I mean finding the right balance between the temporal and the eternal. Saving souls, yes. But not at the cost of sacrificing people to a life of drudgery. There are women in my parish whose lives are very painful, more repetitive and dull than the lives of their husbands who work in the factory. They are religious because they have no other beauty in their lives. They attend Mass because it is beautiful. Have you ever been to a Mass?'

The little man nodded. 'Yes, many times.'

'They struggle, these people, to be good. But their lives are – well, there's very little reward. It's funny, if you asked them they wouldn't tell you their lives were like that, though. I don't think my father thought his life was terrible, monotonous, but there was this anger behind everything he did. I have not been in this cement factory town very long, but I can sometimes hear the desperation behind their words. If you could see the way some of the women glance at the light coming through the church windows when they think no one is looking...'

Father Leo paused, glanced at someone passing along the train corridor outside the compartment, then said 'Why should only some be asked to bear the burden of pain? Why not all of us?'

Father Leo leaned forward again, moved by the passion of his own question, and looked down at his hands resting on his thighs. In comparison to the small hands of the man sitting across from him they looked like ungainly bear paws, hairy and thick. He folded them together and said, 'So my question now is do we want the people to receive the sacraments of the church out of pain – as an escape – or out of love?'

The Buddhist nodded and took a deep breath, then looked out of the window. Father Leo followed his gaze and stared through his own reflection at a stand of trees, a farm and fields, another stand of trees, another farm, more fields.

'Serious questions,' the Buddhist said, then said nothing more. They sat together in silence until the train pulled into the station at Cannes. The little man rose, took his suitcase down from the wire rack above his seat, turned to Father Leo and told him he was glad they had talked, that he had learned many things.

Father Leo stood up, towering over the little man. 'Yes, you were very patient. Thank you.' He was grateful to the man for not trying to answer his final question and wanted to show his gratitude, to shake his hand, but there was no room. They stood there for a second or two, between the seats, the priest's belly almost touching the little man's chest.

Father Leo blushed, unfolded his legs from beneath the robe, stared at his bare feet on the damp floor. He was still embarrassed after all these years.

Why? He'd been so young.

The Buddhist had inched past the priest and opened the door onto the rush of people out in the corridor. As he stepped through the door Father Leo had asked him what he did for a living.

The little man grinned, showing dark gums, and said, 'I sell stained glass.'

They had both burst out laughing.

... and the stained glass seller on the train is a laughing fish...

Father Leo wondered, if he decided to take the train down to Reims tomorrow, would he be able to find that stained glass seller? What would he say to him now? He'd had that conversation when he was under the influence of Liberation Theology in the early seventies, reading Gustavo Gutierrez late into the night – his own luxurious secret – then rising from his bed lamp and standing at this very window, filled with ecstasy, seeing the possibility of a new world, a heaven on *this* earth. Justice and salvation, hand in hand. The beautiful idea that if you overthrow the rich, the ones who are oppressing you, that sin would no longer exist; that sin itself lies at the heart of the exploitative economic system.

... and my father is a fish... and the Holy Father is a fish... and the sea is rising into the sky... and the sky is falling into the sea... and they are both fish...

Father Leo stood up, scrubbed his cheeks with the heels of his palms to get the blood circulating in his face. He stood at the window again, looked down at the cemetery, the gravestones in wet grass. No, unlike wealth, sin is distributed evenly throughout the world, among rich and poor, dark and light. It remains immeasurable, unfathomable, in every human heart.

The grass blades growing up against the stones were long, some of them higher than the crosses on top of the stones, bearing clusters of seeds. The grass around Father Gaspar's grave – the old priest who'd preceded him here in Villon – was taller than the grass in the rest of the graveyard. He'd told the groundskeeper, Nicholas, over and over, about clipping the grass close to the stone, how when it was that high, it looked as if no one cared. Nicholas always stood there, one mud-smeared thigh leaning against a tombstone, arms dangling at his sides, holding a cigarette, nodding and nodding.

Why had he thought the smell of cigarette smoke so wonderful in his youth? A kind of perfume. The smell of Nicholas's smoke now made him feel claustrophobic, shrouded in thick gauze. Nicholas never looked him in the face, just listened and nodded and went about his business as if Father Leo had never said a word to him. Yet another one who was angry at the church because of something a nun or priest had done or said to him in his youth. A ruler cracked on bare knuckles, a blow to the side of the head, a furtive hand sliding inside the waistband, a prolonged kiss stinking of alcohol. Or maybe because he'd been blinded in one eye as a child and blamed it on God?

'The man hates the church for some reason,' Father Gaspar told him when he first arrived in Villon. 'It's an easy way out, I know, to blame the church for everything, but the man is a meticulous worker, very diligent, and very quiet.' Father Gaspar was a meticulous man himself. Always had to have things his way. But Father Leo came to see Nicholas as a man who used silence as a survival technique to maintain his own pride, not as an act of submission. He nodded and nodded as Father Gaspar talked to him, telling him what to do, where and how, and then simply did whatever he wanted.

After a few clashes with Father Gaspar in his first year at the parish, Father Leo saw the value in Nicholas's practice. Look down and nod, then do what you want. Maybe that's why it angered him so much when Nicholas gave him the exact same performance – the dangling cigarette, the head down, lips curled into an almost-sneer – making Father Leo feel ridiculous, an oppressor.

Father Leo placed an open hand against the window glass.

... and Nicholas is a fish swimming inside a globe of dew hanging from a leaf of grass around Father Gaspar's grave... and Father Gaspar is a fish swimming through a sea called Night...

He saw it all too often. Blame. It was this that made me do that, it was that that made me do this. But you can't live your life blaming the sorrow of this world on the church. Or anything else. That German girl Liesl had come asking questions about the factory, the coming rally, what he thought of the rally, and was he bothered by the fact that the anti-dump people had chosen Saint Woelfred's Day for their rally? On and on. She said she was a writer, implying neutrality, but from her questions she was clearly on the side of those against the dumps.

There is no such thing as neutrality. And wasn't she sleeping with Guy?

She had pressed on: What did he think of the factory importing waste from Germany, Austria, Holland, Denmark, Italy, everywhere? Her eyes burned with righteous outrage. He understood. He'd been young once. But he had heard and seen too many things in his time here at the parish to be so quick to judge. He'd listened to her, as patiently as he could, and then had explained that things were not as black and white as she made them out to be.

'You have to understand that the people who run the factory and the people who work in the factory and the people who don't do either, but simply live in this town, all have similar hopes and dreams, similar desires, the same tendency towards greed, selfishness, envy. So, if you are going to try and do something about this problem you must take this into consideration.'

She started to speak, but he raised his hand. 'I know the factory is not angelic by any means – but you must consider that our knowledge, our understanding of things, is so small, limited. We cannot see the larger picture. There are people I know at the factory who have told me about a new technology that will eventually solve the problem of storing the waste, ensuring that the people here will keep their jobs...'

He'd gone on, but the girl's expression had never changed. He wanted to tell her that it was not the bourgeoisie that needed to be overthrown, but sin; not political revolution, but a revolution of the human heart. He knew she would have laughed at him. That was the way of the world. But she would learn. Some day she would look back on her conversation with him the way he looked back on his own conversation with that little Buddhist on the train in Provence.

A crow landed on one of the dead fish lying in the grass

next to Father Gaspar's gravestone. It held tight to the side of the fish with its talons and poked once or twice at the eye of the fish, then jerked up and cawed at another crow that had landed on top of the gravestone. The crow on the stone screeched back, flapped its wings. A third crow settled on the ground next to the fish, made a jab at the carcass. All three screamed at each other.

... and the world is a contest between the fish and the crow... and the crow is also a fish but refuses to acknowledge that he swims through the black water of his own feathers...

There were so many fish in the cemetery and yet the crows all wanted the same one. Maybe that was what he would talk about at Mass.

... and I am a fish... and I am swimming through black waters... and love is a fish swimming through black feathers...

Marie would be coming soon. He wanted to tear himself away from the window, to be somewhere else when she passed below, but he could not. He was addicted to her cold glance. He looked at the alarm clock next to the bed. Eight-seventeen. She usually came around eight-thirty, an hour and a half before Mass. He didn't actually know what she did up there in the belfry during that time. He thought she just needed the solitude. It was probably the safest haven in town, the farthest she could get from Poisson, from her life. On winter nights, when the stars were strongest, breaking through the veil of streetlight, he went up to the belfry himself, to meditate on the extravagant beauty of the constellations, to watch how they moved with such slow precision through the night sky. In those moments he sometimes felt, deep in his own chest, the merciful pity of God.

What was it that Madame Ducasse kept repeating to him, her eyes wide, scared, lying on her deathbed? 'Everyone was so hungry,' she'd said, over and over. Something about the town's hunger rising into heaven and God taking pity, dropping fish from the sky?

... and Marie is a fish... and Marie's fingers trailing across the tops of the gravestones as she passes through the cemetery are fish...

5 The Seer

Marie watched Casimir stand on a chair next to the grapevine and peer over the garden wall into Brunuel's yard.

'What is he doing?' Marie asked Philippe.

'He wants to see if there are fish in Brunuel's yard, too.'

Marie turned from the kitchen window, shaking her head, arms crossed over her stomach. This was not good. She should get home before Emile woke and began to wander. She could see Poisson rising from the cold kitchen floor on one elbow, looking around, one side of his face red and pocked from being crushed against crumbs on cold stone all night. His watery eyes would look around like a newborn, then he'd see her, begin his morning demands. Marie instinctively put one hand up to her ear as she walked across Casimir's kitchen floor to the stove.

Philippe sat down at the kitchen table. He stank of fish.

76

She lifted the kettle off the burner, went to the sink to fill it. The sink stank of fish.

'Do you drink coffee?' Marie asked the boy.

'I'm not allowed,' Philippe said.

Emile drank some of her coffee every morning. They both liked it with lots of warm milk and sugar. 'Why not?'

'Caffeine,' the boy said. 'It's bad for the nerves.'

Answered like a good doctor's son.

Marie placed the full kettle on the stove, turned on the flame. Her feet were so cold. The tile of Casimir's kitchen was as cold as the marble in his front hallway. Almost as cold as her own kitchen floor. Why would a family with money create a house with so much cold stone? Marble, granite, slate, ceramic tiles. Even the blue plaster walls in Casimir's bedroom felt cold, damp. She put her hands out, warmed the tips of her fingers at the fire curling around the bottom edge of the kettle.

Marie looked down at the kitchen tiles. Each one the same: white, with a rose in the centre, bordered with a braid of bluebells. The roses had faded from red to pink; worn down by shoes, constant scrubbing. When she'd washed the kitchen floor that first and only time – down on all fours, knees against the unforgiving cold – she'd thought of the others (maids, mothers) who'd scrubbed the same tiles over the years. A string of women stretching back one hundred years. Women in white smocks, sweat trickling along the ribs.

How many maids had Casimir known in his life?

Casimir had come up behind her, touched her lightly on the shoulder, shocking her out of her thoughts. There had been a sadness, a stark loneliness inside the touch. Since she hadn't seen it coming, didn't know he was behind her, it had swept through her, naked. She'd dropped her scrubbing brush, pulled away, and he had pulled his hand back as if he'd touched a flame, apologising.

He had a beautiful mouth. Full lips. A child's lips. It made her feel ashamed for her own mouth, her small straight lips, her broken teeth. He had the same lips as her younger brother. She remembered the syllables of spit bubbling on the baby's lips, his baby eyes roaming the room, a tiny fist jabbing the air. How she had held him with so much love – and horror wrapped inside that love – knowing he would die within the month. There was nothing she could do, trapped as she always was inside her knowledge.

He stopped breathing one night, as if he had suddenly come to understand something none of the others in the family would ever realise, and simply decided not to continue.

What did you see, little one? she had asked the baby's photo over and over throughout her childhood. Had she seen it, too, but interpreted it differently? The way the grey light of winter rain filled the kitchen until her mother stood motionless over the stove, staring at a blank wall? The way her older brothers wrestled each other, their large hands smelling of rust, muffling each other's cries. Or the way the rainwater puddle in the alley next to the house never cleared, never dried, tiny larvae beneath the surface like fists opening and closing, flexing, hidden from most eyes?

She stuck her finger in that puddle a month after the baby died, sucked the water off her skin. There was a fever. She saw the beasts they call angels circle her, beat her with blue feathered wings, felt them touch their beaks to her lips and scald her.

'You don't have to scrub the floor,' Casimir had said, then held out his hand, to help pull her up.

Fearing to touch him again, she had struggled to her feet on her own.

He had looked her up and down, shaking his head. 'Your dress is all wet.' He told her there were dresses in closets all over the house, would she like to change?

She had said nothing.

He insisted on taking her upstairs, to a bedroom filled with boxes crammed with papers, books, a bed piled with old clothes. He pointed to a small armoire next to a silver radiator. 'There are plenty of dresses in there. If you find something that fits, you can have it.'

He left the room, closed the door. She stood in front of the armoire, stared at the skirts and dresses waiting on hangers. She pulled out a blue dress, somewhat plain, sleeveless, and held it up to her chest. It ended just below her knees. Too nice to wear cleaning. It looked like something her mother would have worn. Were these Casimir's mother's dresses? She put the dress back, crossed the room and opened the door. Casimir was standing out in the hall, leaning against the wall next to the room where he worked on his cabinets, arms crossed, waiting for her.

'No dress?'

'I can't wear them. They do not... who did they belong to?'

'Ah, hard to say,' he said and pushed himself off the wall. 'The world seems to move through this house while I stand still. No matter. You get wet again you know where the dresses are. I have to get back to my birds. There's a fat magistrate from Charleroi who wants his trophy by next Wednesday.' He headed for the stairs. Halfway down the first flight he paused, turned back, and said, 'You don't have to wait until you're wet again, you know. You can have any of those dresses in that room. I

79

have no use for them.' He continued down the stairs. At the bottom, he shouted up: 'And for God's sake, no more scrubbing!'

How could she take a dress home? What would Poisson say? He would want to know what she had traded for it.

Marie opened the refrigerator, looked in. No milk. Some mouldy cheese. No eggs. The boy was playing with the salt and pepper shakers on the table. She was so hungry. It seemed as if she hadn't eaten in days. Maybe it was the pit dug into her stomach by the heavy red wine.

Bread, to soak it up. Did Casimir have any bread?

Marie searched the cabinets next to the fridge. A tin of peaches in syrup. A tin of white beans. A box of stale rye crackers. What did he eat? Nothing. He drank: coffee, gin, Scotch, wine.

'Peaches,' she said to fill the silence for Philippe's sake. She opened the can and dumped the contents into a large bowl. Philippe sailed the salt cellar in wide circles above the pepper grinder, then dived the silver cone towards the table, making strafing sounds. Little white crystals fell everywhere.

Marie put the bowl of peaches on the table and Philippe looked up at her, stopping mid-strafe. 'I'm not hungry.'

'Yes, I know,' Marie said. 'These aren't for you.'

The boy looked hurt. He put the salt cellar back on the table, stood up, dusted salt off his lap and wandered out of the kitchen, towards the front of the house. Marie got a fork out of the silverware drawer and sat down to eat the peaches. They smelled of rust.

She loved to wander through the rooms of Casimir's house, humming to herself, dusting here and there. But she avoided

Casimir's precious Wonder Cabinet room and the room with the jumble of odd artefacts scattered everywhere. All those doll heads frightened her. They resembled the doll heads she'd seen scattered on the banks of the canal and the shoulder of the factory road. It occurred to her that Casimir might be the person who had scattered these heads all over the place, but she never asked.

After several weeks she became so comfortable, she began to sing out loud, unafraid of the echo it made through the front marble hallway. Sometimes, when Poisson was too far gone to watch Emile, she brought the boy with her. The boy pattered behind her, making incomprehensible sounds at the edge of her sight as she cleaned each room. When she sang, Emile would raise his voice too, matching hers, off-key.

One day, working alone, she pulled all the glasses out of the dining room hutch, placed them on the dining room table and dusted them. When she finished she dipped her finger in clean water, ran it around the lip of each one. The music was triumphantly sad, the glass recalling when it was sand, sand remembering when it was stone, stone revisiting the time when it was water, transparent as glass. The resonance of the glass began to vibrate inside the piano next to the hutch and she could faintly make out the ghost of another song deep inside the house.

When she finished playing the glass, the piano continued to resonate at an almost inaudible pitch. The silence that descended into the room after the piano finally stopped vibrating was almost too much for her to bear, chasing her upstairs.

She found herself in front of the armoire full of dresses again. Blue, black silk, cream chiffon, green velour. She fingered the sleeve of one dress, the collar of another, the waist-seam of a third. She took the green dress off its hanger, held it up to her chest. Without thinking, she hurried to the door, turned the key in the lock, and slipped off her brown smock.

She looked at herself in the full-length mirror in Casimir's bathroom. The dress was a little big on her. She ran her hands down over her stomach, brushing the velour darker: the green of a woman who knew how to toss a few strands of hair away from her eyes on a windy, wet street, then tuck it behind one ear, streetlight glistening off the wet cement beneath her high heels. Marie brushed the strands of brown hair away from her face, smoothed the material down from her hips, along the outsides of her thighs. The crush of the fabric became the same deep green as the swathe across her stomach: the green of a woman who knows she is being watched for all the wrong reasons and doesn't care. Marie smiled, turned and looked over her shoulder into the mirror, ran her hand down the back of the dress. The green of forgotten wine, almost black.

Her father had a bottle he found in a cellar in some château in the Ardennes during the war. Her parents opened it on their thirtieth wedding anniversary and the wine came out a greenish-black, thick as syrup. Her father stared at the goop, perplexed for a second, then shrugged, laughed, and opened a beer. Her mother looked over at Marie. She knew what her mother was thinking. She'd heard it so many times. *Everything's a sign, Marie, everything.*

Marie had the urge to go out into the back garden. This dress wanted to be a forest seen from an aeroplane, to dangle fifty feet above the sea floor, slide down the banister in mockery of itself. She knew the woman who had worn this dress had slid down the banister in this house, velour against varnished wood.

82

Marie made her way to the stairs, looked down onto the marble hallway below. If she fell off she'd plummet to hard stone, crack her head open. But the dress wasn't interested in her fear. It wanted sudden speed, to get outside itself, move faster than its own green edges. Marie lifted herself onto the banister. Her heart beat so hard it rocked her slightly back and forth on the thin rail. The dress didn't care.

She launched herself down and sailed into the emptiness at the end of the rail, out over the front hallway, past the glass doors of the living room – flying so slow, so exquisitely slow – with time enough to see the details of the oceanscape above the living room couch: swipes of white paint imitating foam on sea waves breaking against a rock jutting from storm waters in the middle of nowhere. No land in sight.

As she fell, she knew instantly that the painter had never seen that rock jutting up from the middle of that thrashing sea. The painter was a man who lived in a small apartment in Brussels, high above the waves of traffic noise, who only painted at night, the tail lights on the boulevard below bright, ecstatic, auras of red reflecting off the wet street. A red as real as his own brush. *He takes a sip from a glass of beer on the table beside his palette. The brush is a bird. He launches the brush out of the window, waiting for it to sprout wings and fly. Sometimes the brush becomes a pigeon. One time, a crow flapping furiously, stunned by its sudden new form. Other times the brush falls into the traffic below, becomes an eel dodging dark tyres, murmuring curses in a pre-Babylonian tongue. The noise of the traffic crashes over the curses like waves.*

Marie landed on one bare foot, tripped and sprawled onto her stomach. She lay there for a minute, feeling the cool marble against her cheek. The silent aftermath from the Brussels traffic and ocean waves resonated through the empty house. How long she lay there listening she didn't know. At some point, while she was still stretched out on the floor, a figure appeared on the other side of the bevelled glass of the front door and rang the bell. It looked like Casimir's nephew Philippe. She remained still. After a few minutes, the figure turned, ran back down the front steps.

Marie hurried upstairs to change, vowing not to put on the dress again. But the very next week, desperate to be alone with the dresses, she told Poisson that Casimir didn't want Emile coming over to the house any more. Poisson's reaction was expected. 'Isn't my son good enough to grace the idiot's house?' He kept repeating the question to Marie as she dressed, made breakfast, walked out of the front door, as if it was her fault. It was only when she reached Casimir's house, let herself in through the back door, and found herself standing in the centre of that silent house thinking about the dresses upstairs, that she acknowledged that it was, indeed, her fault. She had lied to Poisson.

She wandered through the downstairs rooms, barely dusting, thinking only of the green dress. No, she would not go upstairs. When she went back home after cleaning, she would tell Poisson that Casimir had changed his mind, that Emile was welcome back at the house. No, not that he had changed his mind, but that she had simply misunderstood Casimir. He would, of course, feign disgust at her stupidity, but would be secretly pleased.

Despite her vows, she found herself in front of the room with the dresses again. Her hands were cold, fingers almost numb. She felt the presence of someone on the other side of the door. She turned the knob, entered the room. No one. Only the same boxes. And the armoire with the dresses. She stood in the centre of the room for a few minutes, listening. The hiss of the radiator pipes, slight patter of rain on the window. Fog beyond glass. She approached the armoire.

She only wanted to touch, just one more time –

She stood in front of the full-length mirror in Casimir's bathroom again. This time she wore a beige and cream dress that resembled a veil. The fabric was almost transparent, looked silky, but felt coarse against her skin.

What did the woman wear beneath this so that she was not walking around almost naked? Marie's light blue underwear and white bra (grey from so many washings) stood out underneath the veil-dress, in stark contrast to the delicate folds of cream. There was a brown sash on the hanger that she assumed was a belt of some kind, and she wrapped it around her waist.

She stared at her image in the mirror, embarrassed by her skinny body, so naked, standing straight and awkward – stiff – beneath the transparent cloth. This dress was for a woman who wanted nothing from those who were trying to stare through the fabric, eyes rolling over her skin like cold marbles. This dress wanted her to go outside, wander under the plum trees, under the cover of fog.

She hesitated at the door of the back pantry. The blue marble eyes of a stuffed pelican on Casimir's work table stared at her, accusing. *The pelican feeds its young with its own blood. Same as Christ.* There was a gold pelican on the altar in the national cathedral in Brussels. Five years old, she stood in front of it, holding her mother's hand. How bright it was. How she'd wanted to walk up onto the altar, touch it. 'The pelican is a symbol for Jesus,' her mother had said. 'When there is no food and the chicks are starving, she pierces herself, gives her own blood to her young.'

Marie wanted to cry, not knowing what she should do. But the fog was thick and she could barely see two metres deep into the garden and this gave her courage. She stepped off the cement patio, into the wet grass, barefoot, holding the dress up to her knees. The dress wanted her to climb the plum tree, but the tree was wet and she fought the urge. She stood beneath it, shrouded in fog, the February branches bare above her, stark black against grey mist. No matter how thick the fog, she felt as if all eyes of the town could see her out there, half-naked in another woman's dress. What was she doing?

The woman who wore this dress had dangled from one of the plum tree branches, hung there for a moment, feet off the ground, then pulled herself up into the tree – to feel her nakedness against the nakedness of the tree. Marie jumped, held onto the branch. The entire tree shook, dropping water onto her face. She knew she was going to dirty the dress by pulling herself up and sitting on that thin branch, but who would see? She could wash the dress before Casimir came home. And if she couldn't wash the wet bark stains out of the dress? He probably didn't know exactly what was in that armoire. She could throw it out.

She fell twice into the grass, down on her hands and knees, before she successfully shimmied up the trunk and perched in the first crotch of the tree. She felt like a featherless bird, squatting there, listening to the pigeons coo high up in the gutters of Casimir's attic roof, her hair wet, the dress clinging to her, making her skin itch. But there was a calm up in that tree that she hadn't known since childhood, sitting on the beach at Ostend, watching the waves roll in, the fog descend, seagulls somewhere out over the water, calling to each other, invisible.

She sat in the tree until she began to shiver, then jumped down and hurried back into the house, believing she'd been enchanted, entranced for hours. But it had only been fifteen minutes. She took the dress off in the kitchen, held it up to the light, examined the damage. The sheer fabric was scratched and stained from mud and bark. Too far gone. She had to get rid of it.

The fog was still thick when she left Casimir's house, the cream-coloured dress wrapped in a newspaper under her arm like a fish. Instead of going home, she made her way across the Place, down rue d'Arcy, through the old town gate, and headed uphill towards the factory, looking for a place to dump the dress. A few cars passed, fog lights searched the mist. A cement truck rumbled past and honked, making her jump off the shoulder. She stumbled in the high wet grass along the edge of the quarry until she found the hole the town boys had cut in the fence. She'd found this place on one of her many late night walks after Poisson had passed out at the kitchen table, mid-sentence, eyes fluttering and closing, cigarette burnt out between his fingers.

When she first found the place, she had wondered what the boys did up here, above the quarry. If she were a boy she would have brought a girl up here on a clear summer night, to show her the stars reflected in black quarry water. She would have gone to the edge and stood there, holding the girl's hand, feeling the rush of adrenalin rise through the middle of her body.

One night she had overheard two boys – they sounded like Marc Didier's sons – standing right at the edge, throwing rocks down into the water. They were talking about girls. How one had got his entire fist inside a girl named Marie –

She slipped through the cut wire. The fog hid the edge of the cliff where the quarry dropped to the icy water below. The edge was close. She could feel the water's immense depth through the shifting mist. *Fish the size of houses, scales of black mould, eyes rolling across the quarry walls, looking for a door, a tunnel, the birth canal back. A glowing phosphorescent ball dangles from the lone antenna protruding from their foreheads, lighting their way, casting shadows of other fish onto the limestone walls. They open their mouths. Caves. Caves the smaller fish sometimes enter, thinking they've found the answer.*

She could hear the conveyor belts move through the fog, carrying limestone up out of the water, through the tunnel beneath the factory road, into the factory. She found four fist-sized stones in the grass, tied the dress around them, and took a few careful steps forward, slinging the package into the mist.

The splash sounded so tiny, inconsequential, in such close proximity to the sound of the conveyor belts. She took a deep breath and exhaled slowly, then took off her jacket, laid it out in the grass, and sat down on it, listening to the conveyor belts, the downshift of an occasional passing cement truck. Several cars passed, one after the other, and she thought how Casimir would soon be home, if he wasn't home already. She imagined him rushing up the stairs, heading straight for the armoire, flinging it open –

There was someone standing behind her. She stiffened, thinking it might be one of the Didier boys, but could not bring herself to turn around. Suddenly there was an open hand to her right, fingers spread. The hand closed into a fist, then opened back up. Something dark flew from the opened palm. A bat, a bird, a monstrous insect. She let out a yelp of fear, turned quickly around.

Guy Foulette.

He straightened up, took a step back, eyes wide. 'Marie?' he said, obviously startled. 'I thought you were someone else.'

She had never seen Guy Foulette startled before. He always wore that knowing half-smile. She put her hand up to her mouth. 'You thought I was the German.'

'She's not —' he started, then gave her the familiar smile. 'I'm sorry to have startled you.'

The German girl had come to Poisson's house several times, asking Marie questions about the factory, the quarries, things Marie knew nothing about. And then, that last time, the girl had started asking questions about Marie's broken teeth.

Marie stood, picked up her jacket, hurried off. Did Guy see her throw the dress into the quarry?

The next week she had Emile in tow again, following her around the house with his bat language; the high squeaks echoing in the marble hallway so that she always knew where he was. She kept away from the armoire half the day, busying herself in the bar room at the bottom of the stairs. Unlike every other room in the house, this room was uncluttered, strangely spare. The only pieces of furniture in it were the bar itself, two black vinyl bar stools, and a small refrigerator behind the bar, constantly humming. Opposite the bar sat an old wooden cabinet that housed a stereo. A few album jackets lay scattered on top of the stereo. Always the same ones. Getz/Gilberto: a combination of Brazilian samba and American jazz (Marie had read the inside jacket). And a couple of Miles Davis albums. She wondered if Miles Davis was French. He looked like Jean-Baptiste Monceau, a friend of the family who'd worked on the oil rig with her father and Poisson. Jean-Baptiste was from Martinique. Very black, like Miles Davis.

Above the bar, a fishing net hung from the ceiling, containing several objects from the sea: conch shells, a few small bleached pieces of driftwood, a broken bottle that had been sanded into soft curves by the sea, and a ship's clock (light as the driftwood because all the inner workings had been removed). She got up on the stool, gently slipped them through the net and lined them up on the bar, ready to be dusted. After cleaning the conch, she put it to her ear and listened. There was the same hollow noise that people said was the sound of the ocean locked inside the shell. But this noise resembled the sound of the true ocean, the way the foam on the waves in the painting in the living room resembled true foam. She ran the palm of her hand over the smooth glass bottle, weathered into a reddish brown stone by the ocean, and thought of the green dress upstairs.

It was no use. She would go.

When she'd finished dusting the bar room sea world, she placed the objects back into the net and exited the room. Emile sat on the marble floor just outside the door, talking to the wall or the door or the stairs.

She fed Emile milk and leftover soup that Casimir left in the fridge specifically for that purpose, then sang to the boy on the living room couch, beneath the painting of the battered ocean rock. Emile sang along with her in his incomprehensible tongue until his eyelids grew heavy and he fell asleep.

She pulled the blue dress out of the armoire, the one she had held up to her body that first day after getting so wet scrubbing the kitchen floor. This dress was different from the others she'd tried on. More conservative, a smock almost like the one she was wearing. She imagined an older woman.

In the full-length mirror in Casimir's bathroom she looked

like her mother. All she needed were the beige, wrinkled hose and the black, square-toed leather shoes that her mother always wore. It was so hard to separate the memories of her mother from what the dress desired. This dress wanted to go out into the garden and prune rose bushes. Her mother tended roses, pink roses, white roses, petals folding out into more petals, a labyrinth of pink and white perfumes, lone raindrops on a petal here and there. Her mother would point at a perfect globe of water, touching it with the end of her index finger so that the globe slid from the petal to her skin, then she'd lift it up into the light and say, 'My grandmother told me, a lone raindrop reflects the entire world. Come closer. You see?' Marie would step closer and try to see the world encapsulated in that transparent sphere. She never saw a reflection of anything. More interesting to Marie's five-year-old mind was how it sat on her mother's finger and still maintained its shape. A few days after her mother's death, she found a bottle of moisturising cream in her mother's medicine cabinet called 'Jeunesse'. The label claimed it could make a woman's skin soft as rose petals.

Her mother rarely cut roses, put them in vases. She preferred to let them turn orange, to rust, then sag and fall like too-ripe fruit to the ground. Her father would wander in the backyard when he was home from the North Sea, looking from rose to rose – the rotten ones; the bright, new ones – and say nothing. Sometimes there was a barely perceptible shake of his head, sometimes nothing. Everything's a sign.

When she was seven or eight she woke up at dawn, wandered into the kitchen to eat, and saw her mother, through the kitchen window, bending over a white rose that had gone brown, plucking the petals one by one and eating them, chewing slowly.

This blue dress wanted her outside, pruning, cutting; it wanted symmetry, to wipe cement dust off each petal with a white cloth.

Marie stood in the wet grass with pruning shears she found in the basement (knowing, for some reason, exactly where they would be). This was February and there were no roses. She looked up into the cold grey sky between the bare limbs of the plum tree and closed her eyes.

Who am I?

Emile cried out in his sleep and she dropped the shears in the grass, ran back into the house.

No more, she kept saying to herself as she walked home. Emile hurried behind her, trying to keep up, talking to the stones, the passing cement trucks, the shimmering drops of rain hanging from bare, black branches, reflecting orange streetlight.

No more.

Poisson held up a naked, headless chicken as she walked through the front door, into the kitchen. 'Nothing more to be done,' he said. 'Old Angelina has breathed her last.' Old Angelina was Emile's favourite chicken. Marie licked her dry lips and forced a smile. Poisson smiled back, proud, sucking his great belly up into his chest. He looked almost like the man her father had brought home from the North Sea. The boyish grin, the lock of greasy black hair falling over his forehead into his eyes. He brushed the hair away quickly with his free hand – a jerky, awkward movement – then crouched down to Emile's height, holding the chicken out for the boy to inspect it. 'You see? A feast tonight!'

Marie wondered what had made him so happy. She looked around the kitchen. There was a bottle of vodka sitting on the counter next to the sink. A quarter of it had already been finished off. Poisson followed her gaze to the bottle and stood up. 'Ah yes! Celebration!' He laid the chicken down next to the bottle, grabbed a glass off a shelf above the bottle and poured some vodka for her, turning and handing her the glass.

'What is it the Russians say?'

She didn't know.

Poisson looked down at Emile, who stared at the chicken on the counter, whispering.

'Well, I know what the Greeks say,' Poisson said. 'Do you know what the Greeks say, *petit*?'

Emile kept whispering, staring at the chicken.

'They say "Oopah!"' Poisson raised his own glass and downed the entire contents. He was sweating profusely, even though the temperature in the kitchen was probably well below eight degrees. He hadn't turned on the oven yet.

Emile wandered off into his own room, running the knuckles of one hand along the rough of the stone wall. Marie took off her coat, turned on the oven, and began peeling potatoes. Poisson grabbed her around the waist, kissed the back of her neck. She stiffened, took a deep breath and relaxed, fearing Poisson would become enraged if he felt her resistance to this idiotic chicken celebration.

The bird was scrawny, old, inedible. But Poisson never knew. He passed out before she finished cooking it.

Casimir wrapped his arms around Marie's shoulders. 'What are you eating? Peaches? Where did you find them?' He smelled of fish.

Marie pointed with her fork to the cabinet next to the fridge.

Casimir looked at the cabinet, ran a hand through his hair. 'I wonder how long they've been in there.' He turned back to the table. 'Can I have some?'

Philippe wandered back into the kitchen, holding a small stuffed hummingbird. *Emerald. He will remember the shock of emerald – his fevered face to the white hospital wall – the colour of its wings glittering like the scales of the fish scattered all over town.* The boy caught her staring into him, and quickly looked away. He could feel what she was doing.

'Good God,' Casimir said to the boy, 'how many times do I have to tell you to leave the birds alone. That one is so delicate...'

'I'll take it back upstairs,' the boy said.

'No, no, just put it on the table. Come eat peaches!'

Marie dolloped a few of the peach halves into a bowl and set it down in front of Casimir.

'What about Philippe?' Casimir asked, pointing a fork at the boy.

'He's not hungry,' Marie said.

Casimir shrugged, forked one of the peaches, took a large bite, then spat the contents back into his bowl. 'How can you eat this? It tastes like rust.'

'I saw Poisson near the brasserie this morning,' the boy said, looking at the bird on the table.

'You already said there are fish everywhere,' Marie said.

'*Non, non,*' the boy said, shaking his head, looking up at Marie, a devilish smile on his little face. 'I mean *your* Poisson.'

6 The Illusionist

A dull silver Citroën, coming from the direction of Mons, drove past Guy. It slowed to a stop, then backed up until it was directly in front of him. Marc Didier rolled down the passenger window. 'Guy! What are you doing out here?'

Guy placed his hands on the bottom of the open window, peered into the car. 'Where are *you* coming from so early?'

Marc Didier winked. 'Business here, there.' He pointed at Guy's top hat. 'That what you're wearing to kermesse?'

Guy pointed down the factory road. 'Have you seen the fish?'

Marc squinted down the road.

'There weren't fish on the road coming from Mons?'

'I didn't see any until you just pointed them out,' Marc said. 'Maybe the back of a fish truck fell open?'

'A fish truck driving through Villon?'

'Why shouldn't a fish truck drive through Villon? It must happen. There's no reason why it shouldn't. People toss all kinds of things onto this road. The doll heads...'

'They're all over the fields, too,' Guy said. 'A few live ones in the canal. Huge. They look like they're from the North Sea.'

Marc shrugged. The inside of his car smelled of cigarettes, leather, faint perfume. 'So what are *you* doing out here so early, Guy?'

Guy didn't want to tell him. He knew what would follow. The winks, the innuendos.

'I'm waiting for the bus from Mons. Meeting Liesl.'

Marc winked, predictable as ever. 'Oh ho! That Liesl is something, isn't she? Why don't we have more women around here like that? She reminds me of that American – what was her name? The one who used to live in the Ducasse house?'

'Caryn.'

'Now that was something worthwhile for our little village, eh?' Marc said, digging into the vest pocket of his leather jacket, producing a pack of cigarettes. 'I have dreams about that one sometimes.' He offered the pack to Guy.

Guy pulled a cigarette from the pack, already knowing where Marc was going.

'*Special* dreams,' Marc said and winked again, lascivious. But the eyes betrayed something else. Regret, loss? Maybe he was just tired, from spending all night who knows where with who knows who. That endless round of desire: plunge in, get a brief moment of satisfaction, and then it's gone – transient as thought, as the self, as everything.

Konrad stood in the hall – blue suit, white shirt, red bow tie – holding a bouquet of orange roses. Small and thin, he stared at Guy through thick, black-framed Buddy Holly glasses. Chiqui was going to tower over the poor man. Especially if she wore heels.

Guy let the man in. 'Chiqui will be ready in a couple of minutes.'

He didn't envy this little Konrad. Chiqui was very formal with new lovers, put them through a strict regimen at first, almost as rigorous as his own apprenticeship. Instead of magic, it was etiquette: what flowers were right for a first date, what flowers work for a second, the atmosphere certain kinds of foods create, what wine works with what foods, what clothes go with what weather. He wondered how all the various men who knocked on the door could stand it.

But they all loved her, didn't they? Did whatever she

wanted, desperate to remain in orbit around her. For a while. Eventually they all faded away.

Chiqui walked into the living room, wearing a long, black, sequinned evening gown, and smiled radiantly at Konrad. 'Roses!'

Guy rolled his eyes at the carefully choreographed drama of it all. Konrad gave the roses to Chiqui and she immediately handed them off to Guy, then surveyed Konrad from head to toe.

'Doesn't he look like that silent film star,' Chiqui said, turning to Guy, snapping her fingers, 'the one with the glasses and bow tie, who was always hanging off the hands of clocks above city streets. What was his name?'

'Harold Lloyd,' Konrad said.

Chiqui looked down at the little man, beaming. 'That's the one!'

'Where are you two going?' Guy asked.

'To the movies,' Chiqui said. 'You remember I told you about Konrad's theatre?'

So this little man was the one who owned the theatre that played the silent films. Chiqui had been talking about the theatre for weeks. She was trying to get Konrad to use their act between films.

Guy had been a quick study, practising day and night for the past year and a half, and Chiqui was already letting him perform half of her show by himself. He'd even started using his own trademark trick animal – bats instead of pigeons (though, as Chiqui pointed out, the return rate after the trick was pretty low). She now wanted to put his new skills to use to expand their repertoire – levitating members of the audience, or maybe even an attempt at the dreaded Indian rope trick. For that, they needed to have more control over the space where they worked. Konrad's theatre could be the perfect place.

'Do you have any plans?' Konrad asked Guy. Guy shook his head.

'Come with us!' Chiqui said to Guy, then looked down at the little man dangling off her arm. 'You wouldn't mind, would you?'

'No, no...'

'I'm fine, I'm fine,' Guy protested. 'You two go and have a good time.'

Konrad looked relieved. Then, much to Konrad's dismay, Chiqui insisted Guy come along. Guy sighed. He knew how it would end. There was no arguing when she made up her mind. He'd tried, early on, but she always stood her ground. One time the stand-off went on for so long that her date had eventually jumped in and pleaded with him to come out, please come out with them, just so they could get out of the door.

He went off to his bedroom to change. He was never sure if she dragged him out on her dates for her benefit or his. To shake up her date? He automatically heard her in his head: 'When you get too comfortable, *petit*, you're no longer attentive.'

But who could be attentive every second of the day? Was it too much to ask to get a night of beer and TV, alone?

Memory. Drifting ghosts. The past had no existence. The future was equally non-existent. Thoughts and feelings drift out of nowhere, drift back to nowhere...

All illusion.

'Weren't you and Caryn good friends?' Marc said. 'I always saw you two talking, talking, always talking. Just like with

Liesl. You need to get beyond the talk, my poor Guy, or your thing will wither and drop off. Look at Dehanschutter. Always talking, talking.'

'Dehanschutter is an old man.'

'Shit. Dehanschutter's been old since before we were born. Is that really an excuse? The older I get, the hornier I get. Remember Poisson's father? Standing outside his house, showing us his stiff cock? He was old.'

Guy snuffed a short laugh through his nose. 'We were children. Everyone seemed old to us back then. And I don't remember it being stiff.'

'You should listen to me. I'm only interested in your welfare. The key to success is this: mouth shut, flies open.'

Guy looked over the roof of the car into the high ditch grass on the other side of the road. He wanted Marc to go home, but Marc wasn't going anywhere. Not when he could stay and flirt with Liesl.

'You heard Poisson's started doing the same thing?'

'What are you talking about?'

'My son, Luke, said he saw Poisson wiggling his thing at some girls behind the library. I've had a mind to go over to his place and knock him out. It's sickening. But then, it's understandable if you look at what he comes from. It's terrible what his father did to Ariane.'

Guy looked down the road in the direction of Mons. The bus should have been here by now. An ancient brown 2CV passed. Marc waved at the driver, then took a deep drag off his cigarette and tossed it into the middle of the road. 'Etienne Reecht.'

Guy's crushed foot was beginning to ache from the chill left by the lifting fog. He pressed his elbows on the frame of the passenger window to take some weight off the foot.

'That didn't look anything like Etienne.'

'How would you know?' Marc said. 'Ever since you came back home, you've stayed out here like a gnome. I tell you, Guy, it's not healthy. I heard Etienne got Elise Brunuel pregnant. Or maybe it was her sister Claudine.'

'One of Georges Brunuel's little girls?'

'This is what I mean. You stay out here with your mother and her cow while the rest of life keeps going. They aren't little girls any more. How long has it been since you've seen them?'

At Konrad's theatre, Eisenstein's *Battleship Potemkin* was first on the bill. Workers ran down large stone steps, fleeing Cossack bullets. A woman holding a baby carriage was shot, released her hold on the carriage as she fell, and the carriage bounced down the steps, baby inside, while terrorised people flew by.

Guy glanced over at Chiqui. He could tell she was not impressed. This was definitely not a first date film.

When the lights came up, Chiqui rose out of her seat, walked up the aisle to the bar in the lobby without a word. Guy and Konrad followed dutifully behind. Konrad ordered drinks all around then led them to a small table at the back of the bar. The few people quietly talking and drinking at the other tables kept shooting glances over at them and Guy smiled to himself. He was used to it now. How could they not stare? Chiqui always managed to pull off her extravagant look. There was nothing campy about it. She was the real thing.

'So, do you take all your first dates to a war movie?' Chiqui said to Konrad.

Konrad pulled a pack of cigarettes out of his coat, nervous. 'It's not a war movie,' he defended himself, offering a cigarette

100

first to Chiqui, then Guy. 'Anyway, how the movie is made is more important than what it is about. I mean, it's clearly propaganda. Good sailors versus evil officers. But the form is pure art: the camera angles, the way the film is edited. Eisenstein was trying to edit the film to create the greatest emotional response in the audience.'

Cigarette in her mouth, Chiqui leaned into the candle flame at the centre of the table. She inhaled deeply, exhaling up towards the ceiling. 'But are people really able to watch *how* a movie is made?' she said. 'I was watching the story. Most people watch the story. It's how you watch a movie. And, you have to admit, the story was boring. Propaganda is always boring. How do you separate form from content? Can you really do that?'

'But isn't that what you do when you watch other magicians perform an illusion?' Konrad said, digging himself deeper. 'Aren't you separating form from content? Movies are similar to a magic trick, in a way.' Chiqui frowned and Konrad looked at Guy for help. 'I'm just talking about how Eisenstein performs his tricks.'

'But there's no real story with magic,' Guy said. 'It's just this trick and this trick and this trick.'

'Of course there's a story,' Konrad said, bravely looking up into Chiqui's eyes. 'There's a beautiful woman standing in front of them, weaving a world of magic and desire.'

Aha, so this Konrad had more going for him than Guy had originally thought.

Of course, Chiqui was immediately drawn in. She placed a long, slender hand over Konrad's and they stared into each other's eyes.

'Desire is what keeps things interesting,' she said.

'Funny,' Guy said, trying to break into the silly romantic moment, 'you're always telling me that desire is distraction.'

Chiqui ignored him, held onto her moment with Konrad. But Guy wasn't going to let her off the hook that easily. It was her own fault; she was the one who'd insisted he come along.

'But I thought desire causes suffering,' Guy said. Then he did his best imitation of her low, soft voice: '"Desire blinkers us, *petit*. It conditions what we see, keeps us from seeing what's really there." I thought the point was to let go of your desires.'

Chiqui turned to him. 'You're leaping ahead of yourself, *petit*. Desire *is* distraction, yes. But how can you let it go if you don't even know what it is?'

She turned back to the little man. 'I keep telling him that he can't let go of desire unless he truly experiences it, knows it inside and out, knows what it can do to him.'

Konrad gave Chiqui a lecherous smile. 'I know a place...'

Please leave, Guy said loudly in his head, knowing it would do no good. Marc would wait until Liesl arrived. And Liesl would flirt back. Guy had asked her why she indulged the idiot and she'd told him that being friends with Marc was key to getting the other workers to talk to her.

There was a sudden sharp pain in Guy's right foot. It travelled up his leg, to his groin, spread through the net of nerves from foot to hip. He winced, took a deep breath.

Marc raised his eyebrows and stared at Guy, holding his lighter to the unlit cigarette in his mouth. 'You okay?'

Guy nodded.

Marc lit the cigarette, took a deep pull on it, then said, 'Your foot?'

102

Guy waved it away. 'Comes and goes.'

'Stupid fucking Souzain, eh?' Marc said. 'It's a tragedy, Guy. Whenever I see that man, I can't help but think of your foot.'

'It has nothing to do with Souzain,' Guy said. 'Souzain saved my foot.'

Dr Souzain had been at the factory when the accident happened, had tended to Guy's foot the best he could before the ambulance arrived. Later, it started going around that Guy would have regained the full use of his foot, been able to walk properly again, if Souzain hadn't meddled with it. Guy had no idea where the rumour had started.

'You're a saint, Foulette,' Marc said. 'Or an idiot. Everyone knows Souzain fucked up. You most of all. But, you're right, we should let bygones be bygones. It's Sunday, by god. Saint Woelfred's Day! Kermesse! The rally! Craziness!'

The bus from Mons was visible. Marc looked into his rearview mirror. 'There she is.'

The bus sailed past them. They watched it descend the hill beyond the factory gates, disappear into Villon.

'Looks like the German didn't show,' Marc said.

'She's not –' Guy started, then stopped.

Liesl took the wrong bus again. He had planned on taking her back to the house, making her breakfast, get in a little peace before they were both launched into the chaos of the kermesse, the eco-rally, the levitation. Maybe get a chance to talk to her about what she was going to do after the rally...

Marc leaned across the front seat. 'She probably took the Mézières line. It'll drop her off at the brasserie.' He flung the passenger door open. 'Get in. I'll give you a ride to the Place.'

Guy took off the top hat and slid into the car. Marc tossed

the pack of cigarettes into Guy's lap and put the car in gear.

'Are you hungry?' Marc said, shifting into second. 'I'm famished. I haven't had anything to eat since last night.' He looked over at Guy as he shifted into third, grinning. 'Well, nothing to eat... except...' He wiggled his tongue at Guy and laughed.

Desire.

Guy followed Chiqui and Konrad up narrow stairs to the third floor landing of a terraced house in the Jordaan. The stairwell smelled of patchouli and mould. Konrad made straight for the door at the end of the hall and knocked.

'Nervous?' Chiqui asked Guy.

Guy shook his head, but his heart was pounding. How had he let them goad him into doing this?

Chiqui tapped Konrad on the shoulder. 'You make sure to tell them it's his first time.'

A small man with a shaved head, wearing a studded dog collar, black leather vest and chaps, opened the door. Guy looked over at Chiqui, eyes wide.

She put a hand on his shoulder. 'It'll be okay,' she whispered. 'These people know what they're doing.'

The front room was dimly lit with two candles. Two couches, a wicker chair, a television – nothing S & M about the room as far as Guy could see. The man with the chaps led them down a dark hall to their respective rooms. Konrad gave Chiqui a kiss, entered the first room. The man with the chaps held the second door open for Chiqui. As she kissed Guy lightly on the top of his head, wishing him good luck, he caught a glimpse of two silhouettes inside the room.

Shit, shit, shit.

The man with the chaps led him to the last door at the end of the hall, opened it. Guy couldn't see what was inside. It was too dark. The man with the chaps nudged him forward. 'It's okay,' he said, his voice calm, reassuring. 'They'll take care of you. I promised Chiqui.'

Shadows took off his clothes. Shadows wrapped him in gauze, leaving holes for his nose, his mouth, his penis. Then they lifted him up, set him on a table.

How long did he lie there, nothing happening, before the first touch? Minutes were hours at first, his heart pounding inside his ears. Then, slowly, slowly, as they worked with their soft fingers, tongues, the hours turned to minutes.

Had Chiqui planned this with Konrad from the beginning of the night? Is that why she had insisted Guy come out with them?

Was she out there? Was Konrad?

He was continually brought to the brink, then they let things subside, over and over, wracking his body until all anticipation for an end dissolved and he was nothing but pure, aching desire, the difference between pleasure and pain long forgotten.

Don't stop.

Was that his voice?

7 The Seer

Marie sat down halfway up the stairs, held herself. First the fish scattered everywhere and now Poisson was out looking for her. What would she do if he started banging on Casimir's front door? Hide upstairs while Casimir sent him on his way? And then what? He would still be out there, roaming around.

The fish were a bad sign. An omen.

She imagined her son waking up, no one in the house. She suddenly stood, still holding herself, eyes on the glass of the front door. She had to get home to Emile. The poor boy's drunk father was out hunting the streets for his mother.

And his mother, his mother, what had happened to his mother?

Marie was wearing the green velour dress again, standing in the tiny studio beneath the stairs, next to the basement door, flipping through a book of black and white photos of nude women she'd found hidden in a wreckage of loose papers on Casimir's desk, when she heard the front door open.

She quietly shut the book, switched the desk lamp off, held her breath. Casimir padded softly down the marble hallway, passed the studio door. She exhaled. He had not seen her. Then he stopped a few paces beyond the studio, backtracked until he was looking at her through the doorway. She remained still, heart beating inside her ears.

He broke into a wide grin, full lips open, eyes wide, then felt around inside the door frame and switched on the light.

She felt naked. She wasn't like the woman who had owned this dress; she didn't know how to use the dress as a weapon. She lifted her hand to her mouth, thought of Emile. Where will the money come from if Casimir fires me?

Casimir stepped into the studio, looked her up and down. 'I love that dress.'

She looked down at her bare feet. 'I'm sorry.'

'Don't be sorry,' he said. He took her hands in his, raised her arms out to her sides. 'The dress becomes you.'

'I'm sorry... you said...'

'No apologies. I'm glad you took advantage of the dress. Come.' He led her by the hand through the door, down the hall, into the room with the bar.

'What you need is a drink,' he said and opened the small refrigerator behind the bar, producing a bottle of wine. 'That dress needs some white wine,' he said as he bent down again and searched the shelves of the bar for a corkscrew.

'I should finish dusting...'

'No. No excuses.' He opened the bottle, filled two wine glasses almost to the brim, lifted his glass in a toast. She sat there, unable to move until he impatiently nodded at her glass. She picked it up, nervous, spilling some on the counter, then put the glass back down and looked around for a rag. 'I should clean that...'

'This is a bar room!' Casimir raised his voice, clearly exasperated. 'You are *supposed* to spill in here. For the love of God, let's toast.'

She picked up the glass. 'To freedom,' he said.

She sipped from the glass, placed it gently back on the counter, then put her hand to her chest, feeling exposed in the low-cut dress. She wanted to get back into her smock, go home. No, she didn't want to go home. She wanted to be alone. In this room, drinking wine, alone, all night, playing records.

She smiled at Casimir, then remembered her broken teeth and lifted her hand to her mouth to cover the ugly gap.

Casimir reached across the bar, touched the strap on her left shoulder with the tip of his index finger. 'Do you always wear this dress when you clean the house?'

Marie dropped her eyes again, touched the stem of her glass and whispered, 'The woman who wore this dress. Who was she?'

Casimir finished his wine, poured some more, then topped off her glass, even though it was still three-quarters full. She held out her hand to indicate she didn't want any more, but he poured anyway.

'Her name was Judy,' he said. 'She owned a small art gallery in Brussels.' He put the bottle down, grabbed Marie's hand, and led her into the living room, pointing at the oceanscape above the couch. 'That is a leftover from Judy.'

'She was a painter?'

'No, no. She was a collector. She knew so many fascinating people. This was done by a man who had once belonged to a group of surrealists centred around a magazine called *Osophage* in the mid-twenties. His name was...' Casimir leaned towards the bottom right-hand corner of the painting, squinted at the signature. '... Verginatrix. At least that's what he called himself. Not his real name. He was a friend of Magritte. You know of the surrealist Magritte?'

Marie shook her head.

Casimir knelt on the gold couch below the painting and examined the rock in the centre of the painting up close. 'Verginatrix wasn't as famous as Magritte. Actually, he wasn't famous at all. Never sold a painting while he was a surrealist. Apparently Magritte thought he was a genius. That's what Judy said.'

Casimir stood up. 'Judy found him selling these oceanscapes in a flea market in Brussels. Hundreds of what seemed to be the same painting of waves battering a rock. She did some research and found out that he had become seriously disturbed at some point in his career and covered over all his old unsold surrealist paintings with the same oceanscape. The tragedy of the artist and all that. But Judy saw the ultimate genius in his act.'

Marie didn't understand. She hadn't eaten all day and the wine was going straight to her head. Her feet ached and she desperately needed to sit down.

'It was a moment of genius for both of them, I believe,' Casimir said. 'Do you see it?'

Marie didn't want to shake her head and show her ignorance but she didn't know what else to do.

'The man had heightened the mystery of his paintings by painting over them,' Casimir explained. 'Judy promoted the man as if he'd done this to all his paintings on purpose, taking modern art to some new level. In the end, I think she believed it.'

Back in the bar room Casimir closed the curtains and switched on the lantern sitting on the refrigerator behind the bar, a rectangle of green bevelled glass topped with a brass roof that curved like a Japanese pagoda. Outside, it must have been four in the afternoon; inside the bar, it was two in the morning – the time she usually went out wandering around Villon.

She followed Casimir's lead and quickly downed the rest of her glass. He poured more. Marie didn't raise her hand in protest this time.

'What happened to Judy?'

'She disappeared, the way they all disappear.'

Casimir asked her if she wanted to hear some music and before she had time to answer he was around the bar, fiddling with the stereo. She put her elbows on the counter in front to her, chin in her hands, and closed her eyes. Green light shone through her eyelids.

There was a guitar, a soft male voice, a saxophone. 'Judy introduced me to Brazilian music,' Casimir said behind her. She opened her eyes, turned around. He was moving around the floor between her stool and the stereo. His wiry body wiggled and gyrated, one hand on his stomach, the other raised in the air. She put her hand to her mouth to keep from laughing.

He stopped, held his hand out to her. 'Would you like to dance?'

'You must have loved her very much.'

'Ah yes. For her, I even wrote poetry.' He stood up straight like a schoolboy who had just been called on to recite from memory and closed his eyes.

'The way you move your hand across your face
Brushing the strands and tucking them like lace
Behind your ears...'

Casimir's voice trembled. He stopped, opened his eyes. Marie felt her own body dissolve beneath the dress and she instinctively reached out, touched Casimir on the wrist.

'Judy didn't really like rhyming poems,' he said.

Now a woman was singing. In the same whispery voice the man had used. Casimir took her hands and led her out onto the floor between the stools and the stereo, began dancing with her, holding her close, the bristles of his five o'clock shadow against her neck.

She didn't know why she let him kiss her. It wasn't the alcohol. She hadn't had enough for her to forget who she was, what she was. It could have been the dress, the way he looked at her in that dress. At the moment he kissed her she was – not Marie, not Judy – something else.

When he tried to kiss her again, she pulled away. 'I must go.'

The sun was setting as she walked back to her house. In the middle of the intersection of rue des Ecoles, Lefevbre and Lamaire she stopped, looked out over the Place. She watched as the grey clouds beyond the grey factory stacks slowly turned a leaden blue, heartbroken by the stark contrast between the soft bevelled green night in Casimir's bar room and the sunset.

That night, out wandering after Poisson had passed out, she found herself ringing Casimir's doorbell. As he was opening the door, bleary eyed, dishevelled, it occurred to her that what she had really wanted was to go around through the back gate, let herself in through the pantry and wander around the house in the dark. Maybe sit in the silence of the bar room under the ship clock – stopped at three twenty-two – and watch the movements of her own shadow cast by the green light.

'This is a mistake,' she said.

Casimir shook his head as if to clear it. 'No, no. Come in, come in.' When she was inside, he asked her if Poisson had hit her again.

'He's asleep. Passed out.'

Casimir nodded, looked relieved. 'I'll make some coffee.'

She followed him down the hall, into the kitchen. He told her he'd finished another bottle after she had left and spent the rest of the night correcting tests.

'I have no idea how I graded them,' he said and laughed. 'I probably scrawled on their tests how I actually feel about them. I did it once before.' He pretended to write in the air above the stove where water was boiling. 'Beware Simon, you little bastard, or you will wake up a fat *gendarme* with a fat *gendarme*'s wife snoring next to you...'

Marie smiled. She was too tired to raise her hand to hide her broken teeth.

'It's easy for you to smile,' Casimir said, 'but I was pulled into the headteacher's office after I handed those papers back. Very embarrassing.'

He spooned instant coffee into two mugs, then poured the hot water and pushed a mug across the kitchen table towards her. 'Why did you come?'

She shrugged. 'I can't sleep sometimes and so I walk.'

Casimir lifted the mug to his lips, tasted the coffee and frowned. 'Would you like some milk? Sugar?'

Marie shook her head. 'I don't understand why you hired me,' she said. 'There is so little to clean. And if I can't scrub…'

'This is why you rang my bell at two in the morning?'

'Could you recite one of your poems to Judy?'

Casimir sat back in his chair. 'I only remember the ones that rhyme.'

'I like rhyme.'

Casimir ran a hand through his hair, smiled at her. 'Why not?' He stood up, both hands on the table. 'Let me get my old notebooks. Maybe there's something worth the trip in them.'

He was gone for twenty minutes. Marie sat listening to the water drip from the sink. She tapped her finger against the mug in time with the drops. The light bulb above her buzzed. She raised her face to the light, closed her eyes. Someone touched her forehead and she opened her eyes. There was no one in the room.

Casimir returned wearing black pants and a clean white shirt, carrying a notebook and a bottle of brandy. He poured some of the brandy into both cups of coffee, then flipped open the notebook. 'If we are to read poetry, we must have the proper clothing and the proper libation.'

Marie reached across the table, touched his fingers 'I will not sleep with you tonight,' she said.

Casimir smiled, but his energy, his enthusiasm, seemed to diminish.

'I do not know if I can sleep with you, ever,' she said.

'Ah.'

Marie took a long drink from her mug. The coffee/brandy concoction was terrible. Burning. She coughed, couldn't stop coughing. Casimir jumped up from the table and produced a glass of water for her. 'I'm sorry, the brandy is very cheap. Would you like a whisky?'

'I should go,' she said and stood up, still coughing.

Casimir hurried around the table and began patting her back. He kept apologising, but she wasn't sure what he was apologising for. As soon as she could control the cough, she asked him if she could just sit quietly in the bar room.

'Of course, of course.' He led her by the hand back down the long marble hallway to the bar.

'Would you like me to play some music?' Casimir asked her.

She shook her head and slid down the wall next to the door. Casimir sat down next to her. 'I can make the light brighter or dimmer. Or keep it the same. Whichever you prefer.'

She asked him to turn the light off.

And she sat there, unable to see the hands in front of her eyes for a long, blessed minute. But slowly, slowly, the silhouette of the bar appeared out of the dark, then the odd shapes hanging in the net above the bar. The numbers on the ship's clock glowed green. Three twenty-two.

Casimir's knee and shoulder touched hers in the dark. If she had the green dress on, what would he do? *The floor would open and they would both fall through a long night of stars. A comet would track time beneath them, its long tail shaped like the sloping back of a mackerel with phosphorescent scales.*

Casimir touched her hand and she held two of his fingers. He leaned towards her, breath against the skin of her cheek, and she turned to meet his lips. Thankfully there were no words, only the slow hunt of fingers for buttons, her fingers slipping inside his waistband, his fingers unclasping the top button of her trousers.

He was good. Deft. She didn't know all the buttons were undone until he began slipping her pants down over her hips, gently tugging. Like a thief.

When he entered her, he was only a shadow above her. The luminous numbers of the clock shone above him, over his shoulder. It was so different from Poisson. At one point, he raised her legs up so that her ankles rested on his shoulders and as he moved inside her, he began to kiss with his open mouth the inside arch of first one foot, then the other. At first she was embarrassed, wondering if her feet smelled. Did they taste sour? Why was he doing that when he knew she was on her feet all day? And then she felt the connection between the arches of her feet and Casimir's thumb pressing lightly against her left nipple, beneath her shirt.

Layers of worlds, swinging bridges of light between.

8 The Seeker

February 27th, 1987
Athens

Dear Liesl-the-anti-biologiste,
    Athens is filthy. Dense with diesel bus fumes. It reminds me of Barcelona. I'm looking down into a well of humanity from the

114

edge of my tiny hotel bed: a shaft of windows plummeting seven stories into a tiny little concrete square occupied by a dumpster and a dog. How can the light stand it, having to do so much work to reach the earth?

When I was a boy, I stood on a balcony in a nice hotel in Barcelona, looked down into what now seems like the same dark shaft, windows on all sides. There was a man in the window in the building behind the hotel, sitting at his kitchen table, shirtless because of the heat, five or six kids sitting down the length of the table on either side of him, a wife walking around the table ladling food onto everyone's plate.

That's what I see when I look out of this window. So I'm in Athens physically, but Barcelona mentally. Meaning, I'm nowhere. Floating. Trying to make something new fit into something I already know. And that's the joke – what do I really know of Barcelona? A few images from memory. Practically nothing.

I keep doing this. Playing the same game over and over. Do we ever change? Sitting here, looking down the shaft, I keep coming back to that soldier and his happy trigger finger. Why did I provoke him? He was just doing his job.

When I was a kid living in Villon (up rue Lamaire, two doors down from the boulangerie. Have you gone by it yet? Some day they will have a little bronze plaque on the door announcing 'Here was where Raoul E., poet and genius, lived as a boy.') SHAPE had its own bus system. Still does, I think. Green buses. They went all over the place. To ride one you needed a photo ID that proved you were a dependant of someone who worked at the SHAPE compound. All the SHAPE bus lines began and ended at the building behind the front gate of the compound. Soldiers boarded the bus at the gate and checked IDs. They would stride down the aisles, pistols strapped to their waists, smiling and nodding. But when they reached me they would frown. I rarely had my ID with me. What could they do but haul me off the bus? I could have been a Soviet spy. They hustled me into the guardhouse where I would call my father's office and tell him the situation, and he'd tell the poor soldier guarding me that I was legitimate 'free world' material. This must have happened ten or twelve times! How could the humiliation of having to call my father not make me remember my pass every time I left the house?

Do you see? I haven't changed. I think I liked provoking the guards. The way I provoked that poor soldier. It seems most of us keep doing the same things, thinking the same things, our whole lives. What had Rimbaud's goal been when he wrote poetry as an adolescent? Nothing short of changing reality itself. He thought that the modern poet had to become a seer. How to do this? By a systematic derangement of the senses. In his words: 'All forms of love, suffering and madness.' Debauchery, violent love relationships, absinthe, hashish, starvation, filth. To go so deeply into his own dark desires, allowing him to burn through the illusive veil that he felt shrouded everyone's perceptions, so that he could break through into the great unknown, find the mystery behind all things.

Of course, these otherworldly visions would be impossible to put down in ordinary language, so a new language had to be invented. This was his goal. Do you see? He wanted an art that could not be dominated by fashion, by the whims of this year, of that group. He intended to invent a language that could actually utter the universal mystery. In a sense, it's the old scientist's dream, isn't it? My God, he wanted to put poetry at the head of the march of progress!

But now, sitting at the window of this dingy hotel room, I have the strange and queasy feeling that by abandoning poetry

Rimbaud might have been doing the exact same thing as he wanted to do with poetry. He went to Cyprus, drawn by the lure of wealth from the new colonies opening up in the Middle East and Africa. He worked on a construction crew, became a small merchant, translator, a gun runner, maybe even traded in slaves in Ethiopia. Poetry had not been able to give him what he wanted – a glorified place at the forefront of the modern march towards a new and better age – and so he chose capitalism.

Did he change? Was the new Rimbaud a different creature from the teenage poet? This cycle of not-knowing must end. Athens is Athens, not Barcelona. On to Cyprus.

Raoul

IV

And the Fish Is a Fish of Suffering-that-Comes-from-the-Distraction-Called-Desire...

1 The Stranger

The bus curved around the last sections of the original Mons city wall. Liesl shook her head. She'd caught the wrong bus. Again. This bus would be stopping in every tiny village between Mons and Villon before arriving in Villon's Grand Place. A good hour's ride, at least. She imagined Guy standing by the canal bridge watching the other bus pass, could hear him whisper a soft curse before he started down the factory road towards Villon.

The bus slowed for a red light. One more block and it would turn left, out from under the tram wires of the city, past the little bar with the red Stella sign above the faded green door.

When she'd walked past this bar with Guy during her second week in town, there had been an old man sitting in the window, looking into the wet street, large bags beneath his eyes. A face straight out of a Rembrandt painting. A face like Dehanschutter's. She'd said this to Guy, and he'd given her that amused half-smile, saying something about how Americans saw Europe as one huge museum. She'd argued back that she'd lived in Europe as a child, *and* as an adult, and didn't see everything as if it was a painting from the distant past and – furthermore – it was a fact that Rembrandt painted Dutch faces and Dehanschutter – because of his name – was probably a descendent of some *Flamand* and – another fact – she'd studied genetics and the faces of two hundred years ago wouldn't be that much different from the faces of today – barring another Mongol invasion. Then she'd gone on about immigrants coming into Northern Europe from North Africa, India, Indonesia, how a new invasion was just beginning, and how Europeans were just beginning to understand the strange love/hate relationship Americans and Canadians had for diversity in their own nation.

'I mean, look at me,' she said, stopping on the pavement about a block from the bar. 'I have a past that's this far away from Europe,' she said, holding her thumb and forefinger half an inch apart in front of Guy's face. 'My father is originally from Germany and – apparently – his father was some low level clerk in the whole Nazi scheme of things. He won't talk about it. When my father was seventeen he headed for Toronto, wanting to erase that past, I think. On the other side, my mother's family immigrated to Philadelphia from Russia just seconds before the holocaust. The rest of the family was murdered. You see the confusion? Eventually Belgium is going to be full of people just like me.'

'It already is,' Guy had answered. 'Cambodia, Congo...'

The brick bar with the Stella sign was closed. There was no old man staring wistfully through the glass. The only other passenger on the bus was the woman with the green plastic kerchief, sitting directly behind the driver. She said something to the driver about the rain. The driver looked at the woman through his rearview mirror and nodded, solemn, then downshifted as the bus began the long ascent up the hill towards Saint-Ellon, named after the saint who had been Woelfred's teacher.

'A real saint,' Guy had said, when they'd entered Saint-Ellon on that first walk. 'Do you know the story?'

She told him she'd heard it from Dehanschutter in the brasserie. How Saint Woelfred was taken off the roster of saints by the church in the nineteenth century. 'But what is a saint?' Dehanschutter had said to her, waving his Turkish cigarette dangerously close to her face as he gestured his disgust. 'Nothing but an image in someone else's mind, really.' He had then nodded to the people at the tables behind them. 'They have no idea about her. I know, though.'

Guy shook his head. 'Dehanschutter thinks he's an authority on everything.'

'He told me he was the one who'd done the research that proved Saint Woelfred didn't exist.'

Guy stopped walking. 'What?'

'He said that everyone in the area had forgotten what Saint Woelfred was all about – so he had pulled the plug.'

Guy covered his face with his hands. 'Dehanschutter!'

'He quoted the Bible. At least I think that's what he was quoting: "The Lord giveth and the Lord taketh away." Then he winked at me. Maybe it was his way of flirting.'

120

Guy dropped his hands from his face, looked at Liesl. 'Dehanschutter's a mean, bitter old man, but I've never thought him insane.'

The bus moved across Saint-Ellon's Grand Place, past the First World War memorial, then slowed and stopped for an old couple in rubber boots. She recognised them. The Sempoles. Guy had pointed them out to her in the brasserie during her third week in Villon. 'I want you to see something,' he'd said, then had spun in a slow half circle on the bar stool and nodded towards the tables.

There were only five other people in the room: two boys leaning on the jukebox, scanning the selections, finding them all wanting; a young man playing a video game near the toilet; and an old couple sitting at a table near the window. The old man had a pink bald head, bright pink jowls, and looked over one hundred years old. He sat opposite a woman wearing a grey wool coat. All Liesl could see of the woman was the back of her head. The old man stared into his glass of beer.

'Who are they?' she asked Guy.

Guy raised a finger to his lips. 'Just watch.'

Five minutes went by and nothing happened. The old man lifted his glass, took a sip. The woman did the same. No words. Bored, Liesl started to turn back to the bar, but Guy grabbed her wrist. 'No,' he said, eyes still on the couple. 'You never know when it's going to happen.'

Just as she was about to say 'What?' the old man leaned forward and whispered something into the old woman's ear. The old woman nodded as the old man slid back into his chair. They both took a sip from their glasses at the same time. Guy looked at Liesl, smiling. 'They've been doing that for as long as

I've been coming in here,' he said. 'Sometimes *she* leans forward and says something to *him*.'

'What do you think they say to each other?'

Guy shrugged, turned back to the bar, lit a cigarette he'd bummed off Dehanschutter, squinting as the smoke floated past his eyes, up towards the stuffed birds lining the shelf above the bar mirror.

'Aren't you curious?' Liesl asked.

'I'm not sure if that's important.'

A typical Guy line.

The old couple paid their fare without saying a word to the driver and sat down behind the woman with the green plastic kerchief. The bus chugged and groaned out of the square through a winding one-way street, wide enough for only one car. How the bus squeezed through this particular street was always a miracle to her. Liesl wiped the fog off the bus window, peered out. Walls and windows seemed to scrape right up against the glass. She caught her reflection as the bus passed window after window.

On that first walk she'd had to take small steps up this narrow road so Guy could keep up.

'How can you not support the rally?' she had asked, incredulous at his willingness to sit on the sidelines and watch. 'Activists are coming from all over Europe. Contexture is going to perform.'

'I didn't say I didn't support the rally,' he'd answered. 'I just said that these things come and go. Invasions, wars, cement factories. The sun's not forever.'

'But that's just the point!' she'd shouted, her voice echoing back and forth between the close walls. Her usual hysterics.

Raising her voice. As if that had ever helped get anything through anyone's thick skull. 'It won't go away. New waste is coming in, being imported from all over Europe. This stuff is poison. It will leak into your vegetables, into the soil, for thousands and thousands of years! It *does* matter what we do because if you stop it here and some people in Italy stop it there and then someone in Denmark stops it there – you see? Things *have* to change. If there's nowhere to put the shit, then they have to stop making it!'

Guy laughed, raised his hands in an act of surrender. 'I think – most of the time – people shout on this side and then people shout on that side and then some people way over there begin shouting and no one is really aware of their real motives. It's important to find out the real reason you're doing something so your actions aren't just useless motion. Understand the mechanics behind all the distraction. Do you see?'

No, she didn't see.

She still didn't. If you wait around to map out every single twist and turn of the mind, you'd never do anything.

But, in the end, he'd decided to participate, hadn't he?

Liesl caught a quick glimpse of a young woman in a white tank top and black panties staring out of a first floor window. The image filled her reflection for a second, then it was gone.

Illusion. Guy's favourite word.

But everything is not illusion. Toxic waste, the thin film of fog from her breath coating the glass, these past two months with Guy. Why was it so hard for him to figure it out? She didn't want her time here to end as some kind of hazy memory, another tourist adventure. Pictures stuffed into a box in the closet. *I remember when I was in Belgium... there was this magician...*

Just outside Saint-Ellon, the bus stopped for a man with shoulder-length greasy brown hair and a large, old, brown wool sweater. A pack of cigarettes bulged from a chest pocket underneath the sweater. He fumbled with his change, put a few coins into the meter. The bus driver said something to him and he smiled, shrugged, put some more change in the meter. The driver shook his head, told him he'd paid too much and the man frowned, held a few franc notes up to the driver's face and said 'Again, more?' The driver shook his head vigorously, clearly annoyed, and waved him through. When the new passenger turned to walk down the aisle, he caught Liesl smiling at the exchange and smiled back, deep lines on either side of his long, thin nose. He looked to be in his late forties. He sat down in the seat across the aisle from Liesl, still smiling at her.

He didn't look Belgian. Spanish, French (from the south), maybe Italian? But what did she know? What was Belgian? A patchwork-quilt country, like almost every other nation state, cobbled together from various treaties. You take this piece, I'll take that, and we'll put a fence here.

'Think about it,' Raoul had said, sitting on the edge of his bed back in Paris, pulling on his boots, 'walk up to any imaginary line drawn by any country, walk up to any fence, and both sides look exactly the same. The ground, the people, always the same. There's no difference between the people living on either side of the border between France and Belgium as far as I can tell. The land's the same. Work rises out of the land, so they all have the same history of work.'

'Are you going to Villon?' Liesl asked the man across the aisle in slow French. He continued to smile, obviously unable to make out what she'd just said.

At that moment, the bus jerked forward and great billows

of black diesel exhaust poured from the rear of the bus. They groaned their way up a long, wide avenue, lurching slowly away from Saint-Ellon. Large houses lined the road. Round, voluptuously sculpted bushes skirted the front edge of each lawn. These were the houses of the SHAPE generals, Guy had told her on that first walk.

Liesl inched to the aisle-edge of her seat, one hand on the back of the seat in front of her. 'Where are you from?'

He laughed. A network of wrinkles appeared across his face (mid-fifties?). 'Germany,' he said. 'My French, it's not...'

She switched to German. 'Are you going to the rally against the dumps in Villon?'

'Rally?'

'The kermesse, then?'

He seemed to ponder the question for a moment, staring at a spot above Liesl's head, then said, 'A rally against dumps *and* a kermesse?'

She told him about the factory's plans, about the eco-rally, about Saint Woelfred and her decommission as a true saint.

He pursed his lips and nodded when she finished. 'Interesting. How do they know this saint never existed?'

'She was supposedly a disciple of Saint Ellon, the namesake for the town we just passed. A hermit who lived in the woods somewhere in the province of Hainault. But in the mid-nineteenth century, an ancient manuscript was discovered in a local monastery – the first history of Saint Ellon. It seems Saint Ellon had always been a hermit. No disciples. He'd just communed with the birds and bees. Are you Catholic by any chance?'

The German shook his head. 'No, no. I am...' He looked up at the ceiling of the bus, thought for a second, then said: 'There is always an explanation for things. I tend to believe that Jesus was a man whose fingers were quicker than the eye.'

'I have a friend in Villon who is a magician,' Liesl said. 'You two would probably get along very well.'

A rusted fence ran alongside the road. Beyond the fence stretched half a kilometre of overgrown grass, a few scrub trees – the remnants of what used to be a vast, well manicured estate. At the end of the stretch of grass stood a ramshackle château. The roof was caving in; windows broken, boarded up.

Liesl pointed over the German's shoulder at the château. 'That used to be the house of a man who owned a glass factory.'

She and Guy had ended up in front of the rusted fence enclosing the mansion property. 'I was studying heat shock proteins up in Newfoundland...' she was saying, hands on the fence, still talking to fill in the space between them, staring out across the wet grass, '... stuffing lobsters into small jars of near-boiling water, pulling them out, slapping them on ice. And while they lay stunned, I'd take out these surgical clippers, stab through the carapace...' She'd lifted a hand, clutching imaginary clippers, bringing them down onto the top wire of the fence.

'Then I'd take a sample of the tissue, grind it up, add chemicals, load the proteins into this gel-like substance... poly... poly-something... attach a positive and negative charge to the solution –'

Guy winced. 'Sounds like Frankenstein. And you did all this for what?'

She explained to him how the shock proteins protect an organism when they come under heat stress. 'They keep other proteins in the body from unfolding, dying. My work was part of a research project trying to figure out how to create a solution that would keep transplant organs intact for longer periods of time. Polyacrylamide gel! That's the name! I can't believe I remembered it after all this time.'

'So, you thought you were doing it for the greater good?'

'That's just my point. What's the greater good? Most transplants go to those who can afford them. There's more money spent on research to cure symptoms than search for causes. Diet, everyday living health issues, corporate dumping of toxins into drinking water – science isn't interested in that. It's interested in money. Solving little bits and pieces of the puzzle without daring to look at the big picture. My God, the solution to shutting down the whole toxic dump project is to just stop making the shit. But there's no money in that.'

Guy put his hand through the wire fence, palm up. 'I think it's snowing.' Tiny grains fell into his hand. She looked up into the grey sky. Sure enough, the drizzling rain was turning to snow.

Guy closed his fingers over his wet palm, pulled it back through the gap in the fence, and stuffed both hands into his pockets.

'I went into biology because I wanted to be out in the world,' she continued, 'to be *with* the world, you know? And all that time, while I was boiling lobsters, out beyond the doors of the lab was the entire coast of Newfoundland. Have you ever seen pictures of that coast?'

'Maybe. I can't remember.' He looked up into the grey sky, blinking as the snow grains fell onto his face.

'It's beautiful. Waves beating rocks, spray shooting into the sky, the way the white foam runs down runnels and cracks in the cliffs.' She curled her fingers around the top wire, stared at the château for a couple of seconds, then said, 'So I quit.'

He rested a cold hand over hers.

The snow continued to fall. The smell of rust grew stronger as the grains of snow touched the metal fence and began to melt. They watched the snow for several minutes in silence, then Guy nodded at the château and told her it belonged to a man who owned a glass factory outside Brussels.

'The rumour is that he collaborated with the Germans during the Second World War,' he said. 'The glass works were used in the service of the Reich, of course. That couldn't be helped. It's said that many parties – with members of the German high command – took place in that château. Carousing all night, while the rest of the countryside was cold, hungry. They shipped in prostitutes from Paris. When the Germans left, the factory owner was found murdered in his apartment in Brussels. Throat cut.' Guy swiped the width of his neck with an index finger, stuck out his tongue, and rolled his eyes.

'His family claimed he'd been a spy for the allies and had been executed wrongfully. A tragic mistake. Of course, no one believed the family – a wife and daughter, I think. Maybe there was a son. I don't remember. The place had been badly vandalised right after the war, and fearing for their safety, the family decided to leave it empty for a while. Some time in the fifties the daughter took up residence here. The story goes that she held a séance...'

'You're making this up.'

Guy shook his head, still staring at the château. But there was that smile. 'No, no,' he said, 'it's public record. She hired some medium to come in and contact her father from beyond the grave. They say she was looking to clear her father's name. I have no idea.'

'Through a séance?'

128

'Oh, it gets worse,' Guy said, turning to her. 'The night of the séance, it's said that the sky opened up above the house and angels appeared. Avenging angels, wielding fiery swords, and they lit the house on fire. Poof – gone.'

'The daughter died?'

'Everyone in the house. Gone. Smoke. Their remains were never found.'

'But that's terrible. The daughter couldn't be blamed for anything. Did your mother tell you that story when you were a child?'

Guy shook his head. 'It's just a story that goes around.'

'Sounds a lot like the story of the angels coming down out of the sky with fiery swords during the battle of Mons in 1914, sending the German army into retreat. You know that one?'

Guy smiled and snickered, a kind of quick huff through the nose. Mist shot out of his red nostrils, onto the back of his hands clinging to the fence. 'Maybe they were the same angels.' He nodded toward the château. 'Do you want to go?'

'Interesting story,' the German said to Liesl.

The woman in the green plastic kerchief looked over her shoulder, through the space between the heads of the old couple behind her, directly at Liesl. Liesl tried to remember if she had actually talked to the woman.

The German's eyes roamed down to Liesl's breasts, then back to her face. 'Do you believe that story?' he said, shifting one leg over the other, lightly touching the cigarette pack beneath his sweater with the tips of his fingers, as if he was making sure it was still there.

'I don't know,' she said.

She had followed Guy right through the broken front door into a great empty hall. About three metres from the front door was a wide staircase, ascending to the blackened first floor landing. The carpeting on the stairs was torn, shredded, wet from an opening to the sky in the vault of the high ceiling. Snow grains fell silently through a thin shaft of grey light. She could hear dripping coming from somewhere down a hallway to the left of the stairs.

'Creepy,' she said. Her voice did not echo like she thought it would, but hung like the mist of her breath in front of her face for a second, then faded.

'Yes, but a child's paradise,' Guy said. 'I used to play here as a boy. So many rooms to explore, things to see.'

He took her hand, led her down the hall to the left of the staircase. Boards beneath the wet carpet crackled dangerously.

'Is this safe?'

Guy snickered again – that quick huff out of his nostrils – and the sound sent two birds zigzagging above their heads. He poked his head in each doorway they passed, telling her what used to be in each room. 'This was some kind of study, some books left on the shelves. It looks as if most of the furniture has been taken.'

She followed Guy through the last door at the end of the hall, planting her feet exactly where he did as he picked his way around the holes in the floor, to the centre of the room.

Guy scanned the singed fireplace bricks. 'It's amazing how when a place lies in ruins,' he said, turning in a slow circle, 'it becomes something more. More than it was.'

'More ghosts,' Liesl answered.

Guy shook his head. 'A kind of emptiness that's finally been given a chance to come out and show itself. The original illusion of the place, I think.' He grabbed at something invisible in the air above him, lowered his closed fist to the side of her face, then, giving her that half-smile, opened it.

A bat shot from his palm and sailed crazily this way and that around the room, swooping low over both their heads, disappearing through a broken window. She screamed.

Silence. The dripping, far off. Guy stared out of the window where the bat had disappeared.

'What the fuck was that?' she finally managed to say.

He put his finger to his lips, turned and walked towards the blackened fireplace. His back to her, he crouched and reached into the black emptiness, pulled out a long-stem purple and yellow lily. He stood up, turned to face her, calm, placid – as if what he'd just done was the most natural thing in the world – and picked his way across the rotting floor back to where she stood.

He'd planned this all along. She was elated, frightened.

'So, what is your business in Villon, if you're not going to the kermesse or the rally,' Liesl asked the German. 'Are you visiting friends?'

'Something like that,' he said.

'Who? I might know who it is.'

'Are you from Villon?' the German said.

She had taken the lily from Guy, twirled it once, slowly. 'How did you do that? Will you tell me?'

Guy had shaken his head. 'It's just an illusion.'

Their faces were inches apart and he still had not kissed her. Why the magic show and the lily if he was not going to kiss her?

'But the lily is real,' she'd said and touched one of the petals lightly to his lips.

That first time, he had tasted of creek stones. So cold. Both their lips were cold. And there'd been a hint of iron.

'I'm writing an article, a story, about the dumps, the rally,' Liesl said to the German. 'Interviewing the townsfolk.'

'What paper do you write for?'

'I'm freelance.' She looked over the German's shoulder. His window had fogged up again, but the dark silhouettes beyond the glass looked like the trees at the edge of the property of the Mézières Hotel, across from the chain link fence that surrounded the SHAPE compound. She turned, wiped fog off her own window.

Walking out of the château that day Guy had winced, doubled over, grabbed his right knee with both hands. She'd helped him to the staircase. He told her he just needed to rest for a couple of minutes and then they could head back. But when he stood up again, he stumbled, almost fell, grabbed at her. It terrified her to see someone who'd been in such command only moments before – bats flying out of his hands – almost unable to walk. His arm draped over her shoulders, she held him up as they walked back to the road, towards the Mézières Hotel where they waited for the bus back to Mons.

There were two fences, one inside the other, at the SHAPE compound. The first fence had three somewhat harmless lines of barbed wire at the top. Then, a no man's land where soldiers with automatic weapons walked large German Shepherds. Behind the soldiers and dogs the second fence loomed, topped with jagged razor wire. A group of large, square cement buildings stood beyond the perimeters of the second fence.

Raoul's father had worked in Nuclear Operations inside that compound. His office had been deep below the surface, encased in lead.

The large building just beyond the front gate of the compound housed a little bar, Raoul had told her. There were posters on the wall behind the bar with slogans about keeping silent. Admonitions to the officers and enlisted men who worked within the compound to maintain a code of silence about what they did each day at work. Things like: 'Loose lips sink ships'. She remembered Raoul describing a poster of two men talking over beers while someone at another table was listening in, head cocked towards the two.

Games.

Liesl had rested a hand on Guy's shoulder, feeling the sudden tremor as pain shot up his leg, through his body. Snow fell around them, covering her shoulders, his, the backs of the dogs walking the perimeters inside the compound. What could she do?

'When we get back to the campground,' she'd said, 'I can massage your leg.'

Guy had closed his eyes, leaned against a streetlight pole. 'I should just go home.' He nodded across the street at the bus stop in front of the hotel. 'I can catch a bus back to Villon from there.'

No, don't leave.

Liesl turned back to the German. He had scooted to the aisle edge of his seat. She nodded towards her window. 'That's SHAPE – Supreme Headquarters Allied Powers Europe. Do you know it?'

The German nodded. 'I know someone who went to school

there,' he said and fished the cigarette pack out from beneath his sweater, placing it against his thigh, underneath his hand.

It was dark when she led Guy across the wet campground grass to her tent, his arm still draped over her shoulder. Once inside the tent, they had crawled under her sleeping bag, fully clothed, and held each other, trying to get warm.

'We'd get warm faster if we were naked,' she'd whispered. She'd been serious. Well, half-serious. Impulsive was probably the right word.

Guy had opened his eyes wide, made that snorting laugh through his nose.

She'd laughed back. 'No, really. The heat's trapped inside our clothes.'

Was it strange that first time? It's always strange the first time. His cold cheeks, smooth as stone; the way he gently nudged her, pulled her on top of him, so that even though she was on top, she felt – the next morning – unsure about who had been in control.

Hocusem Pocusem.

She stayed awake long after he fell asleep, watching the shadows of the tiny grains of snow fall through the campground light, onto the tent, then turn to water, and slide.

The bus turned down rue Leopold, the houses appearing farther and farther apart until they descended onto a broken, cobbled switchback that led into the tiny village of Caix, manoeuvring around the small, cobbled Place, passing the open double-wide doors of a stone stable. A boy standing next to a brown horse just inside the stable waved at the bus driver and the driver waved back.

On the opposite side of the Place from the stable stood a tiny, ancient stone chapel. Liesl quickly wiped the fog away from her window again and beckoned the German over, pointing at the chapel just as they passed it. 'That's the shrine to Saint Woelfred.'

It was a small, dark, circular room, lit only with ten or twelve candles, burning on a black iron stand next to an altar. Beneath the iron stand sat two small boxes: a shoebox of white candles and a locked tin box with a coin slot at the top. Flame shadows flickered across the walls, across the two straight-backed wood pews in the centre of the room, across the face of what looked like a black plastic Virgin Mary sitting on an altar built into the far wall, directly in front of the pews.

It reminded her of the cave where a hermit was found, perfectly preserved, in Rocamadour, France, and set up as a shrine to Mary. The houses of Rocamadour were all built into the side of a cliff, facing a narrow switchback road that climbed hundreds of feet into the air, until it reached the cave. Inside the cave were one thousand candles, at least, lighting the glistening rock ceiling, and a thin black stone statue of the Virgin. Liesl stood inside that cave feeling as if, at any moment, one of her ancient ancestors – forty thousand years old, hairy and naked – was going to walk in and begin painting something on the rock. The painted caves of Lascaux and Les Eyzies weren't that far away. She felt a strange continuity, a connection to something far older than anything she could imagine.

Who *was* Mary?

The door of the chapel closed behind her and she stood next to a font of holy water for almost a minute, not knowing what to do. Finally, out of respect, awe, she dipped her finger in the pool and touched her forehead first, then her right breast, her left, and, after hesitating a moment – finger suspended in the air in front of her chest – she touched a spot on her red sweater just above her navel. It was the wrong order, but what the hell.

The door opened behind her and a boy peered into the chapel.

'I'm sorry,' she said, 'am I allowed to be in here?'

The boy seemed not to understand the question. He frowned.

'Am I allowed in here?' she repeated.

'It's a chapel,' he said. 'I thought you were someone else.' He slipped through the opening into the quiet room and stood next to her.

'Is that the Virgin?' she whispered.

He shook his head and whispered back: 'No, no. That's Saint Woelfred. This is her house.'

'But I thought Saint Woelfred didn't exist.'

The boy looked at the statue of the saint, confused again. He pursed his lips. 'But… she lived here.' He looked back at Liesl. 'I thought you were someone else.'

'Can I light a candle?' Liesl asked, still whispering.

The boy shrugged. 'It's not my house.'

She walked up to the candles, fished in her pocket for a coin, produced a five franc piece and dropped it into the slot. The sound of the coin hitting the bottom of the box resounded in the tiny chapel and the flames seemed to flicker in response. She lit a fresh candle, set it next to the others, and sat down on the front pew, directly in front of the altar. The boy sat next to her. The smell of manure from his boots hung

136

in the air around her face.

It was a cold and ancient place. She was glad she had come without Guy. He probably would have made the saint disappear for the boy. Why couldn't he see how the beauty of such a place could draw her in, intoxicate her so. She wrapped her hands in the hem of her sweater.

'Are there a lot of people who come here to see Saint Woelfred?' she whispered to the boy.

He shrugged again. 'No. Mostly the same people.'

'From Villon?'

The boy stared at the altar. 'I don't know.'

'Who did you think I was?' she whispered.

'I don't know her name. She has black hair like you. She brings things.'

'Things?'

The boy nodded. 'She leaves them here.'

'What sorts of things?'

'Stones, mostly. Flowers. Shoes, once. A shell from the sea...' He paused, his eyebrows almost touching in concentration. 'There was a robin's egg.'

'The whole egg?'

It pained Liesl to think that someone was so desperate they'd steal an egg from a bird.

'*Non*, a little blue half-a-shell. My mother thinks she has lost a daughter or a son.'

'That's sad.'

'But the next morning after she comes, the things are always gone.'

'Have you seen who takes them?'

The boy was confused again. 'No one takes them,' he said. 'No one comes, no one goes. I live right across there,' the boy lifted his hand over the back of the pew, pointing in the direction of the stables, 'and I can see the chapel from my bedroom window.'

'Then?' Liesl let the word hang in the air between her and the boy.

His eyes shifted from Liesl to the statue.

2 The Illusionist

Marc spun in a wide circle around the edge of the Place, tyres shaking violently over the uneven cobbles, scattering the crows that had been feeding on all the dead fish. 'I don't think I've been this hungry since I was a child!' he shouted above the whine of the engine.

Guy poked his head out of the window, scanned the roof gutters, checking to see if his handiwork from the night before remained invisible. He had recruited the only person in town who he knew wouldn't talk to help him set everything up for the rally trick. Poisson. The fog had been so thick Guy was barely able to see Poisson's face down at the bottom of the ladder. There were times when the only way he had known the other man was still down there keeping the ladder steady was when the big man had sucked on his cigarette – a faint orange glow through mist.

When they had finished the job, he had given Poisson a bottle of wine. The big man had immediately opened it and offered Guy the first swig. Guy took a swallow, handed it back to Poisson. After Poisson drank, he nodded at Guy, turned and walked off into the fog without a word. The big man hadn't said a word the entire night.

138

Everything looked as it should. Like there was nothing up there. The low grey clouds were perfect cover. But as he'd said to Liesl so many times – too many times – the Place was not a theatre. And he had only performed the trick with Chiqui.

It would be a miracle if he actually pulled it off. What had possessed him to agree to do such a thing?

Marc punched the accelerator, steered the car up rue Lefebvre, towards the three-way intersection where Lefebvre met Lemaire and des Ecoles. 'Food is our first love!' he shouted. 'It very rarely lets us down! It's something a kid can sink his teeth into!'

Guy planted his hands on the dashboard. 'Where are you going?'

'It's right there in his mouth, his belly,' Marc continued, 'eventually sliding out of his ass! Real!'

At the three-way intersection Marc swung the wheel to the left and the Citroën squealed onto rue des Ecoles, bumping over more fish, shooting past Dehanschutter's child coffin display window.

'Where are you going?' Guy shouted again. 'I have to get out!'

'Women are the same as food!' Marc shouted back, weaving back and forth across the road, trying to avoid the fish. He glanced quickly over at Guy. 'If you are denied either, you will soon die. Am I not right?'

'Why are you doing this?'

Marc grinned, downshifted. The pinging and clanging from the strained engine died down. 'Women are something you can actually sink into,' he said. 'Substantial, you know? Too much in life is insubstantial.'

'C'mon Marc, what's going on?'

They sped by a boy standing in front of the school, a fish in each hand. Marc glanced over at Guy again. 'You know what women like? They like a man who goes his own way.'

'I am currently not going my own way.'

Marc rolled his window down, tossed his spent cigarette onto the road. 'Fear not,' he said, 'I'll get you back to the Place in plenty of time to meet the German.' He glanced at the clock above the car radio. 'It'll be at least another hour before she gets there. And what were you going to do anyway with all that time on your hands? Stand around in the Place with the fish and crows? We're only going to Spierry. There's a man there that has something I need for kermesse.'

Spierry was just ten minutes distant. They could easily be back in Villon within a half hour. In time to meet Liesl, wait with her for Contexture to arrive. Guy took a deep breath, exhaled.

The last of the grey terraced houses gave way to fields. The fields gave way to the chain link fence of an abandoned quarry.

'I've got it!' Marc said, rapidly approaching the stone viaduct that marked the westernmost edge of Villon.

'Got what?'

'The fish,' Marc said, pulling another cigarette out of his pack, slipping it between his lips, tossing the pack to Guy. 'It was Poisson. April Fools', one week too late. That'd be just like him. Not knowing the proper date. Fish of April!'

Guy pulled several cigarettes out of the pack, slipped them into his coat pocket for later, then put one in his mouth. 'That's absurd, where would Poisson get all the fish?' He pulled the cigarette lighter out of the console, lit up. 'How did he get them all the way down rue des Ecoles, all the way out to my mother's pasture? He can barely stand at the best of times.'

'Maybe Marie helped him,' Marc said. 'Have you ever noticed that woman's eyes? Uncanny.'

'You're serious?' Guy rolled down his window, flicked ash into the wind as they passed beneath the stone viaduct.

'There's something dark going on with her eyes,' Marc said. 'I wouldn't say it was sinister, but if anyone in town had the ability to create all those fish out of nothing, it'd be her. Of course, no one has that kind of ability.'

Guy shook his head, looked out at the long grass field stretching away from the road as they headed up the long rise toward the village of Caix.

Wait. He checked his side mirror.

'The fish have stopped.'

Marc rolled down his window, glanced out. 'When did they stop?'

Guy exhaled smoke out of the window. 'Must have been somewhere after the viaduct.'

The car crested the hill and Marc downshifted as the first buildings of Caix came into view. Marc pointed at the tiny stone hut that served as a shrine to Saint Woelfred. 'I dropped Liesl off here once,' he said. 'She was hiking out here to see the shrine.' He glanced over at Guy. 'I didn't take her to be religious.'

Guy frowned. Liesl had failed to mention to him that she'd hitched a ride to the shrine with Marc. 'She's fascinated by mystery,' Guy said.

'The mystery of the cross and all that? I thought she was Jewish.'

'She's fascinated by mystery in general.'

Marc tossed his cigarette out of the window, shook his head. 'All that candlelight and penitence and confession and crown of thorns nonsense wearies me. So morbid. Why do you think women are so fascinated by that sort of thing? Remember how my mother was always on her knees in the church. Your mother, too. Everyone's mother. I've often wondered whether they were like that when they were young.' Marc glanced over at Guy. 'But how could they be? What man in his right mind would go anywhere near that sort of thing?

'When they're young they seem free of all that,' Marc continued, 'but they're just hiding it from you. It's been planted like a dark seed inside them by their mothers, by their mother's mothers. A disease of shadows and weeping.' He looked over at Guy. 'Why do you think most men are immune to it?'

'I don't think the mystery Liesl is interested in is about shadows and weeping,' Guy said.

Guy and Liesl stood at the end of the dark hallway of La Mairie, the door to the mayor's office on the right, the town library on the left.

'No, no, no,' Liesl whispered. 'Are you insane? The police could show up any minute.'

Guy pulled a key out of his pocket, flourished it dramatically – the way Chiqui would have done – then inserted it into the mayor's office door, turned the lock, and pushed the door open. He stepped into the mayor's dark office, holding the door for her. She stood her ground in the hallway, arms across her chest.

There was one lone desk below a small shuttered window. Nothing had changed since the last time he'd snuck into the office. The same papers were piled on top of the desk and the same ashtray filled with old butts was still sitting on top of the pile of papers.

'What is so important in here that I have to risk arrest to see?' Liesl whispered, stepping cautiously into the room, still hugging her chest.

Guy moved across the dark room to a cabinet next to the desk, pulled an ornate gold and red wooden box from one of the cabinet shelves, and set it on the desk.

'Holy shit,' Liesl hissed. 'Woelfred's reliquary!'

Using the same key, Guy unlocked the box, lifted the lid, and pulled out a blue velvet sack, tied off with a gold cord, then lowered himself onto the carpet, crossed his legs, and motioned for Liesl to do the same.

'Do you have the lighter?' he said as he undid the cord and turned the sack upside down, dumping the contents of the bag onto the carpet. Liesl fished through her backpack, produced a lighter, flicked it over the sack's contents.

There was a little glass vial, a small fragment of what looked like a finger bone, a cutting of hair wrapped in gold string, and two molars. Guy held the vial up to the flame.

'There's a nail paring in there, I think,' he said. 'It looks more like someone's large toenail than a fingernail.'

Liesl handed him the lighter, took the glass vial, examined it carefully.

Guy picked up the molars, shook them in his hand, threw them onto the carpet in front of Liesl like dice. Entranced, she put the vial down and picked up the teeth.

'These aren't human,' she whispered. 'They're primate.'

Guy picked up the bone fragment, held it next to the flame. 'I took this to Dr Souzain one night,' he said, 'to find out whether it was human or not.'

'You've done this before.'

'He said it was probably dog.'

Liesl held the flame close to his face, searched his eyes. 'Why did you bring me here?' she whispered. Before he could answer she said: 'To show me that all this is a fraud, more illusion? It's not like I believe in saints. You know that, don't you?'

'Nothing like that,' Guy said. 'I just wanted you to see the insides of Villon. Knowing how the trick is done is a kind of magic, you know? It's *my* kind of magic.'

'There are other kinds of magic,' Liesl said, then held the flame over the teeth in the palm of her hand. A minute went by. Was she upset? He opened his mouth, almost told her that he loved her, but said nothing. What did it matter? She would be leaving soon.

Illusions chasing after illusions.

'It's strange, though,' Liesl finally whispered, 'even though the molars aren't human – obviously not from Woelfred – they seem to tingle in my palm.' She handed them over to Guy, then flicked the lighter off.

He sat in the dark, eyes closed, pretending to concentrate on the teeth. After a minute, he opened his eyes, looked up at Liesl.

'If you say it's just an illusion,' Liesl whispered, 'I'll slug you.'

At the edge of Spierry's Grand Place, Marc cut right, down a narrow alley, and pulled in front of an empty shop window. Behind the dusty glass sat a metal shelf full of empty aquariums. Above the window, a small faded sign announced 'Tropical Fish'.

'This is our stop,' Marc said and hopped out of the car.

Guy slowly opened the car door, reluctant to get out. 'You're buying tropical fish?'

Marc peered through the window. 'What's hidden inside this place is far more interesting than fish, my friend.'

144

Guy sighed, slid out of the car.

Marc tried the door and it creaked open. Inside the shop, aquariums were scattered everywhere. Most contained nothing but cobwebs. Some contained a few overturned boxes of bolts, nuts – the spilled contents heavy with dust. A dusty light bulb dangled from the ceiling above the shop counter. On a shelf behind the counter sat a few boxes of fish food. The writing on the boxes had faded from exposure to sunlight – red to pink, yellow to grey, blue to bone.

Marc crouched at the foot of the counter, pulled a dried fish from one of the aquariums and held it up to the feeble light coming through the window, squinting through the brown translucent skin. 'I loved this place when I was a kid. You ever come here?'

Guy lifted a doll head out of an aquarium sitting on a shelf next to a beaded curtain, held it up for Marc to see. Hairless, eye sockets empty, face torn. A patina of grey light rolled across the doll's scratched forehead as he turned it slowly with the tips of his fingers.

'I didn't know this place even existed,' Guy said.

Marc tossed the dried fish into a corner. 'So, I'm curious. Do you love the German?'

Guy placed the doll head back into the aquarium. Did he? Did it even matter if he did?

'I'm not sure that's any of your business.'

Marc laughed. 'Of course it's my business. I introduced her to you at the brasserie. I am responsible for your happiness now.'

Guy parted the beaded curtain, looked down a dark, narrow hall at a closed blue door. 'What is love?'

'What do you mean "what is love?" Love is love. And I know you know what love is. I remember how you used to walk past the Ducasse house all the time, hoping that American would be standing outside.'

Guy let the bead curtain fall back, turned to Marc. 'I was fifteen.'

'I've seen the way you look at Liesl,' Marc said, lifting a faded orange plastic octopus out of the aquarium on the shop counter. 'Love is love.'

Guy lit Marieke's cigarette, then his own, glanced up at the second floor window of the building opposite the backstage door of The Bacchanal. He could see the dim outline of the head and shoulders of the old woman who lived there. Watching, always watching. He had recently started doing tricks just for her amusement during smoke breaks between sets. Sometimes she leaned forward, elbows on the sill, her lined face thrown into relief by the dull blue fluorescent bulb over the backstage door.

Guy reached out, pretended to grab something from behind Marieke's ear, produced a fingernail sized whitish-grey cockle shell, and held it in front of her face. Marieke broke into a big, chipped-tooth grin and clapped her hands. Guy dropped the shell into the pocket of her sweat jacket.

They both had one more performance left. Chiqui was trying out a new trick: floating two fish out over the heads of the audience before making them disappear in a puff of smoke. The trick had initially been rejected by Bakker, the brooding manager of The Bacchanal, telling Chiqui it wasn't sexy enough. 'People come here for the sex,' he'd complained. 'They come here to be entertained,' Chiqui had calmly replied. 'If it's not sexy, then it's got to be funny,' the manager had shot back. Chiqui vowed it was funny.

As far as Guy could tell, there was nothing remotely funny about it. Puzzling, yes. Interesting, yes. Not funny. It would probably be pulled from the act.

Marieke had the last slot of the night, right after Chiqui and Guy's act, appearing on all fours, naked except for some white lamb's ears clipped to her head, a ring of woolly fluff around her midriff. The routine was the same every night: Alain or Jansen would come out of the wings, naked, holding a shepherd's crook, then work themselves into a guilty go at the sheep, eventually thrusting away from behind.

Guy glanced up at the second floor window again. 'You want to get a drink after?'

Marieke nodded, focusing on something at the end of the alley. When Alain or Jansen were busy pounding away, she would sometimes cock her head back, open her mouth slightly, and stare out into the audience with a face so terrifyingly open – the eyes of a child desperate for an answer – that it had once pulled a shocked gasp from someone in the audience.

She fiddled with the shell in her pocket. Guy studied the side of her face under the sickly blue light. She looked so young onstage. Those big, brown eyes. But it was all distraction. Close up, her face was a bit worn – pinched – beginning to show the effects of the alcohol, coke. For some reason he found it comforting.

She pulled the hood of her jacket over her head against the damp air, pointed her cigarette at the trash cans at the end of the alley. 'I saw fox here last night. In garbage.'

'It was probably a dog.'

She shook her head. 'No, fox.'

He couldn't place her accent. Romanian? Bulgarian? Marieke was obviously not her real name. No one ever asked questions of anyone else at The Bacchanal. People drifted in, out. She was probably Greek.

The backstage door opened and Chiqui poked her head out. She glanced at Marieke, then at Guy, the glitter around her eyes sparkling under the wan fluorescent light. 'Can I talk to you for a minute?'

Chiqui led him back to the dressing room, shut the door behind them. The room smelled of new sweat layered on old. She tossed her top hat onto a pile of clothes on a wood bench.

'I like that Marieke,' she said, clearing a space on the bench to sit. 'She's an interesting one.' She sat down, studied Guy's face for a minute, then said: 'Please don't do with her what you normally do with your girls.'

'What are you talking about?'

Chiqui patted the space next to her on the bench, indicating for Guy to sit down. Guy remained standing. 'You keep your distance until they finally give up and disappear on their own,' she said. 'It's an interesting strategy, *petit*.'

'You called me in here to talk about my relationship with Marieke?' Guy said. 'This mother act of yours is exactly the kind of thing that made me move out. What I do or don't do with Marieke is none of your business. You can't have every single last second of my life any more.'

Chiqui smiled. 'I don't think –'

Guy raised a hand to stop her from saying anything more. 'Things come, things go. Days, seasons, the sun, moon, mountains. Even love. Nothing is solid. Isn't that what you've been saying to me for the last four years? "All is illusion, *petit*." Well, I promise I've been dealing with everything with that very thing in mind. You should be proud.'

'You *understand* everything is illusion, yes, but you haven't

148

experienced everything as illusion. The difference between the two is vast. One takes place here.' She pointed at her head with a brilliant red fingernail. 'The other you feel everywhere. When you finally do experience that everything's an illusion, you tend to gain a clearer perception of the self.'

'What – like you?'

Chiqui sighed. 'I'm not perfect. No one is perfect. Perfection is an illusion, too. One of the goals of practising magic the way we do is to see the self as it truly is – craziness, conceits, quirks and all. Maybe even get a good laugh out of it.'

Guy stared at Chiqui's reflection in the mirror. 'Are you finished?'

'What I *say* to you is an illusion. Concepts, words, hot air. It's only through practice, experiencing these things first hand, that we discover anything of value. You're using the *concept* of illusion as a way to protect yourself, *petit*. It's isolating you from those around you. Marieke will eventually start feeling lonely, just like the others, and she'll leave – not because "things come and things go" but because you never show up.'

Guy turned back to face Chiqui. 'What is this about? You want me to spend more time with you? No one to gossip with back home? Lonely?'

'You are a gifted magician,' Chiqui said. 'You have incredible control. But to become a real magician, you must leave all that control behind.'

'Magic *is* control.'

'No, *petit*. Control creates separation. Because you still believe there is *someone* doing the controlling. Because you still believe there is a *thing* outside you that can be controlled. You have to learn how to let all of that go.'

'Are you finished?'

'You want control over your heart,' Chiqui continued. 'There is no control over the heart. Believe me I know. I've been where you are now. There is no control over anything. When you know this – in your arms, legs, your bowels – then everything becomes magic. And when everything is magic, there's no longer any such thing as magic. To become a magician you must let the magician go.'

'Why can't you say anything straight?'

Chiqui stood up. 'As to that...' She shrugged, lifted the top hat off the pile of clothes. 'I don't know how to say what I need to say in any other way.'

'Anything outside of our act is my own concern.'

Chiqui tapped the hat snug onto her blonde wig, nodded at Guy, and left the room.

Guy stared at the open door for a few minutes, unable to move. What had that been about?

Marieke poked her head through the door. 'Is everything okay?'

Guy shrugged. 'Chiqui and I were just talking.'

'Love spat?'

'We're not lovers,' Guy shot back. 'We've never been lovers. We will never *be* lovers...'

Guy followed Marc through the beaded curtain, down the dark hall to the blue door. Marc pressed his ear to the door. 'I hear a television.' He looked over his shoulder at Guy. 'He's probably asleep in front of the TV. It's his only company since his wife died. That and the cats.'

Marc rapped very lightly on the door, listened again. 'I've never seen the point of cats.'

The door knob clicked and the door slowly creaked open,

revealing a bent old man wearing thick glasses. He looked Marc up and down. 'I thought I heard someone out here.'

'I've come for the Romans,' Marc said.

The old man looked confused. 'Romans?'

'It's me, Marc. Marc Didier. And I've brought a friend.'

'Marc! Come in, come in!'

The old man led them down another short hallway, through a room where five orange cats were stretched out luxuriously on a couch, sleeping in front of a television. As they passed through the room the largest of the bunch leapt off the couch and ran ahead of the old man, through a filthy kitchen that smelled of fried eel, into a room filled with boxes.

'You've come at the right time,' the old man said. The cat jumped on top of a stack of boxes next to a small window overlooking an overgrown garden. 'I have an assortment of almost everything right now. I start collecting them in spring for the Americans in July. They love their Independence Day fireworks.'

Marc scanned the piles of boxes. 'Do you have one of those things that turns into a burning snake?'

The old man swept a hand around the room. 'I've got anything, everything.'

'You brought me here to buy fireworks?' Guy said.

'He's a bit irritable,' Marc said to the old man. 'He's in love.'

'Ah, that.' The old man looked at Guy. 'I can remember my first years with Merel, my wife, like it was yesterday. I can't remember what happened yesterday very well, though.' He glanced back at Marc. 'I was a bit distracted, to say the least. A pining fool. But I don't remember being irritable.'

'I'm not irritable,' Guy said to Marc. 'I just need to get

back to Villon.'

'When I was fifteen I used to spend all my time thinking of Merel. Every day was beautiful agony. It's a miracle I didn't walk in front of a bus.' The old man squinted at the doll head in Guy's hand. 'Love expands the world and contracts it at the same time.'

'I think Guy here is starting his contractions,' Marc said.

The old man turned back to Marc, wagging a finger in his face. 'No, no, it's not a joking matter, this love. It's a paradox, pulling you apart. You're young, you must remember it – that feeling that you're not yourself, that you're something more than yourself, that you include another, maybe include everything. Everything becomes beautifully strange. It's like being possessed and yet awake at the same time. Vividly awake. Excruciatingly awake.'

'Like sex,' Marc said.

The fish were shadows floating over the heads of the audience, fins softly swaying. All the faces in the theatre were looking up, their mouths open like village idiots, so filled with distraction that they were unable to see through the illusion. And they would go back out into the street after the final onstage fuck, after that last illusory bleat from Marieke, still unable to understand what was going on; how desire had driven them out to places like The Bacchanal, kept them moving in ever tighter circles, pursuing the next desire, and the next, endlessly searching for something that does not exist. Their houses, their work, their clothes, their wives, their children, their thoughts – all one huge, fucking illusion. And because they believed these things were solid, they suffered. Unable to accept the reality that it was all constantly changing and dissolving around them, they suffered. And that suffering drove them out into the streets again, pursuing more tiny desires to dampen the pain.

Guy looked over at Chiqui, orchestrating the fish-shadows with flourishes from her wand, sending them left, then right, making them circle around each other. She told him to let it all go, don't cling, but she was always clinging to her boyfriends, wasn't she? He could see how she suffered after each boyfriend disappeared. She was even trying to cling to him now that he'd moved out, wasn't she? How had she missed the beauty and force of her own words? It seemed he'd understood what she'd been saying about illusion all this time better than she did.

Marieke stood in the wings to his right, naked except for the sheep ears and woolly midriff. She stared at the fish shadows circling each other with her big, childlike eyes, fascinated. Her fascination was an illusion. She glanced at him – more naked with the sheep props than without – and grinned. More illusion.

He turned back to the audience. They were coming to the moment when the fish would dissolve in a puff of smoke. Nothing from nothing. He could already hear the familiar gasps and sighs.

The two fish were now side by side. It was time. There was the sound of crackling, like burning paper, and the fish seemed to swim from shadow into smoke. Some people gasped, others sighed. Guy glanced into the wings. Marieke watched the drifting smoke, clapping her hands softly together like a schoolgirl.

The audience burst into applause. Chiqui bowed. Guy bowed. The curtain closed. Marieke put her arms around Guy's shoulders, pressed against him, gave him a quick kiss, then helped him clear Chiqui's props before getting down on all fours in the middle of the stage.

Guy stood in the wings, stared at Marieke's ass, while Jansen worked Alain's dick into an erection behind him with some KY jelly. When the curtain opened, Alain quickly moved past Guy with his shepherd's crook, onto the stage. Marieke began crawling around in circles, bleating.

Applause, laughter.

Alain followed Marieke around the stage, poking her with his crook, leering out at the audience. Then he was down on all fours, running his hands over her ass, poking, prodding. Like all the other sex acts onstage, it moved pretty quickly. It was important to get down to business before Alain's erection – or audience attention – began to wane. Marieke pretended to move away from his grasp, blinking out into the audience with her wide, brown eyes, feigning innocence. More laughter. Guy pulled a pack of cigarettes out of his coat pocket, tamped one against the pack.

Alain was now on his knees behind Marieke, spreading her cheeks, eyes wide with surprise. He shot a guilty-shepherd glance over his shoulder, then plunged a finger in, worked it in a circle. Soon he had two fingers in, then three. When he held them in front of Marieke's face, she licked them. Grunts and laughter from the audience. Now things would get going.

Alain slid into Marieke, began thrusting away. Marieke sucked on her own fingers, then circled her nipples with them. Guy looked out at the faces in the front row: slack-jawed university boys, eyes glazed; idiot grins plastered onto the faces of the middle class businessmen. They ate illusion for breakfast, lunch, dinner; were bloated with it.

They were all drifting ghosts. Smoke. Shadow-fish.

Marieke had asked him once after they'd made love if watching her onstage ever turned him on. The question had shocked him for a second. He hadn't understood why she was bringing her work into their little world. 'It's just an act,' he'd answered. 'Yes, but is sexy?' she'd asked again. He tried one more time: 'You're performing an illusion. Just like us.' She'd seemed disappointed in the answer. But what answer could have possibly satisfied her?

The question was an illusion.

Marieke and Alain were now moving towards their choreographed climax. More groans, bleats. Alain thrust faster and faster. Skin slapped against skin. Sometimes she had to take a warm bath at the end of the night, then massage herself with a little Vaseline, to ease the sting.

Marieke raised her face up, looked straight at him, grinned and winked, then looked out into the audience, eyes wide like a lost child, mouth open, and let out a long slow pleasure-groan. Alain closed his eyes, shuddered behind her.

Guy lit a cigarette, blew a smoke ring towards the stage. It floated out past the curtain, dissipated over the couple.

The old man vigorously shook his head at Marc, clearly annoyed. 'No, no, I am trying to explain something serious to your friend and you're talking titillation. Love is...' He looked up at the ceiling. 'Love is...' Ten seconds passed. When he looked back at Guy, his face was blank. He'd forgotten what he was going to say. He pointed at the doll head in Guy's hand. 'I see you've found the heads. A mistake, that. I was expecting shirts from Italy. I open the boxes and inside there's nothing but those strange little faces staring back. What am I supposed to do with two thousand doll heads? You can see what the cats do with them, gouging out the eyes, eating the hair. Cats are naturally evil.'

Marc shot a glance at the cat preening on the boxes next to the window. 'I've never seen the point of cats.'

'Now, whenever I go on errands,' the old man continued, 'I always take a few of the heads with me. I keep them in a box strapped to the back of the moped, leave them on church steps, fence posts, toss them by the side of the road. It's become a hobby, of sorts. Like bird watching or collecting toy trains. I'm sure you've seen them.'

'We came for burning snakes,' Marc cut in. 'And Roman candles.'

'The Romans are an excellent choice,' the old man said, turning to the stacks of boxes, opening one, then another, pulling out various brightly coloured fireworks, holding them up and naming each one, explaining what each one could do.

Marc bought five Roman candles, three burning snakes, and two M-80s. The old man threw in two small boxes of doll heads gratis. Marc protested, but Guy said he would be happy to take them.

Back in the car, Guy asked Marc what he was going to do with the fireworks.

'They're for the rally today,' Marc said, backing the car down the alley. 'Add a little spice to the dull political proceedings.'

'I can promise you it won't be dull,' Guy said. 'Contexture will be there.'

Marc shot a glance at Guy, eyes wide. 'Wait. The ones who got naked at the Vatican?'

'There were flyers all over town. Didn't you read any of them?'

'Of course not, they always say the same thing: bad things

this, bad things that, come and listen to bad things blah blah blah and feel bad. I thought I was all alone in my desire for a good time, but if those naked people are coming, my God Guy, my fireworks will be the perfect complement to all those naked bodies! I shall achieve undying fame! Women will drop to their knees before me!'

On Spierry's high road Marc pointed the car towards Mons.

3 The Player

Philippe sat at the kitchen table opposite Casimir, picked up the hummingbird. 'Why is Poisson called Poisson?'

Casimir reached across the table, snatched the bird out of the boy's hands. 'It's a long story.' He placed the bird back on the table, scanned the kitchen for his cigarettes. When he finally got his money for the Rimbaud poems he wouldn't have to deal with any of this any more. No grubby fingers touching his things. No rusted peaches. No sad, broken-toothed lovers. No hangovers.

He smiled to himself. He could afford to pay someone else to suffer for his indulgences.

'Solfege Brunuel says Poisson is retarded,' Philippe said.

'Solfege Brunuel is retarded.'

Philippe giggled.

'No, no,' Casimir said, 'I take that back. Solfege is just fat.' He leaned forward, elbows on the table. 'Poisson has his own reasons for the way he is.' He scanned the counter between the sink and stove for his cigarettes. 'We all have our own reasons for the way we are.'

'What are Poisson's reasons?' the boy asked, reaching out to the middle of the table, pulling the salt cellar towards him.

'Well, by the time Poisson was about your age, his father was in very poor shape from too much drink.' Casimir lifted his thumb up to his lips, pretended to drink.

'Like you,' the boy said.

Casimir frowned. 'No, not like me. The old man drank like a fish.'

'That's how Poisson got his name, then? Because he drinks like a fish?'

'Not at all. When he was a boy, because his father was so feeble from drink, Poisson had to provide most of the food for the family – for his father and sister. I don't remember his mother. She was gone before my memory begins.' Casimir cocked his head to the left, tried to find some angle that would ease the stabbing behind his right eye.

'So he skipped school to go fishing,' Casimir continued. 'The teachers didn't care. They knew his situation. He'd never been very good in school anyway.' He cocked his head to the right. The pain was the same. 'You can't imagine how jealous I was, how jealous all the boys were, stuck in class, reciting the times tables, while we imagined little Ledoux out having an adventure every day.'

Casimir remembered skipping school one day, making his way out to the canal, hiding underneath the bridge, watching the ripples of light bounce off the concrete, and throwing stones into the water, bored. Poisson had appeared, staring at him, fishing pole on his shoulder. 'This is where I fish,' Poisson had said, simply, plainly, without any menace in his voice. But Poisson was big for his age – large hands, large feet – and then there was the house he lived in – his dark father, his crazy

158

sister – and so most of the boys Casimir's age or younger were afraid of him. But that day, Casimir hadn't been afraid. Why, he no longer remembered. He had not been a particularly brave child, but he'd stood up, dusted off his shorts, and formally introduced himself to Poisson. 'You're the doctor's son,' Poisson had said. It was that simple, how they became friends. For the next six months, whenever Casimir cut school, he'd head to the canal bridge, wait for Poisson.

'So, he's called Poisson because he fishes?' Philippe said. 'Old Monsieur Caillens fishes every day, too, and everyone just calls him Monsieur Caillens.'

'It's a little more complicated than that,' Casimir said. 'Now each dusk, when Poisson would be coming home from fishing, he'd walk through the Place, in front of the old men sitting on the benches outside the brasserie. Since he had no use for books, he used his book satchel to carry his fish. And the old men would cup their hands around their mouths...' Casimir cupped both hands around his lips. '... and call out to him every day, "Eh Paul Ledoux, what do you have in your book sack?" and he'd yell back "Poisson!" and they'd all laugh.'

'That's not complicated,' Philippe said.

Casimir raised a finger. 'Ah, but there's more. It happened so often – him walking through the Place with the fish – that the old men stopped asking him what was in the sack. They'd just poke each other, wink and shout "Poisson!" To tease him at first, I suppose, but then everyone else heard them doing it and the name stuck. After a while we didn't know how to call him anything else. It seemed he'd been born with the name.'

'Poisson waved his *petit poisson* at me once,' Philippe said, fish-fingers sliding all over the salt cellar.

159

'What *petit poisson*? What are you talking about?'

'You know... his pee-pee.'

Casimir laughed. Poisson's father had been accused of the same thing. He wondered if it was all auto-hypnotic-suggestion. What people expected became what they saw. But Philippe seemed too young for that.

'Did you tell anyone?' Casimir asked.

'I told Papa.'

'And?'

'He told me not to talk dirty.'

Casimir shook his head. 'Ah, the good Doctor Souzain,' speaking more to himself than the boy, 'always attentive to the complaints of his patients.' So pompous, just like Casimir's father. Like all doctors.

Was he still jealous at the way his father had fawned over Souzain when Adele had brought him home? Finally, a son to carry on the practice! And then Souzain began to take on the old man's characteristics – especially that tone of voice, so condescending: 'Casimir, you're *so* creative, I can see how practising medicine would have bored you.' And: 'Casimir, aren't you bored by the same routine at the *lycée* year in and year out, it seems such a shame to waste your talents.' Now he couldn't remember whether he'd spread the rumour about Souzain fucking up Guy Foulette's foot by whispering it into Dehanschutter's ear (drunk at the brasserie) or whether Dehanschutter had whispered the rumour into *his* ear. Well, what could he do now? For all he knew, it could have been true. It was so long ago. Water under the bridge. No one remembered it any more anyway.

'I knew Poisson for a time when I was your age,' Casimir said. 'It's hard to believe he waggled his *petit poisson* at you, or

160

anyone. He was quiet. Shy, really. His father on the other hand
–' Casimir picked up the hummingbird, raised it to his nose.
The fish smell was everywhere so it was hard for Casimir to
tell whether it was specifically on the bird or not. 'His father
was a monster.'

Philippe's eyes widened. 'What did he do?'

'Things.'

'What things?'

The boy was too young to be exposed to such things. Or
was he? No one had ever told Casimir anything as a boy. Not
even a hint. Maybe if he'd been given some clues early on the
world would have made more sense.

'Poisson had a beautiful sister,' Casimir said. 'But only half
there.' He pointed to his temple and twirled his index finger.

'She was retarded? Like Solfege?'

Casimir smiled. 'No, not retarded like Solfege. I don't know
how to describe it. Distant. She was distant. She'd walk to
school alone every day, talking to herself, singing to herself.'

'Maybe she was nervous,' Philippe offered. 'I sometimes
sing when I'm nervous.'

Perceptive child. Hard to believe he came from Souzain and
Adele. But then, how had Casimir come from someone like his
father? We are what we are.

'When I was your age,' Casimir continued, 'she would
sometimes sleepwalk – or, at least, that's what we thought she
was doing. She'd walk right out of her house – the same house
where Poisson lives now – in the middle of the night, middle of
the street, down to the Place – like a ghost – and she'd dance
in this sheer nightgown. It sparkled in the streetlight, like it
was made of insect wings.'

'Insect wings?'

161

Casimir spotted the cigarette pack sitting on top of the fridge. He slowly stood up so as not to create any more pain than necessary in his head.

'And you could see right through it,' he said, retrieving the pack off the fridge, bringing it back to the table. 'I overheard a few older boys talking about it and so one night I stole out of the house, went down to the Place for a peek.'

'She had turned into an insect?'

'Her gown would spin out, float around her body,' Casimir said, settling down in his chair, lighting up. 'It was marvellous to watch.'

He would never forget that moment when she had stopped spinning and spinning and had looked over at the shadows beside the church steps, directly at him, smiling, like she knew what she was doing, like she knew he was there, why he was there.

'Nothing like that ever happens around here any more,' Philippe said.

Casimir smiled. 'No, maybe not like that,' he said, smoke dribbling out of his nose, 'but there *are* fish all over my yard and all over Brunuel's yard.'

The boy threw his hands in the air, whether from feigned or true exasperation Casimir couldn't tell. 'But I told you! They're all over town! All the way out to Foulette's field!' The boy jumped off his chair, ran around the table, grabbed Casimir's hand and pulled. 'There are more on the street than there were in the garden!'

Claudine Brunuel, the second oldest in the Brunuel clan – a year younger than Elise – crouched in front of three small fish lying together in a heap at the foot of Brunuel's front steps. When Casimir reached the bottom of his steps, she stood up, smiled at him. She wore a loose blue sweater that hung below her hips and black leggings that tapered down to what looked like blue velour clogs. It had been a while since Casimir had seen the girl. Five, six months? She was much thinner, seemed to have lost that sluggish vacant look that seemed to be the main Brunuel characteristic.

Philippe ran across the street, crouched next to a huge fish lying beneath Dehanschutter's display window: the horror of an open child's coffin, leaning against a thick curtain of dusty velvet.

'I haven't seen you in a while Claudine,' Casimir said to the girl. 'You look good. Healthy.'

Claudine blushed.

How typical that he'd chosen the wrong one. But then, six months ago, this girl probably looked the same as the rest of them. 'What do you hear from Elise?'

'You don't know?'

'Know what?' Pain shot through his skull, behind his eyes. He immediately pressed a palm to his forehead. Was this why the ancient doctors drilled holes in their patient's heads?

'Elise is getting married,' Claudine said. 'My father is outraged.'

'He doesn't like the boy?'

'No, no. She's...' Claudine rolled both hands in the air over her stomach and laughed.

Phlegm oozed down the back of Casimir's throat, poison leaking from his brain, building a long horrible toxic stalactite down to his stomach. He wanted to ask the girl how far along Elise was, but what would be the point? She was getting married. It was done. The chances the baby was his were –

'She's huge!' Claudine said. 'I think she'll have twins. Maybe triplets!'

The way the girl cackled, she was evidently not fond of her sister. He had liked Elise (hadn't he?) and took some offence at Claudine's attitude.

Philippe lifted the head of the huge fish beneath the coffin-maker's window, stared into its open mouth, then scooted down the length of the body and lifted the tail, examining the scales underneath.

Claudine pointed at the fish Philippe was holding. 'Solfege thinks they fell from the sky.'

What did this girl know of his dealings with Elise? It was entirely possible she knew everything.

'That's what Philippe says.'

Claudine looked west down rue des Ecoles. 'It's a brilliant trick, though, don't you think?'

A trick? It would take the entire town to play a trick like this. And for what? 'Who would play such a trick?' he asked the girl.

'The Greens,' she said. 'That's what my father thinks.'

The ever suspicious Brunuel. 'But why would the Greens do something like this?'

She shrugged. 'To show what it will be like to live in a sea of toxic waste? Death everywhere, that sort of thing.'

The fish smell blended with the scent of Claudine's soap. The same soap smell that had been clinging to Elise's skin that night in the attic. Casimir swallowed.

'Elise told me you have quite a collection inside that house of yours,' Claudine said, glancing up at Casimir's third floor bedroom window. He followed her gaze. It would be just like Marie to be standing there, looking down at them.

But no, the curtains were closed.

'Yes, I make little art cabinets. I could show them to you some time if you like.'

164

'Solfege said you have a collection of doll heads, just like the ones that are always scattered along the factory road.'

'Yes,' Casimir said, 'those are the same heads. They didn't originate with me, though, if that's what you're implying.' He needed to sit down.

Dehanschutter's second floor window opened and the skinny coffin-maker leaned out, naked to the waist, dark eyes glaring down at Philippe. 'Get away from my display window. You'll smear fish slime all over the glass.'

Casimir beckoned to Philippe. 'Come on, *petit*, you don't want to mar the maestro's grotesque masterpiece.'

Claudine giggled and Casimir gave her a wink.

Dehanschutter pointed at Casimir with a long bony finger. 'Make fun, Casimir! It's easy for someone like you to make fun. But *I* must make a living.'

'Who says I don't have to make a living, too, old man?' Casimir answered. 'I'm talking about your *display*, not your line of work. It's tasteless, an eyesore.'

'It's not about art,' the old man said. 'It's about business. And what do you know about art, *monsieur expert*? All you do is paste together the crap of the world.'

'I resurrect the trash of this world, old man, and make it live again. All you do is bury things.'

Dehanschutter pointed at Casimir again. 'I'll bury you.' His finger roved to Claudine and then to Philippe. 'I'll bury all of you.' He withdrew into the room, slammed the window shut. Lace curtains fell across the glass.

Casimir flicked his spent cigarette at the window display, then sat down at the bottom of his steps and lit another cigarette. Claudine sat down beside him. Philippe wandered over to the three fish at the bottom of Brunuel's steps.

'I'll bet he's still standing there behind the curtain, looking at us,' Claudine said.

Casimir exhaled smoke through his nose. 'Dehanschutter's probably right. He will bury us all. He was old when I was a boy.' A dull pain throbbed behind his right eye again and he pressed the ball of his thumb between his eyebrows and rubbed.

'Would you like me to massage your head?' Claudine asked.

Casimir looked over at the girl. This was unexpected.

'I'm very good.' Claudine moved to the step behind him and spread her fingers through his hair, moving the tips in slow circles at the crown of his skull. 'I can always get rid of my father's headaches this way. I've had plenty of practice.'

Casimir stiffened – the same hands that were now on his head had practised and honed their skill on that idiot Brunuel's skull?

'Relax, take deep breaths.'

'Is your father worried the rally might actually shut down his new little operation?'

She pressed a thumb to his right temple, moved it in small circles down to his ear, back behind his ear. 'Papa doesn't talk much about work. But he *has* been very tense lately.'

Casimir stiffened again.

'Elise said that your cabinets have some very strange items in them.'

Casimir settled back against Claudine's breasts. Soft. But not too soft. Good. Elise was a bit too soft for his liking. 'What do you mean "strange"?'

'Do you really have a dead baby in a jar?'

Casimir vigorously shook his head and there was a sudden flash of lightning behind his right eye. 'I can't believe Elise would say I have a dead baby in a jar.'

'Deep breaths.'

'It's a death mask,' Casimir said. 'I have the death mask of a Congolese baby. Not the baby, just the mask. There is a world of difference.'

The way some people reacted to the mask, to most of the things in his collection, he might as well have been collecting dead human babies preserved in formaldehyde. One of the strangest things he'd encountered – a two-headed baby goat – stillborn to one of Nicholas Moegge's nannies – he never bothered to show anyone any more. He'd shown it to Louise... Louise... what was her last name? A girl he'd met during kermesse three years ago. He'd shown her the collection after they'd made love, holding the jar containing the goat up to her face, proud. She'd rushed from the room, clutching her stomach.

We still live in the dark ages.

Raoul had reduced the death mask itself to a statement against the Belgian colonisation of the Congo. He'd even lifted it out of the cabinet, run his fingers over the cheeks, the eyeholes. Couldn't the boy tell that the cabinets were arranged, a collage, art? Wasn't he a poet? He should have known better. Would he have reached into one of Joseph Cornell's boxes, fingered all the objects?

Casimir had pulled the mask out of Raoul's hands, placed it back in the cabinet at the proper angle. 'I think, first off,' he'd said to Raoul, 'what you have to understand, is that I collect all these things out of love, not hatred.

'All these things,' he'd swept his hand around the room, 'have been made. There's no going back. It's done. Civilisation is overrun with useless things: doll heads, pieces of outdated machinery, clocks, lizards' tails, tigers' claws, saints' nail-parings, bracelets, glass crosses, marbles, carved Buddhas, little Eiffel Towers, ivory pagodas – you name it – collected from all over the world. It's the price of progress. Go into any house on this street and you'll find the same little talismans on the shelves – souvenirs, precious knick-knacks. You can't stop the proliferation of these things by your disgust or by putting them into a box and labelling it "box of shame". Yes, it's a shame that there are so many idiotic things cluttering up our landfills, but the world of the million things is the only world we know. You may not like it, but it is all there is. It must be reconstituted, rearranged. And that transmutation should be celebrated, not denigrated.'

'Surely you don't mean to include living things in that list?' Raoul had said.

'I do,' Casimir had answered. 'Why not? You walk up a mountain and what do you see? The whole mountain the entire time? Of course not! The whole is broken up into this rock here, that flower there, this tree here. We know the world only by small increments. One thing after another: screwdrivers, incense burners, wine glasses. You can never know the whole. No one can. Maybe it doesn't even exist.'

Raoul had smirked, turned away from him, looked into another cabinet. Casimir had instantly regretted showing him the Rimbaud papers inside the owl. Why had he done that? He was so close to making the sale of his life.

The only one who had ever really truly appreciated his work was Ivette Eseuil. Back when he was twenty or so, when he had first started creating his birds and his cabinets, she had commissioned several of them for the brasserie. Insatiable Ivette. He could still get hard thinking about Ivette's hefty silhouette moving on top of him in the back room of the brasserie. At the time, most of the thrill had come from being able to hear her husband's feet moving around in the bedroom above them while they made love. The close dark of that dusty room should have been claustrophobic, but he'd always had a strange feeling of freedom in there.

The pleasure underground. Panties beneath velvet curtains.

But nothing lasts forever. One night they heard the footsteps creaking down the stairs. 'Ivette? Ivette? Are you down there?' She quickly hopped off him, pushed him out of the back door before he could find all his clothes. Still hard, he stood out in the cold fog behind the brasserie, naked to the world. But he had not panicked. Instead, he felt himself expand and expand through the fog, out to the perimeters of the entire town. Then, he ran. He ran down every street in Villon as fast as he could, naked, beautifully naked, flauntingly naked. As if he was the first person to have opened his eyes in a newly created world of fog. As if he was the last man on earth. As if he was both at the same time.

Casimir opened his eyes. 'Where did the boy go?'

'He went around the corner.'

Casimir called the boy's name and Philippe came running around the corner, holding a fish the length of his skinny forearms by the tail. He ran up to Casimir, held it in front of his face.

'It's got an antenna!'

Casimir pressed back into Claudine's chest, trying to get away from the smell. 'Get that thing away from my face!'

Claudine tapped Casimir twice on the top of his head. 'I need to get up.'

He reluctantly leaned forward and she stood, stretched, then crouched next to Philippe and examined the fish. 'It looks so ancient...'

'Ancient or no,' Casimir said to the boy, 'I don't want you to end up making a pile of fish at the bottom of my steps here like you did in the backyard. No more collecting fish.'

Philippe pulled the antenna taut, let go. It waggled back and forth like a thin rubber tube.

Claudine touched the fish's snout. 'If I knew how, I'd preserve something like this. It's so strange.' She looked at Casimir. 'Wouldn't you?'

My God! What had he been thinking? He struggled to his feet, pried the mouth open, peered at the row of teeth. He lifted the fish, rocking it back and forth in his hands so that the scales caught the grey morning light. Teeth! Scales! Antenna! Fins! Snout! Eyes! Fish parts!

'What an incredible idea!' he said to the girl, then pointed at the three fish in front of Brunuel's steps. 'Pick up those fish and take them inside. We're going to freeze as many as possible!' He hurried across the street to retrieve the huge cod beneath Dehanschutter's display window.

When he spun around, cradling the fish, he suddenly remembered Marie. He looked up at his bedroom window again. The curtains were still closed. Shit, shit, shit, if Claudine saw Marie inside that would probably end any possibility of manoeuvring the girl into his bed. At least for today.

Well, Claudine was in the house now, no getting around that. He hoped Marie had enough sense to stay hidden. He'd have to stay with both Claudine and the boy in the back kitchen as long as he could, give Marie time to slip out of the front door.

He ran across the street and bounded up the front steps two at a time.

4 The Seer

Marie leaned against the door of Casimir's cabinet room, eyes closed. Moments before, on her way to the kitchen to get a glass of water, she'd overheard Casimir telling the boy about her sister-in-law's body. Poor Ariane. Terrible Ariane. Why would Casimir tell the boy something like that? Didn't he know where that woman was now?

Poisson wouldn't even go and see his sister. He'd stand outside the institution, hands in his pockets, like a schoolboy, while Marie went into that horrid place. The cries, the stares of the patients, lost in a confusion of drugs. There were so many drugs swirling inside them to erase the pain that pain was all that remained. And she would follow the attendants through those rooms, past all the caged windows, trying not to make contact with anything. She wouldn't even touch poor whispering Ariane – so old and sunken-faced from fighting the confusion – because she knew what touching her would mean.

There was no shame in Casimir's house. How had she let herself become a part of a house with no shame?

Marie leaned over the pelican on the window ledge, looked through the lace curtains, down into the street. The stuffed pelican fell off the ledge, landed on the floor with a soft thud. A blue marble dislodged from one of the eyes, rolled slowly across the floor, and disappeared under the bed.

A bad sign. It would have made her laugh if she didn't know that Poisson was already up and wandering around the town, looking for her. Leaving Emile all alone.

She had to get home.

Marie picked the half-blind bird up, unconsciously stuck an index finger into the empty eyehole. *Skimming low over waves,*

1 / 1

the fish in her belly still alive. Wind beneath, lifting up against her, the sea inside. She turned her finger slightly to the left. *The sun, grey through overcast skies, smooth as moon through fog. Sleet. Leave the shore behind for open sea. The one flying below lifts its beak, pierces her side.*

Marie dropped the bird, touched the place beneath her left breast where she felt a sudden pain. She lifted a knee onto the ledge, one hand pressing the curtain to the glass, the other clutching the place below her breast, eyes closed. The pain sharpened, subsided. She pressed her forehead to the curtain, opened her eyes, and caught some movement down below in Dehanschutter's second floor window. A figure behind lace. Dehanschutter? It looked like a woman. Smaller, round. Dehanschutter was thin, a ghost.

A year ago, she'd gone into the brasserie searching for Poisson, and Dehanschutter had offered to buy her a drink. She'd declined and he'd nodded, saying something about how she had to keep the household in balance. Then he'd lifted one of those small Turkish cigarettes to his thin lips and leaned close to her face.

'I see you out walking, small one,' he'd whispered. 'I know where you go on your midnight rounds. But it won't do any good.' He had grabbed her wrist, pulled her closer. *Where there are houses there once was forest. Do you see it, small one? Dark. The dark was luxury. Then came the waves of hysteria. People wandering away from their villages, starving themselves, praying – whispering, whispering long into the night. How sleep with all that whispering? One night I went out wandering and there she was. Alone, in her stone hut. I came to her and knew her and in knowing her I knew myself –*

Before she could jerk her arm away, she felt grains of sand

shoot over her skin, through her body, her skin peeling back, revealing another skin, until that raw skin was peeled back, revealing another, another, on and on, the sand whittling her down until she was naked to everything, invisible as air.

She'd screamed and the coffin maker had let go. The others in the brasserie had looked at her for a second, frowning, then returned to their conversations. She knew what they were thinking: Poisson's wife. She ran out of the brasserie as fast as she could. It took her days to get the feeling of being skinned to nothing out of her mind.

After that, she avoided the old man. Whenever she saw him she walked to the other side of the street or simply turned around and walked back the way she had come. If she went to the *boulangerie* and saw him through the window – waiting in line – she kept walking – maybe down to the Grand Place or over to the park – until she'd given him enough time to get his bread and go home. She wanted to ask someone in town, anyone, what they felt when they were near Dehanschutter. But who? After four years in this town, there was still no one to ask such a question.

Marie parted the curtains a few centimetres. No, there was no figure behind Dehanschutter's curtain. Feeling steadier, she slid her foot off the ledge, turned to the bed. She had to find the pelican's eye, then get home.

On her hands and knees, she lifted up the sheets and blankets hanging over the side of the bed. They smelled of Casimir's cologne. He'd sprinkled some on her when they'd first crawled into bed last night. Then, after they'd made love, he'd unscrewed the stuffed owl on the mantel, pulled out that packet of papers, jumped back on the bed, penis flapping, breathless, telling her how valuable the papers were, how there was a man in Paris who was going to pay him millions of francs just for the privilege of keeping them hidden forever, all to himself.

A couple of minutes after he'd crawled on top of her for the second time, he passed out. Poisson had never done that. She'd rolled Casimir off, curled up under the blue sheet at the edge of the bed, eyes fixed on the pelican. How many hours before she put on Casimir's flannel robe and slipped out into the hall? She ended up on the first landing, looking down the last flight of stairs, at the marble hallway. What could it be like to be alone all the time in such a house? All these rooms waiting night after night, like spiders' eyes in dark grass, lit by the moon.

She descended the stairs quickly, the momentum sending her skidding across the marble at the bottom. The hallway shifted back and forth for a second and she took a few unsteady steps back to the banister and held on. Such smooth oak. She lowered her face to the varnish, slid her cheek against it. Cold. But not as cold as marble. There was a give to it, a softness. *An old woman's skin, rubbing the wood. Back and forth, worrying, her other hand nervously playing with a button of her blouse. She stares through the bevelled front door glass. Shadows, falling. Snow? Flakes large and dark as fish.*

Marie lifted her hand from the banister, turned and stared at the front door. Streetlight through bevelled glass, pale orange across white marble. She stepped away from the banister, stood just inside the bar room. The white shells hanging from the net over the bar seemed to glow in the dark, as if there was a secret light rising from inside them. She giggled, then quickly raised her hand to her mouth.

No, Casimir would sleep till morning. She could scream and he wouldn't wake. But she didn't want to break the spell. She tiptoed to the bar, reached up to the fishnet and touched

174

the face of the ship's clock. She could do anything she wanted. She opened the fridge behind the bar and pulled out a bottle of beer. After a minute of fumbling around behind the bar looking for the bottle-opener, she sashayed around the room, humming to herself – what she remembered of the Brazilian tune about moonlight on water.

She could dance naked if she wanted.

She undid the belt of the robe, let it fall to her feet, then tiptoed across the hall and stood in the centre of the living room, facing the picture window. Casimir had forgotten to lower the blinds and there was nothing between her and the streetlight but a sheer curtain. She had no idea what to do next. Spin? She tried to pivot on one foot, but only managed to stumble off balance, facing the dining room. Her shadow, cast by the streetlight, stretched through the glass dining room door. She raised one hand over her head, then the other. The shadow responded. She took a step forward, a step back, raised her right knee up slowly, arms out, like she was balancing on a high wire. She lost her balance instantly and stumbled forward again, stopping inches away from her own reflection in the glass.

Wild hair, wild eyes. She curled her hands into claws, bared her teeth. An idiotic, harmless gargoyle leered back at her. She put a hand to her mouth, stifled a laugh, then leaned forwards and bared her teeth again.

Less like a demon than a forlorn toothless monkey.

Marie closed her mouth, stuck her tongue into her upper gums, and lifted a hand to scratch an armpit. 'Oop-oop.' She hopped chimp circles around the living room until she finally exhausted herself and sank to the ground, lying spreadeagled on the carpet, all the empty rooms in the world whirling around inside her.

175

There was a noise in the direction of the kitchen. Mice? Marie exhaled and giggled, then automatically put her hand to her mouth. Poisson? No, Poisson was passed out on her kitchen floor. Like Casimir, there was no waking him till morning.

Thief? Let the thief mess with Casimir's things, what was it to her?

She sat up, listened. There it was again – a rustling, like pigeons in the attic. It was definitely coming from the kitchen.

Marie slowly rose to her feet, concentrating on the sound, tiptoeing out of the living room, down the long cold marble hallway. When she passed Casimir's study she stopped, held her breath, and listened again. The sound was clear now: air rushing through a crack in the kitchen window. But there was no crack in the window. And no wind. Only fog.

It's probably nothing.

But if there is someone in the kitchen?

She cupped her throat with one hand, touched her mouth with the other, took a step, stopped, listened, took another step, stopped. The sound didn't change.

When she reached the kitchen entrance, she pressed her back up against the wall. The shock of the cold plaster sent a ripple of goose bumps across her entire body. She held her breath again. Still that soft rush of air. She inched one eye past the doorframe, hoping to get a glimpse of the whole room through the reflection in the kitchen window.

In the glass she saw an old woman standing at the stove, stirring a pot.

Who? And at this hour? In the neighbourhood where she grew up there was an old woman – the grandmother of Thérèse and Paul Loitte – who would leave the house, heading to the *Bon Marché* for groceries, and end up in some stranger's

176

kitchen, humming to herself, cooking supper, thinking she was at home.

How to confront her? Naked, Marie would probably scare the old woman out of her mind. She padded to the bathroom next to Casimir's study, grabbed a towel off the rack, wrapped it around her, then tiptoed back to the kitchen, stepping quietly through the door.

The woman was gone. The right front burner of the stove hissed. The small blue flame faintly illuminated the wall behind the stove. Marie let out her breath, stepped cautiously up to the stove and turned the burner off.

Madness. She was seeing things, like Poisson. Casimir must have come down here some time during the night, turned on the burner to light a cigarette.

Marie looked at the door to the pantry, slightly ajar. If there was an old woman, she could have slipped through there, disappeared into the backyard. The hair on the back of her neck stood on end. She ran from the kitchen, the towel slipping off halfway down the hallway.

Are pelicans' eyes blue? All the pictures Marie had ever seen of Jesus portrayed him with blue eyes. She fished the marble out from under the bed, rolled it around in the palm of her hand. When she first met Poisson, his eyes were a curious and strangely intense blue. Sky blue, just before night fell. She stood up, eyes fixed on the marble.

When her father had brought Poisson home, the first thing she'd noticed was the eyes. He'd stood at the entrance to the kitchen, shy, smiling. But the eyes, they had studied everything – her face, hair, hands – with an intense longing. When she'd smiled at him he'd dropped his eyes to the floor, pursed his lips, dug around in his pockets for a cigarette. But the gaze stayed with her. Everything touched by his gaze had changed. Her mother's kitchen was no longer her mother's kitchen. The pots, the stove, the cupboards, the cross, the calendar, the dim light above the kitchen table, all had shifted, become strange.

Marie slid the marble back into the empty eye socket and stepped back to see how it looked. Casimir would probably notice. He was so exact with his birds, his cabinets. This goes here, that only goes there, don't touch this, be careful of that. Casimir's voice drifted up from the street below. She parted the curtains again. Casimir was talking with one of the Brunuel girls on the pavement.

Was it Elise? Casimir had told Marie all about Elise. How Elise had pursued him, knocked on his door at all hours, almost begged for sex. When he had told her about Elise, she'd thought of how she herself had shown up at his door at two o'clock in the morning, and blushed. He'd reached across the kitchen table and stroked her cheek. 'Oh, no, not like you. I don't mean to denigrate all knocking on doors late at night. It depends on who it is. You are always welcome.' Then he continued the story, telling her how he'd made love to Elise out of sheer exasperation, hoping the girl would finally leave him alone. He'd even described how the girl played with her own nipple while he made love to her. Marie had listened, saying nothing, feeling ashamed and embarrassed – for herself, for that poor Brunuel girl, for Casimir.

Why had he told her that? Why did he think she had wanted to hear that?

Marie leaned closer to the glass. No, it was not Elise. This girl was younger. And much thinner than the older sister. Out of the corner of her eye Marie saw a movement behind

178

Dehanschutter's second floor window curtain, then suddenly there he was, swinging the window out, pointing down at Casimir. Marie instinctively pulled her hand back and the curtain closed. Sour liquid – from the wine or the peaches – rose up from her stomach, into her throat. She made a fist, pressed her knuckles against her abdomen and swallowed.

No more time to waste, she had to go and get Emile, head to church. Maybe Poisson would still be out hunting for her when she got home.

She threw Casimir's flannel robe onto the bed and pulled her smock off the brown ceramic lamp on the bedside table. One of her buttons caught at the top of the lampshade and the lamp crashed to the floor. Ceramic shards and glass from the bulb scattered across the wood. She slipped her smock over her head, crouched down, and started picking up the pieces of the lamp around her feet, panic rising up from her stomach.

She didn't have time for this. She stood up, scanned the room for her shoes. One was sitting on the fireplace mantel, next to the hollow owl. She folded her fingers over the small pile of ceramic shards in her hand and picked her way around the bed. What was her shoe doing on the mantel? She deposited the shards in a little pile next to the owl and lifted the shoe. The inside was red. Wine. Last night Casimir had poured wine into it, pretending to drink from it. The wine had rolled over his closed mouth, down his naked chest. She had laughed and laughed.

The shoe stank of wine. How could she wear it home?

Bile shot up from her stomach, into her throat again. She raised her hand to cover her mouth, but it was too late. She doubled over and vomited through her fingers, onto the floor next to the bed.

Broken glass on one side of the bed, vomit on the other. She sank to her knees. Down on all fours, she stared at the ragged peach scum on the cold wood floor, the top of her head against the side of the bed.

All she had wanted was to be lonely in a way she herself chose.

She closed her eyes. 'Woelfred.'

She could hear Casimir shouting at Dehanschutter down in the street.

'Woelfred,' she said again, lifting her head, looking across the bed at the pelican on the window ledge. 'Please.'

Was she a child, a fool, for believing?

Marie pressed a hand down onto the mattress and struggled to her feet. The room began to spin and she lowered herself onto the bed, face down in the sheets. Somewhere, far down below the bed, in the street, Casimir was talking, talking. She slid the shoe up to her face, touched a finger down onto the inside heel. It was still wet.

Why would Casimir do such a thing?

She squeezed her eyes shut and a lone tear rolled from her right eye, over her cheek. The smell of stale wine mingled with the stink of her shoes. She raised herself up on one elbow, struggling to get away from the smell. It was so strong it seemed as if it was rising from inside her. She threw the shoe against the wall next to the window and it hit one of Casimir's masks. Dead centre. Both mask and shoe fell to the floor together. A ghostlike silence flowed up from the mask – like the sound of crow wings on a still day – then dissolved into the stench of peach-vomit.

How could she ask Woelfred for anything? Why did she bother?

180

Marie stood up on the mattress – slightly off balance – and scanned the room for her other shoe. It hung from the outstretched hand of a tall wooden monkey next to the closed bedroom door. She hated that monkey; its red plastic eyes staring, staring; had demanded that Casimir leave the bedroom door open whenever they made love, to keep it covered, out of sight.

Marie stepped off the bed, into the mess of glass slivers and lamp shards. Maybe she would cut herself and the blood would cover the wine. She carefully slipped the shoe off the monkey's paw and put it on. Then she hobbled over to the wine-soaked shoe lying next to the mask and slipped her foot into it.

She picked up the mask. It had a thin, hairline crack running from the left eyehole down to the mouth slit. *Long palm fronds shuddering under a pounding rain. Eyes on the trail ahead, eyes at the back of the head. Everything breathing. Scent of the man running, already wounded by some other beast. Soon. Eyes that hear, teeth that see, ears reaching into the dark beneath the flat, broad vine leaf, leaping through the pincers of a scavenger beetle. Then suddenly, there, on the trail ahead: Casimir, clothes torn, running.*

Marie let go of the mask and it fell to the floor and shattered.

She opened the curtain again. Casimir was sitting with the Brunuel girl, the back of his head pressed against her chest, the girl massaging his head. Marie stepped away from the window. A burning liquid rose to her throat again. How was she going to get out of here if he sat there on the front steps with the Brunuel girl all morning?

'Woelfred,' Marie said, 'how do I –' She froze. Her underwear. Where was her underwear? She moved around the room in a panic, lifting the sheets, flinging them onto the monkey, scattering the dusty boxes and papers underneath the bed, sifting through Casimir's clothes on the floor, pulling the dresser away from the wall, checking behind it, shaking out the blankets, dropping them onto the floor at the end of the bed.

There is no way out.

Marie shook her head to clear it and surveyed the room. An unholy disaster. Maybe Casimir had played a joke with her underwear. She rummaged through the drawers of the desk next to the fireplace. No. She lifted the owl off the mantelpiece, untwisted the head from the body, and looked inside: nothing but that dead poet's papers, wrapped in plastic. Frustrated, she threw the headless owl at the bed. It bounced off the side of the mattress, hit the floor, and rolled to a stop in front of the fireplace, next to her feet.

To remove yourself from God's love brings on suffering, her mother had told her, again and again.

There is no way out.

Marie put her hands to her ears. 'No!' She closed her eyes and began the prayer: 'Woelfred with flowers, Woelfred with fog, Woelfred with satin, Woelfred with grace...' A singsong prayer she had made up on one of her night walks to the shrine in Caix. Whatever she saw, she used in the prayer. '... Woelfred with masks, Woelfred with wings, Woelfred with owls, Woelfred with underwear... please help me find my underwear.'

She opened her eyes, stared at Casimir's chest of drawers. She might get away without Poisson noticing her wine-soaked shoe, but there was no way he'd let pass the missing underwear. She could see it all: how he would stand in the bedroom doorway while she changed for church, watching with those sad, bloodshot eyes. And when she slipped the smock over her head?

Casimir had so many women. He had even saved poor

Judy's panties, sealed them behind velvet in a cabinet up in the attic. There must be something she could wear in one of those drawers. She pulled open the top one. Nothing but socks, a scattering of condoms, a few envelopes with Casimir's name written on them. She tried the second drawer. Undershirts, some handkerchiefs; at the back, a lace bra. She was getting close. She pulled open the third drawer. Notebooks, journals. All sizes. She grabbed a stack and dropped them on the floor, making room for her hand to search the back of the drawer. More papers. Useless. She wanted to scream 'Fuck you!' at the notebooks, the socks, the underwear, but she only moaned, a hand in front of her broken mouth. If she screamed, someone would hear. She had so little time. She needed to get home before the town woke up. How was she going to get past the Brunuel girl? What was Casimir thinking? Had he forgotten that she was still in the house?

Down on her knees, she opened the next to last drawer, mouth set, grim. And there she found, like a vision, a pair of women's panties. They were stuffed between two sweaters at the back of the drawer. She pulled them out, held them up to the light and they unfurled like a huge yellow cotton flag. They were big. *Listen to him pant. Such a great amount of trouble and now here I am legs spread, ass on cold wood. I thought at the very least we'd do it in his bed. Was it Jeanette Lausch who said all it took for the professor to go down on his hands and knees was to brush past him in the hall, breasts against his arm? Listen to that breathing. He must be having such a good time. How many days did I have to stand out in the garden, waiting for him to spot me from the attic window? Listen to him groan! Is that delight? It's not what I expected; to make love to a man my father loathes. But next time Papa hits me, I won't even flinch. Is there delight? At least this old one knows what he's doing. Circling down, circling down. Not like Etienne or Jac – the way they thrash for a few minutes and finish, like it's a race. Listen to him breathe. I should at least look like I'm enjoying myself.*

Elise.

Marie crumpled the panties in her left hand and held it close to her chest. Her heart beat against it. 'Bird in a cage, bird in a cage, bird in a cage,' was what her mother said whenever she pressed her cheek to her daughter's chest. Marie lifted the panties up again, stretching the elastic waistband with her fingers. So big. He had had no idea who Elise was, what she wanted. Marie let the underwear drop to the floor in front of her, stood up.

Woelfred was right, there is no way out.

She heard voices downstairs in the hallway. Casimir's voice, the Brunuel girl's voice, Philippe.

'Fuck Casimir!' she whispered and kicked at the under-wear. It lifted off the floor, landed on the owl. A headless owl with yellow panties. Marie put her hand to her mouth, giggled through her fingers. The giggles quickly degenerated into a coughing fit. She held both hands in front of her mouth until the coughing subsided. She needed water. She needed to get out of there before the girl heard.

What difference does it make if the girl hears?

'Fuck Casimir!' The sound travelled a few feet in front of her, over the bed, then died. Why was it so hard to be loud? No one could hear. She raised shaking hands up to her face, cupped them around her mouth, took a deep breath and listened. The voices were now coming from the back of the house, probably the kitchen.

'Fuck Casimir!' she shouted and stepped back into the chest of drawers. 'Fuck Father Leo! Fuck Villon!' The clack of the chest of drawers against the wall seemed louder than her shout. The nausea returned, passing up through the middle of her body, her mouth, into her head. She took a few steps forward.

It didn't matter now. She would go home without underwear. She would walk out of this house, walk right under Dehanschutter's window without underwear. How funny. And if she passed the Brunuel girl on the way out? She would blow her a kiss, Judas to Judas.

Marie walked around the bed and surveyed the room from the bedroom door. What would Casimir do when he saw this? She stepped out into the hall, closed the door behind her, turned the key in the lock and slipped the key into the front pocket of her smock. That would give her a little more time. He would think she was still inside, sick or afraid. She cocked her head and listened. The voices were small now, far away. She walked to the top of the stairs, stood next to Casimir's cabinet room.

There was something else.

She turned the knob, went in. Grey morning light shone through the window, across four cabinets standing in the centre of the room, each one facing a different wall. On the floor, scattered around the cabinets, all the bric-a-brac Casimir used to make his cabinets: wire, glue, the usual doll head, a stone Buddha, a few records stacked next to a small portable phonograph, ashtrays filled to the brim with butts, three paint-splattered sweaters, a pair of trousers, a stapler, crêpe paper, animal bones.

Marie found what she was looking for in the cabinet facing the window: the dead baby mask. She untangled it from several strands of silver wire, held it up to the dim light.

Fly through the crown, into the sky; fly through the crown, turning, turning; fly...

Mask tucked under her arm, she moved quickly, silently,

down the stairs. At the bottom, she leaned over the banister, glanced down the hall in the direction of the kitchen. She could hear Casimir talking, talking. He was always talking.

She opened the front door, looked up and down the street. No one out in front of Brunuel's house. Good. She descended the front steps, taking them two at a time. On the pavement, she looked up at Dehanschutter's second floor window. The dark silhouette was back behind the lace curtain.

She lifted the mask to the window and the figure behind the curtains melted away.

As she crossed the three-way intersection at the end of rue des Ecoles, she glanced down into the Place: a massacre of fish, strewn over the cobbles. And crows. So many crows.

5 The Lover

... and mystery is a fish... swimming beneath the surface of the waters...

Desire for coherence. Everyone wants the world to be coherent. It was his job to make the world coherent for his parishioners. But what could he say about the fish? If Marie was still talking to him, what would *she* say about the fish?

When she first came to the church that night, six months ago, her mouth bloody, broken, he thought she was yet another one of the women in town clinging to the church out of pain. He had helped her up to his room. Crying, crying, so much crying. The noise of it was more shocking than the mucus and blood dribbling from her mouth because he had never heard her utter anything above a whisper.

He had settled her in his bed, dabbed her poor mouth with a cold, wet cloth, then stood up, telling her he was going downstairs to call the police. Eyes wide with terror, she had clutched at his leg. 'No, no, please no.' Such pain, fear. Reluctantly he had sat back down on the edge of the bed with her, held one of her tiny hands for a while, listening carefully for any suspicious sounds downstairs – maybe Poisson had followed her, was still sneaking around – but all he had been able to hear was the dripping of the sink behind him and Marie's laboured breathing.

Her hand had been hot, clammy. He had reached out to feel her forehead with the back of his hand, thinking she might have a fever, but she had pulled her head away from him. The familiar move of the mistreated animal. 'I think you have a fever,' he said. She nodded, but did not answer, holding the cloth to her lips, those black eyes roaming slowly around the room. 'Would you like me to put out the light so you can go to sleep?' She frowned and he took that as a no.

How long did he sit there, holding her hand? It seemed like hours. Eventually she turned away from him, curled into a foetal position, and fell asleep. He spent the night praying for her protection and guidance, periodically nodding off into a light sleep.

... and God is a fish... ripples on the surface of the water...

There was a tentative knock. Father Leo stared at the door. Like all the mornings for the last six months, he wanted it to be Marie, wanted her to stop at the priory on her way to the belfry, say something, say anything, break her dark silence. Forgive. But he knew it was only Michel Clouet, his best altar boy.
'Come in.'

The door opened and Michel's face appeared in the opening. The boy had the eyes and lips of an angel, the mouth of a devil. How that little one could swear. Father Leo had overheard the boy walking by the church with his pack of friends. F– this, F– that. The great American contribution to the language. Father Leo had even heard the boy swear when he was alone, practising his newly learned words on the crows down in the cemetery. He would probably end up becoming a priest.

'Have you seen the fish?' the boy said. He was holding a small fish in either hand. The room filled with the thick green scent of the sea. 'Is the world coming to an end?'

'No, the world's not coming to an end,' Father Leo said, frowning at the water dripping off the fish onto the hall floor.

'Will there be Mass today?' the boy asked.

'Of course, Michel,' Father Leo answered, 'there will always be Mass.'

Michel's face fell.

'Go and take those fish back outside before they stink up the entire priory,' the priest said.

Michel looked down at one fish, then the other, clearly disappointed.

'Then you can go and get something to wipe up this mess. There are rags under the kitchen sink.'

The boy turned, ran out of the door.

Father Leo poked his head out of the bedroom door and shouted, 'And if they aren't under the sink, there's a box of rags down in the cellar.' But Michel was already gone. He could hear him opening the door below, running across the alley. He hoped the boy had enough sense not to take the fish into the church. He sat back down on the edge of the bed. Again he thought about what he was going to say about the fish at Mass. Did he need to say anything? Hadn't he learned his lesson with Marie?

Mystery should be left alone.

... and Michel is a mystery equal to the fish... a mystery carrying a mystery... in a church surrounded by fish...

At dawn the next morning Marie had tapped him on the shoulder and he had instinctively jerked into an upright position, eyes wide. 'What? What?' She had jumped back onto the bed, hand to her mouth. 'I'm sorry, Father.' Her voice was thick, muffled. Before she lifted her hand to her mouth, he'd seen the two yellowish-white nubs where her front teeth had been, the puffy, bruised lips. Such incredible sorrow in those eyes, looking at him over the edge of that hand.

He had immediately raised his hands, palms out, as if she was an abused dog, showing her he had nothing in his hands to beat her with. She'd turned and pointed at the pillow, hand over her mouth still. 'I'm sorry about the blood.'

He ran a hand through his hair, blinked a few times to clear his vision. 'It's not your fault. No need to apologise. How do you feel?'

Marie shrugged. 'I'm sorry you had to sleep in a chair. I will go.'

'No.' Father Leo held out his hand. 'You mustn't go back. Not right now. I will call the police.'

Marie shook her head, eyes frightened. 'Please, no police.'

'But why?'

Marie looked down at the pillow, shook her head. Okay, it was too soon to deal with the outside world, he thought. This room was her refuge for the time being. Maybe after she'd eaten some breakfast. But with those broken teeth –

'You will have to see a dentist, I think,' Father Leo said. Marie closed her hand tightly over her mouth, stared down at the pillow, ran a finger across the blood stains. It had been the wrong thing to say.

It was too bad. She hadn't been a beautiful woman, but she'd never been hard to look at. A bit thin. Probably because there wasn't much for her and that son of hers to eat. Her son! What was his name? He always saw the little boy toddling behind her as she made her way home from the *boulangerie*. Always talking to himself, humming.

He rose, put some water in the kettle, set it on the hotplate to boil. 'I admit I love English breakfast tea,' he said, 'so that's all I have at the moment.' He kept quiet while the water boiled, hoping to give her enough space to gather her thoughts, begin to talk, but she remained silent.

When he handed her the mug she looked at it as if she didn't know what it was. 'Tea,' he said. She shook her head. 'It's warm, you should drink something warm. Would you prefer broth?'

She held both hands out like a dutiful child and he gave her the mug. She sipped and winced.

'Wait until it cools down a little,' he said. After more silence – the dripping tap behind him growing louder – he broached the subject of the boy.

'I have just remembered your little boy – what is his name?'

'Emile.'

'Emile, yes. Don't you think I should go over to your house and retrieve him?'

She looked up from her mug. 'No.'

'But Poisson?'

'Emile is not part of this.' She said it so forcefully he took a step backwards, towards the sink. As if she was reprimanding

190

him for thinking such a thought. 'Poisson would never strike him.'

'I don't want to do anything that makes you feel uncomfortable, but...'

She looked back down into her tea. 'I'm sorry.'

'There's no need for you to apologise. You have suffered. Right now you need rest. We can think about these things later.' He took a sip of tea. 'Would you like milk, sugar?'

Out on his rounds later that morning, he saw Poisson and Emile fishing in the creek that ran along the alley behind the brasserie. Poisson looked him up and down, and turned back to his fishing rod, looking as innocent as his young son. The boy seemed fine, sitting there in Poisson's lap, squinting into the sun on water, babbling his baby nonsense to himself. Odd.

When he returned to the priory, he found Marie asleep. He stood at the end of the bed, watched her face, listened to her breathing. A little wheezy, but more or less regular. Her eyes darted back and forth underneath her eyelids. She moved her bruised, swollen lips every once in a while. Dream conversations. He tried to imagine the Poisson he saw with Emile down by the creek lifting a fist against this woman. What could have provoked him? Drunkenness? But he was drunk all the time.

Marie stirred, opened her eyes, saw Father Leo and raised the blanket up to her nose, covering her mouth.

'How do you feel?'

Marie stared at him, said nothing.

'Some chicken broth?'

Her black eyes moved from his face to the open door, then back to his face.

'Well, I'll just go and make some in the kitchen and you can continue sleeping...'

He checked the tins that lined the shelf along the wall next to the fridge, found the chicken broth, opened it and dumped the contents into a pot on the stove. As he stirred the yellow liquid, he thought again of Poisson and Emile down by the creek. The boy had looked so contented, sitting there in his father's lap.

He set a bowl of broth on the bedside table. 'You don't have to eat if you don't want. But me, I'm a big man, I have lots of space to fill.' He sat in the chair next to the bed, raised his spoon. 'I hope you don't mind?'

Marie picked the bowl up off the table. After she had finished about half the bowl, he broke the silence and asked her, as delicately as he could, why Poisson had struck her.

'If you do not wish to talk about it, I understand... only...'

Marie lowered her spoon gently into the bowl and placed the bowl on the table. 'I was out walking,' she said, looking down at her hands.

'He hit you because you went out walking?'

Marie shook her head. 'No. He doesn't know I go walking. I wait until he passes out, then I go.'

'Ah,' he said, as if he understood. 'You go out walking alone? What about Emile?'

'He's a heavy sleeper like his father,' she said, still looking at her hands. 'But this time he didn't sleep through the night.'

'Emile?'

'Poisson. He must have woken up in the dark – he doesn't like the dark, has nightmares – and was wandering around half-asleep, afraid, when I came back into the house. He must have thought I was an intruder.'

'That's why he hit you? Because he thought you were a thief?' Father Leo sighed, lowered his spoon into the broth, settled the bowl in his lap. 'Didn't you scream? Tell him who you were?'

192

Marie shook her head. 'He hit me once. Then I ran.' Tears ran down her cheeks, dropped into her open hands. 'He was frightened, alone.'

Father Leo didn't know what to say. Why was she protecting Poisson? Maybe he would just let it rest for a while.

'Where do you go when you go walking?' he asked.

'There is a hole in the quarry fence...'

Father Leo nodded. 'I know it.'

'... I used to sit on the edge of the cliff there.' Marie looked up, stared past Father Leo's face at the window behind him, then looked down at her hands again. 'I like the feeling I get when sitting next to such a drop.'

'Did you ever...' the question had to be asked, '... think of throwing yourself off?'

Marie looked up at Father Leo, eyes wide with shock, shaking her head vehemently. 'No, no. It was the space. It's so dark you can't see the water below and it looks as if you are looking down into the sky itself. But a group of boys started going there, so I –'

'Did they... bother you?'

'No, no, I just wanted to be alone.' Marie began to pick at her left thumb with the nail of her right thumb.

'I understand the desire,' Father Leo said. He wanted to reach out and clasp his hand around both of hers, stop her from picking her own flesh. 'I sometimes go down into the church late at night and sit.'

Marie nodded, hair hanging over her eyes. 'I don't usually think about where I'm going to go, I just walk,' she said. 'The canal, the park, everywhere.'

Father Leo put his bowl of broth next to hers on the bedside table. He could feel her eyes on his hand as he placed the bowl – as gently as he could – on the wood. He sat back in his chair and smiled at her. She attempted a smile, then dropped her eyes back to her hands. Picking, picking. As if to counter the image of her busy hands, he folded his in his lap.

'But, in the last few months,' she continued, 'I've been gone longer and longer. I know it's not right, but I can't stop myself.'

Ah, here it comes. The desire that drives us on and on. He'd heard the same confession so many times.

'Where have you been going?' Father Leo asked.

'Caix,' Marie said, barely above a whisper.

'Caix? But that's five kilometres from here! What's in Caix?'

'Saint Woelfred's shrine.'

... and Saint Woelfred is a fish called into existence by the dark eyes of Marie... and Marie is a fish...

What was taking Michel so long with that rag? Father Leo walked to the window, looked down at the gravestones. Michel was bending over a large cod at the foot of Father Gaspar's grave. Father Leo unlatched the window, shouted down at the boy. 'Michel! Bring me a towel to wipe up the fish water you dribbled all over my floor! Right now!' Michel stood up straight, faced the window, arms at his side like a soldier standing at attention, then saluted. 'Never mind the theatrics,' Father Leo shouted, but the boy was already gone, back through the kitchen door, into the priory.

Father Leo waited a few minutes, listened for Michel's feet in the kitchen below, but heard nothing. 'If you don't find the rags under the kitchen, there's a box in the cellar,' he shouted.

No response. He shook his head and walked to the bathroom, grabbed a roll of toilet paper, brought it back to the bedroom and began swabbing up the stinking water. The paper soaked through immediately, and he ended up swishing the water around in circles with wet balls of gummy paper. Useless.

... and the trees are fish, circling into the earth... and the earth is a fish, circling around the sun...

A leaf, a flower, a stone. These were the things Marie would pick up on her way to the saint's shrine. And one time, she confessed to him, she had left her own shoes.

'Your shoes? Why your shoes?' The poor woman couldn't have owned more than two pair of shoes.

'I wanted to show her that I –' Marie lifted a hand to her eyes, pinched the bridge of her nose. A tear ran down her thumb, across her thin wrist. She dropped her hand back into her lap and looked at Father Leo. 'I want to love. To be able to love. Do you see?'

Her eyes were so black, fierce. To walk night after night to a saint's shrine, and not ask for shelter, protection, healing? Tears welled up in his eyes. He met her gaze, his lips trembling. Marie quickly looked back down at her hands. He rose off the chair, knelt by the bed and took her hands in his.

'I do see,' he said to her. 'I do.'

... and Saint Woelfred is a fish... consuming Marie... and Marie is a fish... consuming me... and I am a fish...

Father Leo poked his head out into the hall again and listened. Still no sound. What was the boy doing? He wondered if the boy was afraid of going down into the cellar. The light switch for the cellar was, for some perverse reason, at the bottom of a flight of steep stone stairs.

Father Leo picked up the balls of wet toilet paper, dropped them into the bin under the sink. Would Marie be afraid? Marie's faith could easily light the way down those very stairs, and what had he done? Knelt by the bed, held her hands, lowered his forehead onto those cold, cold hands, then looked up at her and said, 'You are proof that Saint Woelfred does indeed exist.'

Marie had slipped one cold hand from his grasp. 'What do you mean?'

'I mean that it doesn't matter if Woelfred lived or didn't live, that the love you find is surely the true answer.'

She had then slipped the other hand from his. 'I don't understand.'

'Didn't you know that Woelfred was no longer a saint?'

Marie shook her head. 'But the shrine –'

Father Leo pointed to his heart: 'History can't compete with the heart. You are the proof that makes Woelfred real.'

Marie lifted a hand up to her pale throat, clutched it. 'She did not exist?'

It was only then that he understood his mistake.

'That is not important, what's important is –'

Marie's eyes cut him off. Black grief. Betrayal. 'Tell me yes or no,' she said, her hand inching up to cover her mouth as she spoke. 'Was she real or not?'

What could he have said to her? It was not a yes or no answer. 'It doesn't matter,' he said, leaning towards her, reaching out to touch the hand in her lap.

'No,' she whispered, but she didn't pull her hand away.

'You are so cold,' he said. 'Maybe I should heat up the broth?'

'I must go.' She swung her legs over the opposite side of the bed and sat there, hunched, her back to him.

'Please don't go,' he said, wanting to stall her, keep her there, until he could think of a way of explaining to her what he had meant to say. 'It might not be safe.'

'I need to be alone,' she said, looking down into her lap.

'Yes, I understand that. Sometimes I go down into the church, light a candle. Would you like to do that? You shouldn't go out walking in your –'

'Why is there a shrine if she doesn't exist?'

Father Leo shook his head. It was too complex. 'I don't know,' he said.

Marie stood up. 'Where are my shoes?'

Father Leo produced them from under his chair, handed them to her across the bed. She took them without looking into his face.

'I think it would be a good idea if you sat in the church for a while,' he said. 'There are many answers that come to me when I sit in solitu –'

'If you would like me to sit downstairs and pray, then I will,' Marie said. 'But then I must go home.'

'It's not about what *I* want, it's about...' The end of the sentence drifted away from him as he followed her out into the hall. They were both silent descending the stairs. At the bottom he rested his hand on her shoulder, guiding her through the dark kitchen. She pulled away, walked ahead of him across the alley, into the dark church.

'Would you like me to light a candle for you?' he whispered, his heart sick.

'No, I'll sit in the dark,' she said.

He quickly kissed the top of her head and whispered 'You are beautiful. And true. Know that.' Then he retreated back to his room.

The next day he went to her house. Poisson answered the door, looked him up and down, wondering aloud if the priest had lost his way. Father Leo asked to see Marie. The monster Poisson continued to stand there in that cold kitchen while Father Leo asked her if she would take a job ringing the bells each Sunday. He couldn't pay much, but...

Poisson had laughed. 'Charity? The church is offering charity?'

Marie did not want to take the job, but Poisson insisted.

It did not go the way Father Leo had planned.

Marie's black eyes had burned through him. Black as a crow ripping into a fish next to a grave. If Poisson hadn't been there, he would have dropped to his knees and begged her forgiveness. But would she have understood? Better to have left it alone.

... and love is a fish inside a fish inside a fish...

Where was Michel? He probably ran off, the belief in this fish-chaos stronger than any other authority at the moment. Why not? If fish fell from the sky then everything the boy had been taught in school – at least, on the surface – had been proved false. Why listen to anyone? Why not go off and play?

What was he going to say at Mass? That Ducasse woman, lying there on her deathbed, had she seen into the future, had she seen this chaos? Or had it been a memory?

He walked downstairs, crossed the alley, entered the church, stood behind the altar. Red and blue light streamed in through the upper windows. There was a rustling up in the eaves. No, it came from the back of the church, near the door.

'Michel?' Father Leo's voice bounced off the stone.

Pigeon wings flapped, were still. He retreated back to the priory.

Back in his own kitchen he opened the cellar door. 'Michel?'

What was he thinking? Why would the boy be down there in the dark? Well, he might as well go get the rags himself.

The stairway was steep and he proceeded slowly, hands against the cold stone on either side to keep his balance. When he reached the bottom, he felt around for the switch, thought he touched something cold and wet. Fingers? No, more like a fish.

'Stop it,' he said to himself. The mouldy dark absorbed his words the instant he said them. He squinted around in the dark, thought he saw a figure in the direction of the furnace room. No, that's the furnace. He blinked, looked quickly into the storage room and saw the same figure. No, those are boxes. He found the switch, flicked it on. The feeble bare bulb blinded him for a second. When he opened his eyes, the cellar looked like it always did. He hurried into the storage room, bumped his shins against the ping pong table, found a couple of rags, turned off the light, and scrambled as quickly as he could up the stairs. At the top, he turned and looked back down. The same figure stood in the dark at the bottom. More tricks. Why did he do this to himself every time he went down there?

He shut the door, made his way back upstairs. When he reached the bedroom, he got down on his hands and knees and began swabbing the floor. The rags were greasy and didn't absorb the water. Father Leo shook his head and laughed, then sat back against the wall next to the door.

What was he going to say about the fish? Maybe everyone in town will do like Michel did – abandon themselves to the chaos. Why go to Mass when the laws of nature have been reversed? Go straight to kermesse.

Madame Ducasse's eyes had been so bright with fear. That black intensity. Like Marie's. The old woman had clutched at his wrist with her bony hand, whispering 'They fell like snow.' And all he had thought right then was 'Your money can't save you from death.'

Father Leo closed his eyes, shameful still after all these years. If that old woman appeared to him now, he would prostrate himself before her, apologise. He opened his eyes, looked at the rags. He could at least take comfort in the fact that he no longer judged the world in the same way. That had been so long ago, when he knew so much more than he did now.

Madame Ducasse had then whispered to him that everyone in the village thought God was rewarding the town for all the pain suffered during the war. Fish falling from heaven.

He had nodded, smiled, wondering which war she was whispering about.

She had responded to his smile with a violent shake of her head. 'No, no. You must understand. They had a great feast in the centre of town,' she had said, taking deep, horribly painful breaths between the words. 'Music, dancing, and do you know? Everyone got sick as dogs. Some died.' Then she had let go of his wrist and bunched her arthritic fingers around a white linen handkerchief embroidered with her initials. 'Why had God given such a gift, only to mock?'

… and water is a mystery to fish… and fish are a mystery to water…

Father Leo heard the sound of running on the stairs and he struggled to his feet. Maybe he would talk about Madame Ducasse at Mass. On the theme of judgement. Who are we to judge what is a gift from God and what is not?

Michel appeared in the doorway, eyes wide, pointing back at the stairwell. 'Poisson's beating on the door of the church, looking for his wife!'

6 The Seeker

March 5th, 1987
Lemesos, Cyprus

Dear anti-biologiste,

There's a medieval castle here that looks out over the clay roofs, the port. Richard the Lionheart shipwrecked here, they say – on his way to the holy land to kill some Muslims – and ended up marrying Berengaria of Navarre in the castle chapel. I went through it yesterday. The usual paraphernalia: armour, cannons, swords. I wonder if this museum was here when Rimbaud came through one hundred years ago. Probably not.

Yesterday I caught a ride with a couple from Philadelphia (isn't that where your mother lives? Small world), up into the Troodos Mountains. They were driving around hunting for painted Byzantine churches. I told them about Rimbaud, his journey from poète maudite in Paris, a genius before his time, rejected by the great poets of his day, to construction worker in Cyprus, and they ended up helping me get to the old Governor's summer residence where Rimbaud had worked. He'd been a foreman on the site. There are rumours he 'accidentally' killed one of the workers here and had to flee to Egypt. We found it (an unimpressive building, really) along with a plaque that reads: 'ARTHUR RIMBAUD poète et génie français au mépris de sa renommée contribua de ses propres mains a la construction de cette maison.'

The plaque exists because Rimbaud wrote poetry in his adolescence. But who was the man that was foreman here? The same person? (I know, I know, I keep coming back to that. I thought in Athens that he was essentially the same person all his life, but I have changed my mind. How easily the mind seems to change in a different landscape, a different climate, a different culture – a bit like a derangement of the senses. Now I'm beginning to see that after all those years of travel, Rimbaud couldn't possibly be the same person with the same desires that he was in his youth.)

While looking at the plaque, I suddenly heard all the scholarly noise and gossip about Rimbaud that's occurred between my life and his. One hundred years of speculation about the man. All based on his poems. Poems he stopped writing when he was twenty-one.

Why did he stop writing? Why did he go to Cyprus? Why Africa? One hundred years of scholars and biographers and poets and rock stars (Jim Morrison was a big fan) all trying to get a clue about who they are by attempting to solve the mystery of who Rimbaud was...

I'm no different.

For some, he's the original punk rocker, with that tousled hair, his vicious pranks, and his angelic boyish looks. For others, he's the dark gay poet, having an affair with the poet Paul Verlaine, then breaking it off and getting shot in the wrist by the spurned poet in some fleabag Brussels hotel. Or is he the visionary, the synaesthetic, who assigned a colour to every vowel, believing poetry could change the very face of existence?

Then again, is he the skinny, violent foreman of a construction crew here in Cyprus? Or the failed capitalist who tried to sell guns to Menelek, King of Shoa, in order to make a killing and return home to France a rich man?

What is it that makes us who we are? Our physical pattern? That changes. Our memory? That changes, too. What is it that holds the person we call 'Rimbaud' together from beginning to end? What makes Rimbaud Rimbaud?

Last night I woke up feeling some presence in my hotel room. I looked around and saw a silhouette next to the door. How long did I stare at it, frozen? I watched it for what seemed hours – fascinated, terrified – and, after a while (I think I became somewhat hallucinatory), I imagined I could feel some kind of vibration coming off the silhouette, attaching itself to a lost part of my own mind. I eventually fell asleep and woke as the sound of traffic began down in the street. The silhouette had been the curtained window. It seems hysterically funny now, but it was so real last night. I looked at my hands, shadows in the grey morning light coming through the curtain, and thought: 'Who do these belong to?'

I'm losing myself. As Rimbaud once wrote to Georges Izambard, his teacher at the Collège de Charleville when he was a teen: 'I is another.'

Some time this week I'll be taking a ferry to Cairo, figure out how to get to Yemen from there. After that, maybe Harar in Ethiopia – the walled Muslim town where Rimbaud lived for ten years. We'll see.

Raoul

V

And the Fish Is a Fish of the Desire-for-the-Cessation-of-Desire-which-Causes-Suffering...

1 The Stranger

In the centre of Spierry, Nicholas Moegge, the large, powerfully built old groundskeeper of Villon's church, got onto the bus, holding the hand of a little boy who looked to be five or six. While the groundskeeper fished around in the front pocket of his canvas trousers with his free hand, searching for change, the boy looked down the aisle at Liesl. She smiled at him and he quickly pressed his head into the thigh of the groundskeeper.

She had interviewed Nicholas about his opinions on the waste dumps right after she had interviewed Father Leo. His take on everything was in complete opposition to the priest's: cynical, venomous, giving no quarter to anyone. He had leaned against a gravestone, crossed his arms, and squinted down his red bulbous nose at her with his one good eye, explaining to her that, yes, the factory was evil, but what was that in comparison to nuclear devastation, now that Ronald Reagan was playing cowboy, his trigger finger on the button? 'The world is poison,' he had said, then pointed at the church. 'The poison started with the church. They say "In the beginning was the word..." but what they mean is "In the beginning was the lie..." Be good, do as you're told, then go to heaven. My God, the factory couldn't *exist* without centuries of their lies softening the people up like veal calves.'

Nicholas picked the boy up, carried him down the aisle and deposited him on the seat in front of Liesl, then hitched up his trousers and lowered himself, groaning, onto the edge of the seat next to the boy. When he was settled, he glanced over at Liesl, asked her if she was ready for the big rally.

'You're going to the rally?' Liesl asked, surprised.

'I will be there, yes. I'm supposed to be taking my sister's grandson here to Mass, then kermesse.' He twisted around, looked at the boy. 'He has a lifetime of sad penance ahead of him, I'm afraid.' The boy stared out of the window, into a field of long grass, one lone cow chewing near the fence line next to the road.

Nicholas turned back to Liesl. 'I fear he hasn't the strength to resist the poisons of the church. He's already been infected with holy water.'

Liesl laughed, but Nicholas's face remained stone. He pointed a huge, thick finger at the German's cigarette. 'I agree with him,' he said, producing a crushed pack of cigarettes from inside his old brown leather coat, raising one to his mouth.

The German looked over at Liesl. 'What did he say?'

'He wants to smoke with you.'

'Isn't it forbidden?'

'*Verboten*?' Nicholas repeated the German's word, then said to Liesl: 'He is German? Your brother?'

Even though there was no fog she still felt the damp inside her bones. The factory lights made tiny jagged stars in the dark quarry water.

'Are you the German who's been asking those pesky questions about the dumps?'

Liesl spun around. 'I'm not –'

Guy.

'You startled me,' she said. 'How did you know I'd be here?'

Guy gave her his half-smile, took her hand. 'I didn't.'

He looked down into the water. 'When I was a kid I imagined there were great beasts living down there. That the dredgers would one day cut too deep, break open some ancient limestone cave that was the lair of some monster, releasing it from its million year sleep.'

'It's a kind of truth,' she said. 'Digging this deep obviously has consequences. Maybe not monsters from the deep, but they've released some kind of monster.'

His hand was cold.

'Cement,' she said. 'Making walls to keep people out, to keep people in; horrible high rises that alienate everyone who lives and works in them; dams that torture rivers into doing our bidding, harnessing water power to make more electricity that creates demand for more walls and high rises and dams.'

Guy led her away from the edge of the cliff, took off his leather jacket, laid it on the ground, motioned for her to sit. Even with the leather jacket between herself and the wet grass, she was cold. Had she ever been completely warm since she'd arrived in Villon? Certainly not in her tent. It had been constant fog, snow turning into that never-ending drizzle.

Guy sat in the wet grass next to her.

'You'll catch cold if you sit in the wet grass,' she said. 'You can't afford to be ill for the rally. Contexture...'

Guy waved her worries away. 'If I am ill Contexture will still be able to perform. They've been doing it for years, long before I learned my first trick.'

'Do you *want* to get ill?'

He laughed. That huff through the nose. 'I realise that according to your personal understanding of psychology I might induce myself to be ill in order to avoid failure. But I have no such intentions.'

'I'm not saying you're trying to get out of anything, I just don't want you to be ill my last week here.'

'This is not our last week together,' Guy said. But he didn't look her in the eye when he said it.

Nicholas lit a match, cupped it around the end of his cigarette. The driver looked in the rearview mirror, yelled something. Nicholas yelled back.

The German leaned into the aisle, asked Liesl what they were saying.

'I have no idea.'

After a few more shouts between the driver and Nicholas, Nicholas turned back to Liesl. 'Tell your friend he can smoke. It's okay now.' He handed the German his cigarette lighter.

Liesl wiped fog off the window, looked out at the wet fields, a line of scrub trees lining a distant stone wall. The bus was now descending the narrow cobbled road that eventually turned into rue des Ecoles at the edge of Villon.

'Ask the German where he's coming from,' Nicholas said to Liesl.

The woman with the green kerchief coughed, waved her hand in front of her face, said something to the bus driver, and he glared into the rearview mirror at Nicholas. Liesl asked the German Nicholas's question.

'Marseilles,' the German said.

'Marseilles!' Nicholas repeated, planting huge hands firmly on his knees, leaning forward into the aisle. The boy behind him looked over his shoulder, blinking like he'd just woken from a nap.

'I'm coming back from the Middle East,' the German said to Liesl. 'Kuwait, Saudi Arabia.'

'Merchant marine?'

'I worked in the oil fields. But no more. You hang in there for six months, a year or two, do nothing but work, then you piss it all away in a matter of months. Drinking, women. I'm done with that.'

Liesl turned to Nicholas, told him what the German said.

Nicholas nodded, cigarette poised inches from his lips. 'Did you know Poisson worked oil rigs in the North Sea? That's the only way he could ever have found a girl who would stay with him, you know. Far from here, where no one knew him.'

'What is he saying?' the German asked Liesl.

'He says one of the men in Villon used to work oil rigs in the North Sea.'

The German looked at Nicholas, nodded and raised his cigarette in a kind of toast. 'To the poor bastard, then.'

Without waiting for a translation, Nicholas raised his cigarette to the German in return. The boy draped his arms over Nicholas's shoulders, laid his cheek against the big man's bristly red neck, and stared at Liesl. Liesl winked and the boy quickly slid down Nicholas's back, out of sight.

'Speaking of Poisson,' Liesl said to Nicholas, 'I heard there were fish scattered all over Villon this morning.'

208

'Fish?' Nicholas repeated, looking at the German. 'What fish?'

The inside of the bus grew dark for a few seconds as it passed beneath the old stone viaduct that marked the beginning of rue des Ecoles. The driver downshifted and the bus shuddered. Everyone suddenly jerked forward, then fell back into their seats. The driver tried for the gear again and there was a terrible screech of metal against metal. The bus lurched on for another few metres, then abruptly stopped.

Nicholas turned to Liesl. 'I think we just threw a rod.'

The driver tried the ignition, produced another shriek of metal. In the silence that followed he stared through the windshield, both hands on the wheel, shaking his head.

The German looked over at Liesl, frowning. 'What's going on?'

The driver announced that the bus had broken down. They could either wait for the next bus, scheduled to pass in an hour, or walk to Villon.

'I think you've thrown a rod,' Nicholas said.

The bus driver told Nicholas he wasn't interested in what Nicholas thought, then walked off the bus, pulling a pack of cigarettes out of his vest pocket as he did.

Nicholas's grandnephew pointed out of the window. 'Fish!'

2 The Lover

... and the world will be consumed by a fish... and the universe will be consumed by a greater fish... and that fish will be consumed by the Lord of the waters of heaven...

Father Leo was halfway down the nave, lumbering towards the front of the church when Poisson burst through the church door. The priest rushed at the drunk, but Poisson easily tossed him aside, and made straight for the door behind the apse, screaming his wife's name.

The priest struggled to his feet and followed the drunk into the priory. In the kitchen he grabbed a rolling pin from a drawer next to the sink and padded carefully into the living room, pin raised high. Poisson's footsteps resounded on the floor above.

Father Leo moved as quietly as he could up the stairs. When he reached the top, Poisson suddenly appeared from around the corner and pulled the pin out of his hand.

'What are you going to do without your sceptre?'

'You must leave at once,' Father Leo said, his voice shaking.

Poisson raised the pin as if to strike the priest and Father Leo covered his head with his arms, waiting for the blow. Poisson laughed. 'Idiot.' He grabbed the priest by the back of the collar and pushed him back down the stairs. 'I'm sick of all you people sneaking in and out of my house at night, taking whatever you want.' When they reached the bottom, Poisson leaned over the priest's shoulder. 'Don't think I don't know what's going on. I know she's here.'

'I understand,' Father Leo said, holding his hands up in a gesture of surrender. 'You want your wife. But she is not here.'

'You're a thief, *monsieur*,' Poisson said. 'And you are going to show me where you've hidden her.' He pushed the priest forward, through the kitchen door, across the stone path, back into the church.

3 The Illusionist

'I'm not going in with you,' Guy said as Marc slid out of the car. 'I have to get back to the Place *right now.*'

He knew it would do no good to say it. He'd been saying it ever since they'd left the tropical fish shop and Marc had pointed the car towards Mons, insisting they go to some *patisserie* on rue d'Havre, babbling on about women and food, food and women. But the *patisserie* was closed. Marc had then decided what he really needed was a new cigarette lighter, but since all the shops in the centre of Mons were closed, they'd had to drive out to the Delhaize on Chaussée de Roeulx. They'd wandered the vast, lonely aisles of the giant supermarket for a good fifteen minutes – Marc poking through the frozen meats, vegetables, still talking about love and food, the obsessive quality of both, forgetting all about the lighter – before Guy had finally shouted that the tour of Mons was over, that it was time for Marc to get back home to his wife. This seemed to have broken Marc's spirit and they'd headed back to Villon in silence.

But no. Just as they were passing a strip of new houses along Route de Villon – the factory road in sight – Marc had brightened and slowed the car, pulling to the curb in front of the house at the end of the row. The house of an old lover, Marc told him. She made the best omelettes he'd ever eaten. They might be able to procure a little breakfast.

'I have an appointment!' Guy shouted.

Marc shut the door behind him, walked a few paces across the tiny gravel yard, then turned back to the car. 'Your Liesl's not going anywhere,' he said. 'She came to cover the rally, so she'll be at the rally.'

'It's not just about Liesl,' Guy said. But Marc wasn't

listening, he'd already turned, lost inside his own churning wheel of desire.

If Guy didn't have time to walk the dancers through the trick, show them their marks, how was he going to pull it off? What had ever made him think he could pull off the trick by himself? It was going to be impossible without Chiqui.

And Liesl –

Marc rang the buzzer.

Liesl touched Guy's left fist. He opened the hand – empty. She touched the right fist. He opened it – empty. He closed his hands into fists again. She was about to touch the left one again, but shook her head, giggled to herself, and picked the right. There was a small Turkish cigarette in the centre of his palm.

'You're stealing from Dehanschutter now?'

'I don't have many,' Guy said. 'We'll have to share.' He fumbled through his coat pockets, looking for a match, pulled out two marbles, a couple of coins.

Liesl grinned at the marbles, cigarette between her lips. 'You didn't steal matches?'

He dropped the marbles and coins back into his pocket, defeated, then glanced across the Place at the church. Light flickered in the windows. 'There's candles and matches in there.'

He made his way as quickly as he could across the Place, up the church steps. He tried the door. Locked. He pressed his ear against the wood. Silence. The Father was probably praying. Or sleeping.

He raised his hand to knock, turning to Liesl: 'When the good Father comes to the door, I want you to tell him that you were out walking and suddenly you wanted to pray... for... for...' He snapped his fingers, hoping it would produce the excuse.

'What are you talking about?'

'You were out walking and you saw something... something...' He snapped his fingers again. '... A shadow in the alley next to the brasserie...'

'Even if you don't believe in all of this,' Liesl said, waving a hand at the church door, 'don't you think you should respect... I mean, how would you like it if you were meditating under a bush and –'

'I've got it,' Guy said, ignoring her. 'You were out walking and thought someone was following you, you saw the light in the church window, but now that you've knocked you think it was only your imagination. You get him to step out, look around, while I slip in and grab some matches.'

He rapped on the door and moved into the shadows.

'Fucker!'

Marc rang the buzzer again, looked back at Guy and smiled. A man opened the door. Marc began talking, pointing back at the car, down the road, laughing, nervous, an endless stream of nonsense coming out of his mouth.

Guy's stomach clenched. Did Marc think he could talk his way into the house?

Guy hurried up the centre aisle towards the candle stand, felt around for the box of matches beneath it, patting the dusty stone floor with the flat of his hand, finding nothing. The voices behind him were growing louder.

She's coming back inside with Leo?

He looked over his shoulder. Two figures at the end of the centre aisle. What was she doing coming back inside with the priest? Just then, his hand found a long thin cardboard box.

Matches! He grabbed the box and quickly crawled behind the column closest to the stand.

Liesl and the priest stopped in front of the candle stand, their eyes reflecting the flickering light.

If only Liesl could see this vision of herself. It would probably put her over the edge, send her into the arms of Mother Church.

'Are you sure you don't want to sleep on the couch in the priory?' the priest was saying. 'It gets rather cold in here – especially right before dawn.'

Liesl shook her head. 'I think I'd like to stay out here, if you don't mind.' She looked back at the candlelight. 'It's so beautiful. And I'd like to... think.'

Father Leo ran his hand through his hair, making it stand out above his temples. He looked like a tired owl, as if he'd fallen asleep during his prayers.

'I'll go get some blankets.'

The priest moved off into the darkness behind the altar. A door opened, closed. Liesl took a few steps backwards, whispered Guy's name. He stepped out from behind the column.

'What's going on?'

'I couldn't help it,' she said. 'He offered to wait at the bus stop with me and I panicked, told him there were no more buses for the night. He insisted I stay. What could I say?'

4 The Stranger

They were everywhere, scattered all down rue des Ecoles. Huge fish with glazed eyes, stinking of the sea. Cod, sturgeon,

214

flounder, haddock. And one huge eel, black eyes reflecting the morning light, draped over a stone wall. On the road in front of Liesl, Nicholas's grandnephew ran from one fish to the next, poking them with a stick, jumping back, then running ahead to the next fish to repeat the same performance.

She stared down the long road, a row of houses on either side, the cement-dusted doorsteps. Would she miss all this? The narrow country roads with massive cement trucks rumbling through, the old women looking at her suspiciously under the perpetual grey light. Last night, walking out in the back pasture with Guy, she'd asked him how he could stand it – the smallness, the sameness of it – after all those years living in Amsterdam. He had walked in silence for a minute, then said: 'The people I knew in Amsterdam, they were just like the people here. I don't think they knew anything more than anyone living here. The only difference I can see is in the work. Here, it's cement; there, it was sex and magic.'

'But you never would have met someone like Chiqui in a town like this,' Liesl had protested, trying to get him to understand that she was leaving, that she wasn't going to stay here, that she couldn't stay here. Did she need to shout it at him? How could they do anything about their situation if they never discussed it?

'I met *you* here,' Guy said, slipping an arm over her shoulder. 'When I was a child, maybe seven or eight, wandering around in the fog, I saw a naked man – stark naked – run past me in the Place. He had his clothes bundled under one arm, sprinting as fast as he could go. It all happened so fast that after he was gone I wasn't sure if I'd seen him at all. I stood there, completely at a loss, for minutes, wondering if it had been a vision. I never saw anything like that in Amsterdam.'

'The only people with the resources to do something on this scale would be the factory,' Nicholas said, crouching over a fish with faded red scales in the centre of the road.

Liesl translated for the German and he nodded, looking back down the road, at the old woman with the green kerchief clucking and mumbling to herself as she steered a path through the fish, trying to keep as far away from them as possible.

'In Kuwait, a man from Australia told me he'd seen fish rain from the sky when he was a boy,' the German said to Liesl.

Liesl crouched down beside Nicholas, translated what the German said. Nicholas looked up at the German. 'These probably got flushed out of an aeroplane. Some NATO military test that went awry.' He squinted into the grey sky.

'This is a redfish,' Liesl said. 'Found in the Atlantic. The North Sea.' She looked at Nicholas. 'He's partly right, you know. There's been recent research into the phenomenon of animals falling from the sky. The theory is that they get sucked up into a waterspout or tornado during a storm, pulled to high altitudes. Which explains how they can be carried for large distances. Frogs, fish, jellyfish and snakes have all been recorded falling from the sky. Even spiders. Sometimes the animals that fall are completely frozen, which supports the thesis that they've been pulled to vast heights.' She touched the side of the redfish. Cold, but not frozen. 'But for the hypothesis to work, the animals usually have to be small and light. And the animal rain is usually preceded by a storm. There wasn't a storm last night. Only fog.'

She looked up at the German, translated what she'd just said.

'Spiders?' Nicholas said. 'Just spiders?' He squinted up into the sky again.

Liesl stood up. 'The odd thing is that it's usually only one species that falls. One kind of fish. One kind of frog. One kind of jellyfish. If a waterspout or tornado scooped up an area of the sea or land, it would probably grab everything.'

'Well, that rules out your hypothesis, then,' Nicholas said, standing up, searching the road ahead for his grandnephew. 'There are many different kinds of fish on this road.'

'It's not *my* hypothesis!'

'Another time I was wandering down on the canal, near the factory and I heard this sound – it was incredible – like a wounded animal.'

'What was it?'

'Ariane Ledoux, Poisson's sister. She was squatting on the pavement, her skirt hiked up to her waist, hand between her legs.'

'You're so making this up!' Liesl said, laughing. 'First a naked man in the Place, now a naked woman down on the canal! You're just trying to make this place look more interesting than it actually is.'

'She looked up at me and smacked her lips together,' Guy continued, ignoring her. 'It was shocking. It's still shocking. More shocking than anything I ever saw in Amsterdam.'

'That's absurd. You performed magic in a sex club, for God's sake.'

'It's different,' Guy said. 'Think of it this way – if some poor slob wandered drunk out of a sex club after watching a bunch of people going at it all night, then turned the corner and was greeted by a naked woman squatting on the pavement, diddling herself, you can bet there would be some kind of shock. He'd be stripped just as naked. Like I was with Ariane.'

The performers on stage are not naked. Never naked.'

Liesl touched her head to his. 'It's still hard for me to see you in a place like that.'

'So many things I never would have seen, done, without Chiqui...'

'There have been reports of fish falling from the skies throughout history,' the German said to Liesl. 'All the way back to the Bible.'

Liesl translated for Nicholas and he turned on the German, shouting that the Bible was a pack of lies, nothing but religiously induced mass hallucination.

The old woman in the green kerchief walked past the German, still clucking and mumbling to herself.

The German turned to Liesl, confused. 'What is he saying?'

5 The Lover

Light filtered through the stained glass, bathing the aisles of chairs in a wash of purple. Father Leo stared across the altar, sick with helplessness. What could he say? No matter what he said he wouldn't be believed.

'Why would I hide Marie from you?'

Poisson poked his ribs with the end of the rolling pin. 'She's not yours,' he whispered. 'No more passing her from house to house, night after night. Do you think I don't know what's going on?'

The priest pulled away from Poisson's stale alcohol breath. This was what Marie lived with day after day?

'I don't know who you are talking about, Poisson,' the

priest said. 'No one is passing your wife back and forth.' He took a step back, glanced over his shoulder. If he ran, would he make it to the front door before Poisson? They were both big, lumbering men. But Poisson had already tossed him aside without a second thought. 'I think you should be less concerned with imagined lovers and more concerned with the fact that Marie has not –'

'Lovers!' Poisson shouted, then touched the end of the pin to the priest's nose. The priest swallowed. 'This isn't about love. None of you know anything about love.'

Poisson grabbed Father Leo's shoulder, spun him around, and pushed him towards the altar, up the five creaking steps to the pulpit.

'Turn on the microphone,' Poisson whispered.

Father Leo turned it on.

'Now tell her to come out of her hiding place.'

The priest looked over his shoulder, shook his head. 'But she's not –'

Poisson pressed the pin into the priest's spine. 'Do it!'

Father Leo leaned into the microphone, looked out into the empty dark church. Was it going to end like this? Twenty years in Villon – deaths, births, confessions, graduations, arguments, reconciliations – all of it passed through his mind like a school of fish – the way they flowed together as one –

... and Madame Ducasse is a fish...

a beautiful pattern – how they all turned at once, flashing in the sunlight filtered down through blue water –

... and Pierre Caillens is a fish... and Theo Brunuel is a fish...

and now it was going to end like this? Speaking to an empty church and then – when Marie doesn't appear – beaten to death by a madman with a rolling pin?

'Marie?' Father Leo said into the microphone, eyes closed, his voice shaking again. The name – that beautiful name – echoed off the walls. What had Poisson done to her?

'Are you out there?' The question echoed back to the priest. Then, a blessed silence. Father Leo opened his eyes.

... and Silvie Foulette is a fish... and poor pregnant Elise Brunuel is a fish... and Mariette Culer is a fish...

Poisson pressed the rolling pin into the priest's spine again. 'Tell her you don't love her... that you have never loved her.'

Father Leo shook his head. 'But –'

Poisson pressed the pin deeper and Father Leo whispered into the microphone: 'I have never loved you.'

Poisson eased the pressure off the priest's spine. 'Now tell her it's all over, she can come home, everything will be different.'

The priest paused, straining to hear something, anything, beyond the church. But he heard only crows. Arguing over fish. He pressed his lips to the microphone and said in a flat monotone: 'It's over now, Marie, you can go home. Everything will be different.'

Poisson grabbed him by the collar, pulled him down off the pulpit. 'Now we wait,' he whispered into the priest's face. And they stood, side by side, Poisson holding the rolling pin into his ribs like a gun, waiting for a phantom to appear out of the purple gloom.

... and Adele Souzain is a fish... and her son Philippe is a fish...

Five minutes passed. There was a point, staring out into the dark church, when Father Leo could have sworn he saw something move. Michel? Marie? Had she come into the church while he had chased after Poisson into the priory?

Insanity.

'If you leave now,' Father Leo said, trying to keep his voice steady and firm, 'then I will not press charges. It's obvious that Marie's not –'

At the mention of his wife's name, Poisson exploded. 'Don't!'

The word bounced around the church. Father Leo winced. 'I'm only trying to say –'

'Don't!' Poisson screamed again.

... and Father Gaspar is a fish... and blind Georges Cacques is a fish... and my father is a fish...

'You are filth and you want to make her filth, too,' Poisson yelled. 'You all do!' He turned around to face the rows of chairs. 'Every last one of you!'

How could he possibly reason with this man?

Poisson grabbed Father Leo's collar again. 'Tell me where you have her tied up.'

Enough of this craziness! Enough! He had to do something. 'Why would I have her tied up?' he shouted into Poisson's face.

Poisson took a step back, blinking like a newborn for a second, looking around the church as if he'd suddenly arrived there out of a dream. He blinked again and the wild, fearful eyes returned.

'Back to the house,' Poisson said. He raised the pin up to the priest's face again, touched his chin with it, pushing him backwards. 'We're going to go back and check behind every single door in your little love nest.'

6 The Seer

Marie turned the corner off rue Demesne, up rue Grand Caisse, and almost bumped into Madame Culer. The old woman was standing over a large fish at the bottom of her doorstep. She squinted at Marie.

'Is that you, Marie Ledoux?'

Marie stopped, said nothing, holding the mask of the dead baby tightly to her chest.

Madame Culer swept her hand in a wide arc, wonder on her ancient face. 'They're not just in this street. They're everywhere.'

Marie stepped off the pavement, into the street, walked slowly around Madame Culer, keeping her eyes on the old woman's face.

'Been out walking all night again?' the old woman said, her eyes narrowing as she looked from the mask to Marie's face.

Marie nodded.

'It's no wonder, with Poisson the way he is.' The old woman looked down at the fish again. 'I wouldn't be surprised if he was the one who did all this.'

Marie stopped.

'There's no reason for you to protect him,' the old woman said. 'Something must be done. And soon. Look at what he did to your mouth.'

222

'Poisson doesn't even know his own name,' Marie said. 'How could he have done this?'

'It's just as Madame Seguie says,' Madame Culer said. 'You keep protecting him. But who does it hurt? If you don't care enough about yourself to do something, fine. But that beautiful boy of yours...'

Anger shot through Marie at the mention of Seguie. Monsieur Seguie was always peering down into Marie's tiny backyard from his second storey bedroom window. It was Monsieur Seguie's favourite pastime to shout at Poisson whenever he went to the outhouse, trying to drive Poisson into a rage. 'Eh, Poisson! I heard your father fucked his own chickens!' No matter how many times she told Poisson not to pay any attention, that if he didn't answer back the old man would get bored and stop, Poisson would always respond in kind.

One time he had picked up a chicken, heaved it at Seguie. The bird had arced over the garden wall – squawking crazily – and hit the Seguie's house with a horrible thwack while Monsieur Seguie pointed and laughed from his second storey perch. Another time Poisson had opened his fly and wiggled his penis at Seguie, shouting obscenities about Seguie's mother and sister. Seguie had loved this even more. The last time, leaning on his windowsill in his T-shirt, beer on the ledge next to him, Seguie had taunted Poisson about his sister. 'Eh, Poisson! Do you know how many blowjobs your sister gave me when I was in school?' Poisson had screamed like the monster he was supposed to be, a frightening shriek that tore the smile off Seguie's face. Then he had picked up a chicken and bit right through the neck, blood spurting all over his face. Seguie had immediately slammed the window shut without another word. It was a horrible thing to witness, but there was a part of Marie that had felt glad, that

Poisson may have finally vanquished his tormentor.

'Don't speak of Emile,' Marie said to the old woman. 'Don't talk about him.'

Madame Culer looked offended, as if she'd been misunderstood. 'But I am on the boy's side. He should be taken from that forsaken house.'

'No!' Marie held the mask out in front of her, at arm's length, the face of the dead baby staring at the old woman.

'What is that?' Madame Culer said and took a step backwards.

'Do not speak!' Marie said, backing slowly away from the old woman, mask raised. Madame Culer stood transfixed, mouth open. When Marie reached the corner of rue Dienne, she lowered the mask, turned, and ran. She slowed down at the mouth of the alley on which she lived, suddenly thinking of Poisson. Out of breath, she peered around the corner and almost smacked heads with Pierre Clouet, the Mayor of Villon.

'Whups!' Pierre shouted.

Marie raised a hand to her mouth.

Pierre's shocked, thin face stared at Marie for a few seconds before he said: 'What are you doing? You scared me half to death.'

'I was...' What was *he* doing here? Monsieur Clouet lived on the other side of the Place, on rue d'Arcy. 'I live here,' Marie said.

Monsieur Clouet looked Marie up and down. 'I'm out examining the fish,' he said. 'They seem to be everywhere. A very elaborate practical joke.' His eyes settled on the mask for a second. 'I suspect it has something to do with the rally today. Have you been out long?'

Marie tightened her grip on the mask.

'I only ask because you might have seen someone, something...'

'I must get home,' Marie said.

The tall man pointed at the mask. 'I am curious. What is that?'

Marie held it up in front of Pierre Clouet's face. He stepped back, frowned, then leaned forward, pushing the frame of his black horn-rimmed glasses up the bridge of his long nose. 'My God.'

'A child,' Marie said and edged around the man, still holding the mask out at arm's length.

Pierre Clouet turned with Marie as she circled around him, his eyes fixed on the mask. 'Yes,' he said, 'but where did you get it? This looks like something Casimir –'

'No!' Marie shouted. The word bounced between the walls on either side of the alley. There was movement behind a curtain in a second storey window above. She turned and fled.

'Wait!' Pierre called after her, but when she reached her own door and turned to look back down the alley, he was gone.

7 The Illusionist

As Guy had predicted, it wasn't going well. Marc was gesturing wildly, flinging his arms this way and that, shouting about how all he wanted to do was see an old friend, why was that such a problem? The man at the door was matching Marc gesture for gesture, shout for shout, furious, his peaceful Sunday morning quickly slipping into oblivion.

A woman appeared behind the man at the door. The ex-lover. She began to shout at Marc, too. A neighbour pulled back the curtains of the second floor window next door, looked down at Guy. Guy raised his hands, shrugged. The neighbour rolled his eyes, disappeared.

Could he cancel the trick? If he didn't have time to walk the dancers through the illusion, what else could he do?

He fished a cigarette from his coat pocket, lit it, but it did nothing to calm his nerves.

Guy spooned against Liesl's naked back under the priest's blankets, watched the candle flame shadows flicker across the stone columns that framed the chancel. It was cold, so cold, but he didn't want to put his clothes back on. Not yet.

'This would be a good place for a levitation,' he said. 'Imagine Father Leo floating between those columns, giving a sermon.' He glanced up at the dark ceiling. 'It would be hard, but it's possible.'

'I don't know if that would bring in more people or drive them away.' Liesl pulled the rough blanket over her shoulders.

'We once levitated two people fucking,' Guy said. 'It was one of Chiqui's last big tricks.'

'*That* would bring people to Mass.'

'She'd stand behind Marieke and Alain going at it onstage, then raise her wand, and they'd begin to rise, spinning slowly until their feet were pointing out at the audience, giving the tourists a shot of what they came for. Then she'd wave the couple out over the audience, two metres above everyone's head.'

He pressed closer to her, feeling the warmth between her legs radiate onto his thighs.

'Of course, they weren't really fucking. Alain couldn't stay hard when he was up there like that, so he'd just lie on top of Marieke and try to keep as still as possible.'

'Sounds almost beautiful. In a weird, creepy sort of way.'

226

The candle flame popped and cracked.

'If I'd had a teacher like Chiqui when I was back at university,' Liesl said, 'I think I might have stayed.'

'Someone to teach you how to make a lobster disappear?'

'You know what I mean. Chiqui wasn't just teaching you magic, she was using it to teach you about everything, about life. You were very lucky.'

Had Chiqui been a good teacher? She had certainly been a master magician. But the rest of it? He felt unfinished. He couldn't go back to the way he'd seen the world before he met her, but he couldn't seem to find his way into seeing the world the way she had wanted him to see it.

Liesl turned to face him. 'You're going to hate what I just thought.'

'You want to convert to the Holy Roman Church?'

She kissed him. 'You should do a levitation at the rally.'

The man at the door had Marc in a headlock and the woman behind him had switched from shouting at Marc to shouting at her new lover to let go, just let go. Marc stamped the man's foot and he howled with pain, but did not let go.

It always ends. That's how things work. How could they not have understood that from the beginning?

Guy pulled an M-80 out of the box of fireworks at his feet and got out of the car. He stood watching the three wrestling and shouting for a minute, then lit the fuse with his cigarette and gently tossed it into the yard halfway between himself and the melee.

The sound of the explosion sent the three jerking into the air, landing apart. They blinked at Guy, dumb.

'It's time to go.'

227

Guy kissed Liesl lightly on the forehead, slid out from under the blankets, and dressed quickly in the dawn cold. He headed for the front of the church, leaving his coat on top of her for extra warmth.

Heavy wet flakes fell through the streetlight at the edge of the Place. A thin white cover had accumulated over the cobbles, black water glistening in the seams between stone. Marie Ledoux appeared out of the alley next to the brasserie and Guy retreated back into the shadows of the church door. She walked slowly, holding herself. Under the streetlight at the entrance to rue Demesne she looked up into the sky. Snowflakes fell into her open mouth.

He could almost taste them himself. Rust, ice.

Marie closed her eyes, unfurled her arms, and began to spin.

8 The Lover

Father Leo took one hesitant step down the cellar steps, then another. Poisson followed close behind, prodding him on with the pin. As they got closer to the bottom, the darkness began to press against the priest's lungs. He switched on the light at the bottom of the steps and Poisson blinked, blinded for a second, then looked around at the chaos of boxes in each room.

'Marie?'

They went from room to room, Poisson examining each dark corner, looking behind anything where a person the size of Marie could possibly hide, calling her name. 'Marie?'

Father Leo wondered if that was the voice Poisson used after he beat her, apologising.

... and I am a fish... and Jesus is a fish... and Marie is a fish...

When Poisson was finished searching the cellar, he turned to the priest: 'She may not be here, but I know who you traded her to. Do you think I don't know?'

Father Leo kept his mouth shut.

Poisson tapped the side of the priest's head with the end of the rolling pin and chuckled. 'You people think I don't know the shell game you play with her, night after night?' He stepped backwards onto the first step at the bottom of the stairs and whispered 'Do you think I don't know?' Then he ran up the stairs. At the top, he turned around, told the priest not to forget to turn off the lights.

The priest stood there, uncomprehending, for a couple of seconds. He listened for Poisson's breathing, some movement. 'Poisson?' No answer. He took a step up. 'Poisson?'

Was Poisson just waiting at the top, ready to bludgeon him as soon as he appeared in the doorway, sending him tumbling back down into the dark?

Father Leo left the light on and cautiously ascended the stairs. Between each step, he cocked his head and listened. Nothing. At the top of the stairs, he slowly poked his head through the doorframe, his heart racing, expecting a sudden blow. Nothing. No one was in the little hallway. He went outside, breathing in the cool, wet morning air. A few crows opened their wings, croaked once or twice, then returned to the fish carcasses they were standing on.

... and the crow is prophet of the coming of the fish...

Father Leo rushed back into the church, eyes roaming through the gloom, into every corner.

'Poisson?' The name echoed off the stone walls. 'Poisson!'

He ran into the chancellery. The door that led to the belfry was open. Heart racing, he walked slowly, cautiously, up the stone steps. Quiet, quiet. To his relief, no one was up there.

But where was Marie?

He looked at his watch. Half an hour until Mass? He ran down the steps, flying across the church, out into the alley, through the door of the priory, and called the police.

... and chaos is a fish... and the bells are fish... and chaos is a bell that must precede the coming redemption of fish...

9 The Illusionist

Singing from inside the church drifted across the Place. He had missed her. Liesl's bus had come and gone and he had missed her. All because Marc had taken him on a wild goose chase, searching for – what? An excuse not to go home to his wife. What can she have thought, standing around in the Place waiting for him? Most of the town would be suffering through Woelfred Day Mass so they could enjoy the kermesse that waited for them afterwards. *Frites* vendors, mask vendors, ice cream vendors, waffle vendors, all were busy setting up along the perimeter of the Place. It was traditional for them to set up during Mass. He remembered that giddy feeling he used to get as a child when he walked out of the church doors after Mass, into a Place suddenly full of jugglers, puppeteers, carnival booths.

The Place was also filled with people Guy had never seen before, those who had shown up to see Contexture. They milled around in rubber masks: Fidel Castro, Astro Boy, Henry Kissinger, King Kong, François Mitterand, Margaret Thatcher, Spock. Some had already started drinking.

Where *were* Contexture? How was he supposed to perform the trick if they didn't arrive in time to practise?

Had they come and gone while he was out wandering with Marc? But where would they have gone?

He heard Chiqui's gravelly voice; distant, failing: 'You have to be prepared for the unknown, *petit*.'

'But how can you prepare for the unknown?'

'Precisely.'

A crow in the centre of the Place, standing on top of a large cod, cocked one eye towards Guy, then cocked an eye at two men dressed in brown coveralls – one in his twenties, the other in his fifties, with a bushy white beard and flowing white hair – setting up a small wooden stage in front of the brasserie. Guy recognised the older one. He'd been performing at the Villon kermesse since Guy was a boy – the usual plays about Charlemagne (with the intrepid, drunken, down-on-his-luck puppet Tchtantches leading the charge against the Saracens and making his usual asides to the audience of children) or the Belgian revolution of 1830 or – once – a little play about how Saint Woelfred was stripped of her sainthood by an evil bishop, with Tchtantches trying to protect the poor saint's honour by beating the pompous bishop with a broom. Guy remembered his mother had been slightly offended by the anti-clerical nature of the piece, but also pleased that Woelfred had been presented as the victim and redeemed.

The younger puppeteer pointed at the crow perched on the cod. 'What are all the fish about?'

Guy shrugged. 'They appeared in the night.' He needed a

cigarette, something to stifle the rising panic inside him.

'They appeared in the night,' the older puppeteer repeated.

'Alloo! Guy!'

Philippe Souzain rode his bicycle across the Place, weaving in and out of the milling crowd, slicing by the fish, sending the crows flying, and stopped in front of Guy, breathless. He pointed at Guy's top hat. 'Are you going to perform at kermesse?'

'I was supposed to meet someone here,' Guy said, 'but I'm too late.' He nodded at the church. 'I fear the church has swallowed her whole.'

'The German?'

Guy smiled, weary. 'Yes, the German.'

Philippe pointed at the two small cardboard boxes at Guy's feet. 'What's in those? Magic tricks?'

'Look inside,' Guy said.

The boy jumped off his bike, knelt down, opened the lid of the top box. He looked up at Guy, eyes wide. 'Where did you get these?'

'Do you want them?'

Philippe looked back down at the doll heads, then at Guy – solemn, serious – and nodded.

'Then they are yours.'

Philippe immediately pulled two heads out of the box, one in each dirty hand, and stuffed them into his pockets.

Guy desperately needed something to take his mind off the fact that Contexture had not yet arrived. He leaned down beside Philippe, nodded towards the puppeteers. 'Shall we show them how it's done?'

'How what's done?'

'Do you remember what to do for the flying fish trick?'

Philippe's eyes widened again. 'But –'

232

Guy pulled a doll head from the box, held it up in front of Philippe. 'We'll use this instead of the papier mâché fish, okay? You remember what you're supposed to do?'

Alain had called him, said Chiqui was waiting for him in the alley behind The Bacchanal. He found her standing in the snow in rubber boots, a long down coat hanging from her bony shoulders, smoking. Her fingers trembled as she took the cigarette from her red lips and exhaled.

'You shouldn't be smoking,' he said. 'You should be in bed.'

'I have something to show you.' She pulled a long red swathe of silk from her coat pocket, turned and held it up to the second floor window across the alley. The old woman was sitting just inside the window as always, watching.

'Why are you doing this?' he said. 'Do you want to die?'

He'd had to retrieve her from so many different places in the past few weeks. Phone calls from old friends of hers in the middle of the night, telling him she'd appeared at their door, performing tricks in a bathrobe and top hat.

Was it the drugs? She'd been this way ever since she'd started chemo.

Chiqui opened the rectangle of silk, showed the old woman one side, the other, then beckoned Guy closer, asked him to take the cigarette from her mouth.

'You shouldn't be smoking,' he repeated, taking the cigarette.

Chiqui threw the silk out in front of her and it hung there, motionless, draped over some invisible shape. Blonde wig slightly askew, her face beaded with sweat – a sick face; a gaunt, old man's face – she grabbed the bottom hem of the silk and pulled it, revealing a small fish hanging mid-air. Flicking her fingers up, up, the fish slowly rose. When it reached the second

233

floor window, Chiqui majestically swept a trembling finger in an arc towards the end of the alley. The fish followed her summons and shot into the shadows beyond the backdoor light.

Guy looked up at the silhouette in the second floor window. Chiqui must have collaborated with the old woman to pull off such a trick. All that work. But why?

'I'm so sorry to leave you dangling,' Chiqui said, taking the cigarette back from him with a shaky hand. 'I had hoped I would be there for you all the way through your training, help get you through this terrible halfway place you've reached. But...'

She sagged against him.

'What are you talking about?' Guy said. 'You're not going anywhere. You'll outlive me.'

'Things have no existence by themselves, *petit*,' Chiqui said into his ear. 'Not you, not me, not anything. It's important for you to remember that.'

Guy helped her to the back door. She was so light now. Nothing but twigs and feathers.

What was he going to do?

'Nothing exists as a separate thing,' Chiqui repeated. 'It's all an illusion.'

The doll head floated in mid-air between Guy and Philippe. Applause, whistles. More people had gathered around to watch: a few vendors, an Astro Boy, a John Wayne with a cowboy hat, two Ronald Reagans, along with Madame Eseuil, watching from the doorway of her brasserie. Guy pointed his index finger at the doll head and feigned concentration, then swung his finger to the right. The head floated to the right. He swung his finger to the left and the head followed to the left.

He made the plastic head rise up, up, then floated it gently down, next to Philippe's head. Now it was the boy's turn.

Philippe ran his hands above the head, below the head, made a circle with his arms and moved around the head exactly how Guy had shown him so many weeks ago, making it look as if there was no possibility that any string or wire could be attached. Guy nodded his approval, then once again raised the head up, up. Philippe stepped directly beneath it, just as he'd been taught, and Guy lowered the head down into the boy's waiting hands.

More claps, whistles. Philippe looked down at the doll head in his arms, then over at Guy, and grinned.

A dented blue Renault sedan moved slowly through the Place, honking people out of the way, blaring something disco-like from the car radio. When it rolled to a stop next to the puppet stage all four doors opened and a group of men and women in skin-tight skeleton costumes began to roll out. The older puppeteer counted them off: 'Six, seven, eight! Nine! Like a clown car!'

The skeletons began dancing with masked revellers, the disco beat thumping across the Place. Half the people in the Place were twisting and writhing, bopping up and down.

Madame Eseuil stood next to Guy, swaying with the music. 'These ones have spirit!'

Contexture. Nobody but dancers could look so good in those skin-tight suits.

'They're here for the rally,' he said to Madame Eseuil.

'Those are the ecologists?'

The younger puppeteer leaned towards Madame Eseuil: 'They're the ones that got naked at the Vatican!'

Madame Eseuil nodded, but looked confused, obviously

having no idea that anyone had ever got naked at the Vatican.

Guy walked up to a small female dancer gyrating with Astro Boy in front of the passenger door. 'I'm looking for Stephanie Mertz.'

The dancer put her hands to her ears, shook her head, then shouted for someone to turn the music down. Another skeleton slid into the car, switched the radio off. On cue, all the skeletons withered to the ground, played dead.

'I'm looking for Stephanie Mertz.'

'Stephanie's behind us,' the dancer said. 'About a half hour behind, I think. And who are you?'

Guy offered his hand. 'Guy Foulette.'

'The magician!'

'He's quite good,' the older puppeteer offered. 'I just saw him float a doll head in mid-air.'

Madame Eseuil looked even more confused. 'The people who dance naked at the Vatican are ecologists who know Guy Foulette?'

'Guy is going to help us perform something at the end of the rally,' the dancer said to Madame Eseuil. 'Something about the Garden of Eden.'

The younger puppeteer leered. 'Will you be as naked as Adam and Eve?'

'We will be what we will be,' the dancer said, then winked at Guy.

'I have nothing against nakedness,' the older puppeteer said to Madame Eseuil, 'it has its time and place, but,' he looked at Guy, then at the dancer, 'there will be children.'

10 The Seer

'Emile?' Marie whispered. She took a step towards Emile's door, stopped. 'Emile?'

No answer.

Blood roared through her ears. Ocean waves. It was hard to hear. Cradling the mask in her left arm, Marie gripped the edge of Emile's bedroom doorframe with her right hand and peered into the little boy's room. The window above the bed was open and Emile was stretched out on top of the blankets. 'Emile!' She stepped into the room.

Not Emile, but a huge cod. Dead, mouth open. One eye stared up, through the wood beams of the low ceiling above the bed.

Marie turned and ran into her own bedroom. No Emile, no Poisson. She hurried out of the back door. And there he was. Crouching over another large cod in the middle of the small dirt enclosure, humming to himself, one of her old sweaters draped over his shoulders. She crouched down, placed the mask at her feet, rested her cheek against the back of his head.

The chicken coop roof had caved in. Two large fish lay in the straw at the bottom of the coop. There was another large fish lying on top of the outhouse roof, its dark mouth open.

'Where did they come from?' Marie whispered into Emile's ear. Emile stopped humming, started to whisper. Marie leaned closer to the boy, her face over his shoulder, trying to hear what he was saying. A soft hush poured from his mouth, the sound of a wave retreating back into the sea, rattling broken shells.

Marie pointed at the fish. 'Have you ever seen such a thing before?' she said to the boy. The smell of the sea was strong. She could taste it in her mouth, feel it coat the inside of her nose. The boy continued to whisper. Marie thought she heard the word fish.

'Yes, such a fish, such a fish,' Marie said.

Still whispering, Emile touched his tiny index finger to the eye of the cod.

'That's the eye,' Marie said. 'Can you say that? Eye?'

The boy giggled, curled his index finger into his palm, then pulled his hand back to his chest, balled into a fist. Marie smiled, nuzzled her cheek against his, then placed a finger gently on the eye of the fish. 'Eye –' *Black-water fog soaks it off the surface of the sea. Other fish – mackerel, cod – swim in the haze, suspect nothing. Occasionally, they slap into the faces of dead sailors. The sailors stare through them, unsurprised. The fog rolls inland. Whiting skirt the edge of black fields, rub against fog-soaked grass, search the crevices of stone walls for food. Herring circle the chimney pot of a barge house on a black canal, touch their lips to sheet metal – one by one – then dart away. Mist thickens over pink-orange streetlights, fish spiral around the metal poles. Large fish follow small fish. Small fish follow the dim red tail lights of four a.m. trucks. The cod finally swims through the open window of a stone house, following a boy room to room, circling over the kitchen table while the boy crouches next to his father, passed out on cold stone. The boy reaches out, almost touches the big man's naked chest, withdraws his hand. The fish follows the boy to the back door, circles above him while he pees from inside the shelter of the doorframe, dribbling all over his bare feet. 'Marie? Marie?' The boy's father lurches past the boy, into the backyard, scattering chickens in the tiny hallway. 'Marie?' The cod detaches itself from the boy, follows the man, circles above him as he pisses into the rosebush next to the outhouse. Halfway through, the man raises his head, stares into the eye of the passing cod, and screams.*

'Marie!'

238

11 The Seeker

March 21st, 1987
Cairo, Egypt

Dear anti-biologiste,

I wander and wander, listening to the sounds of the city mingling with the sounds inside my own head. Sometimes there's no difference between the two. Why am I here? I saw a man standing next to a McDonald's yesterday staring into the madness of the passing traffic. His shirt was torn, his pants dusty, like he'd been walking for days and days in the desert. I don't know how long I stood watching him – half an hour? – but the whole time he didn't move. I couldn't take my eyes off him. Maybe he mirrored my inner situation.

For some reason I keep coming back to a night in Villon as a boy. I went looking for a pen in my father's study (he used quite beautiful pens – I have inherited the same fetish). On his desk I found a memo. I can't remember the exact wording, but it was about the development of a new weapon that would disrupt weather and communications. I immediately understood that I was reading something top secret and so, of course, devoured the rest of the page. It was all about heating the ionosphere with some kind of magnetic charge. This was followed by crazy apocalyptic descriptions of the disruptions such a weapon would cause. Something like: 'The sky would turn into sea and the sea would become sky.' I'm sure that's not what it said, but that's how I remember it. Up until that time I had never really thought about what my father did for a living. Planning World War III? I rushed out of the room, saw my father fast asleep on the couch in the living room.

Lost, lost.

239

About two months later I got up the courage to ask him about the memo. He acted as if he didn't know what I was talking about at first, then burst out laughing. Apparently the memo was a form of Nuclear Operations humour.

I wandered in the old city today and stopped in front of a mosque (no idea which one) and studied the patterns on the ornate door. I thought how the person who carved that door was probably driven with a purpose – a spiritual purpose – that allowed him to feel something, be something, greater. Something beyond his own pitiable self. Rimbaud was trying to break through to something greater, see the inner meaning of the world and the heavens, with his poetry. Become something other than his confining self. Failing that, he abandoned the whole project.

Standing there in front of that door I felt so sad for the poor boy. I suppose I'm really just feeling sad for myself. What am I looking for?

Maybe Rimbaud was running from the very thing that made him what he was. He was born a poet, it was in his cells. (You once told me all the cells in our body are completely replaced every seven years. And yes, the atoms that make up our structure are constantly mingling with all the atoms around us. What then is the true line that divides things? What remains to make us this thing that thinks and remembers and rejects poetry for a wandering life in remote outposts?) Maybe the cancer that eventually ate away Rimbaud's leg was his own body crying out, rebelling against his decision to abandon his art. His silence might have been the very thing that killed him.

Everything is constantly mingling, changing. All borders are a lie. Maybe I am finally feeling it and that is what is making me feel so lost.

The sea is becoming sky, the sky becoming sea.

Raoul

VI

And the Fish Is a Fish
Trapped Inside the Wind...

1 The Stranger

The smell of *frites* from the vending carts out in the Place drifted through the church, mingled with the incense. Liesl's stomach grumbled. She hadn't had anything to eat since last night's dinner at Guy's house. And there hadn't been much of that. Madame Foulette had cooked chicken even though she knew Liesl was a vegetarian.

Father Leo was speaking about a town similar to Villon – in some vague past, during a time of starvation, of war. One morning, the townsfolk of that other town woke to find fish all over their streets. After so many years of hardship, they believed the fish had come from Heaven. They thought the fish were a kind of reward for everything they had suffered during the war. Some cooked and ate the fish. Some got sick. Some died. Was God mocking them?

Liesl stared at the point on the floor beneath the pulpit

where she and Guy had spent the night. She imagined getting off the train in Paris, alone, the echo of voices in the station around her, people rushing by, embracing each other...

'Maybe God had given the fish to those poor people as fertiliser for the soil,' Father Leo was saying. 'And so – as with any miracle, with any mystery – we must be patient. Till the soil... and an answer will eventually arise...'

Liesl's stomach rumbled again.

'... and Jesus is a fish... and Saint Woelfred is a fish... and we are all fish...'

Was that from the Old Testament?

2 The Player

'Who else could it be but the Greens?' Casimir said to Monsieur Caillens.

The old man twisted around on his bar stool to face the table where Casimir and Claudine sat, and waved the idea away. 'Absurd. Why would they kill fish as some kind of – what did you call it?'

'A performance piece,' Casimir said. 'Don't you see the symbolism? The fish symbolise the massacre that will take place once the factory brings in the waste. The dancers who are going to perform today, Contexture – have you even heard of them?'

'Should I have?'

Casimir shrugged. Caillens wasn't interested, wouldn't understand anyway. He had his version of the world. It would never change. Casimir looked across the table at Claudine and winked, then lifted his snifter of cognac, took a sip. Claudine raised her glass to him.

She wanted to know what he knew, what her sister knew.

A pudgy man with a walrus moustache wearing blue under-wear, blue vinyl boots, and a blue cape pushed through the brasserie door. He grabbed the hem of his cape, flung it dramatically over his left shoulder, shouted something about the end of the world.

'You can't come in here half naked!' Monsieur Caillens shouted back.

The blue man dropped the cape, announced that he could smell the coming fire of the end, then turned and plunged back into the crowded Place. Casimir stared out of the open door: men in masks; women in veils, feathers, trench coats; painted women swirling in a painted crowd.

All the happy crazies of the world were tumbling past. All waiting to see Stephanie Mertz take her clothes off again. What a brilliant woman! The Lady Godiva of the Green movement! How many boys and men had seen her naked in front of the Vatican and instantly fallen in love?

This was the world he wanted to join. Beautiful, full of appetite. He had been away from it for far too long. *Too many nights with that brooding, dark Marie.* Always sorry for this, sorry for that. Casimir swirled the cognac in the snifter, looked at Claudine's form through the glass.

When Marie came to clean on Tuesday, he would tell her that he was sorry but it was over.

3 The Stranger

The last of the people coming out of Mass streamed around Liesl, down the church steps, into the busy Place. So many people! Masked musicians honked on tubas, clarinets, saxophones, danced around revellers carrying aloft papier mâché replicas of Saint Woelfred, Jesus on the cross, even Ronald Reagan (an ICBM poking out from between his legs). A group of children stood laughing at two puppets whacking each other with sticks in the middle of a small wooden stage next to the brasserie. On either side of the entrance to rue d'Arcy sat two television news vans. One of the reporters stood in front of a camera, holding a microphone, looking into a small compact mirror, combing her hair.

How was she going to find Guy in this crowd?

A cry went up from the direction of rue Demesne and suddenly, there it was, the reliquary of Saint Woelfred. The box was held aloft by four sturdy wood poles carried by what looked like the local *gendarmes*.

Would she stay in Villon if there was no Madame Foulette to contend with? No. Yes. She didn't know. But if she stayed –

The crowd surged forward, gathered around the reliquary, pushing against the *gendarmes* holding the box. Cymbals crashed, tubas honked, horns bleated. The procession stalled as the crush of bodies forced the *gendarmes* to retreat a few metres. After a minute of stalemate the reliquary broke through the wall of bodies and began to move in a slow circle around the edge of the Place.

She couldn't stay. How could she stay?

'Are you ready to dance behind the saint?!'

Liesl turned. Marc Didier. In a rumpled blue suit, black tie. He nodded at the crowd, moving counterclockwise around the Place. The bodies blended, retreated, congealed. 'It's not kermesse unless you dance behind the saint!' he shouted above the noise, then took her hand and pulled her down the steps

244

towards the edge of the crowd.

She descended a few steps, stopped. The box was now passing close to the church steps, the *gendarmes* shouting for people to get out of the way. No one did. Marc tugged at her arm and she relented, moved with him down to the wall of people at the edge of the Place.

Marc shoved, bellowed, managed to make a small space in the mass of bodies, and pulled her through. Bodies pressed against her thighs, ass, back, breasts; shoes clipped her heels, stepped on her toes. People spun and writhed into the gap between her and Marc until she could no longer hold on to his hand and he slipped out of sight.

4 The Player

Madame Culer stumbled through the brasserie door, shut it fiercely behind her, eyes wild, hand over her heart. Casimir leaned towards Claudine: 'It *must* be the end of the world if Culer is in the brasserie.' Culer-the-heartless, all the boys had called her, when she used to be secretary to the Mayor – years and years and years ago – good God, before Claudine was born. The woman had been haughty and disdainful, a perfect bureaucrat. Then she had retired and disappeared off the face of the earth.

It happened to them all, ground to dust before they were even in the grave: Dehanschutter, Caillens, Madame Eseuil, Doctor Souzain, his mother, his father. Everyone. Even his sister Adele. Philippe, soon enough. But it would not happen to him. He wouldn't give them a chance to say, 'Old Casimir used to be good looking, had almost every woman in Villon, but look at him now, jabbering away at no one, off in his lonely corner next to the jukebox.' Because he wouldn't be here. Rimbaud – that wonderful, wily, eccentric teenage poet – would save him from that kind of dust. He would be dust in the grave eventually, yes, but not before he was dead.

He looked around the room at all the faces. This could be his final time in the brasserie. Soon he'd be off to the south of France. He raised his snifter to Claudine. 'To kermesse!'

Madame Culer approached Casimir's table. 'People grabbing, grabbing,' she said to Claudine. 'These skeletons grabbed me, pulled me in...' She placed a hand to her throat. 'I lost my purse. It's madness.' She glanced at Casimir. 'These are the people who come to see Saint Woelfred now?'

'They aren't here for kermesse,' Casimir said, trying to clarify the situation for the old bat. 'They came to protest.'

'Protest? What is there to protest in Villon?'

'The toxic waste dumps.' He looked across the table at Claudine. 'Do you think anyone out there really cares about getting rid of toxic waste?' He shrugged, raised the snifter to his lips. 'It's just another party to them.'

The old woman shifted her gaze to the door, bewildered. 'How am I going to get home?'

Claudine looked across the table at Casimir. 'We should take her home.'

That was fine with him. Rescuing the old hag would get him back to his house with Claudine that much sooner.

'I think I can arrange something,' he said and went to the bar. Madame Eseuil nodded to him. 'Another cognac?'

He shook his head, beckoned her closer. 'I've got a favour to ask.'

Madame Eseuil raised one eyebrow, looked over at Caillens,

shifted her eyes back to Casimir. 'Yes?'

He swallowed. It would be the first time since he had been pushed out of the back door naked – what had it been, twenty-five years ago? – that he'd acknowledged something had once happened between them.

He nodded towards the old woman. 'Old Culer needs to be taken home. But I don't think she'll be able to make it through the crowd in the Place. So I was wondering if I could help her escape through... the back?'

Caillens lifted his head from his beer. 'There's a *back way* out of this place?'

5 The Stranger

Liesl fell backwards into a sea of hands, masks. Someone in a gorilla mask to her left growled something in Flemish. A woman to her right with deep blue eye shadow leaned into her face, sang something in Spanish, then disappeared between two men dressed like The Village People. Three bearded men passed her on the left, banging tambourines, wearing buckskin.

Saint Anthony? Saint Ellon? Hippies?

More masks, feathers, beer breath, skeletons. She was shoved into a stream driving in the opposite direction, spinning her around, pushing her north, towards rue Demesne. Henry Kissinger grabbed at her breasts. Astro Boy pressed up against her thighs. The smell of cigarettes, shampoo; the sweat of people who eat pork. And the faint trace of fish, rising up from the cobbles. She stepped on something, looked down, desperate not to see a body, bloodied by hundreds of feet.

A brown leather purse.

She looked out over the rolling sea of heads, saw someone in a top hat – waving, waving (was he waving at her?) – standing at the top of the church steps. Guy? Someone grabbed her shoulders, shoved her violently to the right, further into the centre of the Place, and she caught another stream of people moving back south, towards rue d'Arcy. The reliquary bobbed in the air to her left, over the heads of the crowd, somewhere in front of the brasserie. Someone stood in one of the open windows above, watching the chaos through a smooth porcelain Venetian mask.

What was she going to do about Guy? What could she do?

Nicholas loomed to her right, carrying his grandnephew on his shoulders.

'How do we get out of this mess?' Liesl shouted at him.

The large man glanced down at her with his good eye. 'I always dance behind the saint!'

'I thought you didn't believe in any of this!'

Nicholas frowned, put a huge callused hand to his ear. The cacophony was rising. Drums, howls, the repetitive honking of that damn tuba. Nicholas and his grandnephew disappeared.

It wasn't all illusion, was it? Was Guy the one actually facing the reality of the situation? How could they possibly stay together?

Someone poked her in the back, kept poking her in the back with something hard, sharp. Two skeletons moved past her, chanting something in Italian, heading in the opposite direction. Liesl spun around behind them so she could get a good look at the one poking her.

'Philippe Souzain!'

The boy waved a small fish at her, the rubbery antenna protruding from its forehead bobbling back and forth.

'Hey German!' the boy shouted. 'Where's Guy?'

6 The Lover

... and all the fish are turning... a flash of fins, towards the mouth of a bell... and the bell is a fish...

Father Leo stood at the bottom of the belfry stairs, palms pressed against the stone on either side, holding himself up against the deafening waves of sound rolling down from the top. Beneath his hands he could feel the stone walls vibrating from the incredible thunder Poisson was making.

Was Poisson strong enough to rip the bells from their beams?

Beneath the ear-murdering sound Father Leo could hear Poisson laughing and hooting. Was Marie trapped up there with that madman, waiting for the bells to break from their moorings, crash on top of her?

He was on his own. The police were all out in the Place with the reliquary.

... and Marie is a fish... and the fish is a cross...

Father Leo stuck his index fingers in his ears, took a few careful steps up towards the belfry. The bell cacophony slammed into him, tore through him, like thunder in the mountains. The last time he had encountered such a sound was the summer storm he'd experienced on retreat at a Benedictine Abbey in the Haute Savoie area of the French Alps on his way back from Rome. The piercing lightning was out there, beyond the monastery, too far away to hurt him, but the thunder seemed to be coming from the centre of his own body, exploding out, tearing him to pieces, making him forget who he was, why he was there. It was relief, terror. Both.

But there was no relief this time. It was all terror. Because he knew what he must do when he reached the top. There was no one to do it but him.

... and the cross is a fish inside a bell... and the bell is a fish... and chaos is a cross riding a fish...

The thought of Poisson having already beaten her so badly that she was lying unconscious on the belfry floor, blood pooling around her head – right here, in her only sanctuary – kept him going.

He bounded up three, four, five more steps, his hand sliding against the curve of the stone. Almost there. The bells clanged inside his head, fierce, maddening, the voice of a giant trying to imitate the voice of God. The beams creaked. Poisson shouted. Father Leo pushed himself off the stone wall and ran up the last ten steps to the door.

7 The Illusionist

Guy was talking to a half-circle of skeletons in the alley behind the brasserie, explaining something, making gestures, pointing up, pointing down. Marie pulled her head back around the corner, looked down at Emile, held a finger to her lips. 'We can't go until the skeletons go,' she whispered. The boy held a finger to his own lips. 'That's right,' she whispered, 'not a sound.'

Marie counted to one hundred, then looked around the corner again. The skeletons were shaking Guy's hand, patting him on the shoulder, breaking away from the half-circle in twos and threes, walking back down the alley towards the chaos in the Place.

When the skeletons were gone, Guy took off his top hat, looked inside. He looked sad. He took a deep breath, dipped his hand into the hat, pulled out a string of scarves tied together. He cracked them like a whip and they disappeared.

Marie strapped the mask of the dead baby onto her face, took Emile's hand and stepped out from her hiding place. She slowly walked towards Guy. He stared at her without saying a word.

She stopped in front of him, said his name. He remained immobile, silent, scared. She touched the brim of the top hat he held in his hands. *Guy is flying towards a woman in a red-sequinned dress, calling her name as she dissolves, becomes small, smaller, a tiny fish swimming out of the German girl turning and turning.*

She unstrapped the mask from her face, gently placed it on the hat. Then she took Emile's hand and walked down the alley in the opposite direction to the Place.

8 The Seer

A tall, thin woman, face painted white, smelling of lilacs, enfolded Liesl within her open trench coat. Too tired to struggle, Liesl slowly turned in a circle with the woman, the crowd swirling around them. She caught a glimpse of the reliquary floating past the church steps; the entrance to rue d'Arcy with the long television antennae poking up towards the windows on either side of the street; masked people standing at open windows (one in a Nixon mask, making victory gestures, then turning around and wiggling his ass at the crowd); followed by the windows and walls of the south end of the Place; balloons swaying above a sweep of heads – red, blue... wasn't it her mother who told her that Death had the smell of lilacs (something her mother read in some occult book – or was it just something some character said in a movie she'd seen?).

The woman bent down, whispered something in Liesl's ear. A soft, scented whisper. How strange to be turning, turning, embracing this strange woman – no clue as to what she was saying – nodding and nodding while the woman threw back her head, eyes closed, and laughed – a high shrill sound blending in with the shrieks and honks rising up from the people, hands waving over heads, musicians playing a crazy merciless din.

Was Guy seeing all this?

They turned and turned; the brasserie slipping by; the one with the Venetian mask still standing guard at the window above the bar; turning, turning, past the grey space where the alley next to the brasserie winds down along the little creek; turning, turning, past the windows of the house on the other side of the alley where that woman – Madame (what was her name?) – sat Liesl down in a front parlour that looked out across the cobbles and asked her about America – she knew America, her daughter lived in Baltimore – and showed Liesl pictures of a middle-aged woman with tired eyes, two sullen children at her feet holding their hands up to their eyes to block the glare of the sun; turning, turning, past two kids in a first storey window – both wearing animal masks – a deer with short antlers and a monkey face – waving at the crowd; turning, turning, past an angel inching up the streetlight that marked the beginning of rue Demesne, waving at the crowd, crossing himself, waving again, feathery wings bobbing up and down; turning, turning, as the woman with the white face pulled Liesl closer; turning, turning, past the long wall of stone between rue Demesne and rue Lefebvre, the woman whispering softly into her ear again, the noise of the crowd stealing the words; turning, turning, as she followed the woman's turning lead like they were dancing; turning and turning, scanning the heads rising and falling in waves across the entrance to rue Lefebvre.

She was at the centre.

She was at the centre, turning past the front of the church, where a red balloon had freed itself from the sea of heads near the church steps. She watched it rise, turning, towards the grey sky. Three metres above the crowd it stopped, bounced a few centimetres back towards the earth, still turning, then rose again, and stopped, suspended, rolling against some invisible ceiling.

Guy!

The balloon hung suspended for a minute, turning and turning, then found some unseen hole in the air and rose again, climbing up into the low clouds, heading west. The church bells began ringing, cheering the balloon on, while Liesl turned and turned.

9 The Stranger

He had done his duty, escorted the old woman to her front door, and now it was time for his reward, for what he'd been anticipating all morning: Claudine in his bed. He led the girl down rue Lamaire by the hand, through the masked stragglers tossing confetti at each other. Everything was perfect. The church bells were now clanging, so he knew Marie was no longer in the house (poor Marie... he would send her some money once he was settled in France).

Everything would soon be possible. Everything he had ever desired. How did Arthur Rimbaud say it? 'All is permitted.' Claudine was going to be a perfect send-off.

They raced up his front steps laughing, the bells clanging and clanging above him, through him, electrifying his muscles, his nerves, bones, as he pushed open the front door.

There was a long crack in the mirror above the walnut hutch next to the living room door.

He let go of Claudine's hand, ran into the living room. The oceanscape above the couch had been pulled off the wall, the canvas torn, tossed onto the couch. The couch had been slit, crumbs of yellow foam scattered across the carpet.

He ran into the dining room. The contents of the boxes he'd left on top of the dining room table had been thrown around the room, books and papers strewn everywhere. He shot upstairs. Doll heads and broken jars were scattered on the first landing outside the room where he kept his collection. 'No, no, no,' he kept repeating up to the second landing, hearing the anguished repetitive word as if it came from someone else, somewhere further up the stairs. He reached the second landing and stopped, stared into the bedroom. The African mask had been ripped off the wall, lay shattered on the floor.

No, no, no –

He ran around the bed, crunching over broken glass, found the stuffed owl on the floor in front of the fireplace. No, no, no. He plunged his hand inside.

Empty.

Casimir stood up, heart racing, and surveyed the wreckage. The pelican lay on the bed, its head twisted off. Claudine stood in the doorway, staring at him, eyes wide, both hands over her mouth. Shouts of the people passing in the street below rose up past the bedroom window. The church bells kept clanging, pounding against his head.

He saw it all: Poisson thrashing through the house, screaming his wife's name – finding Marie in here, cowering on the bed – and Marie, to save herself, had offered up the poems.

'Poisson,' Casimir whispered.

'Poisson?' Claudine repeated.

'Poisson!' Casimir screamed and threw the owl across the room. Claudine fled downstairs as the owl slammed into the far wall. Dark feathers flew everywhere. He slumped to the floor, head in his hands, the sound of the bells clanging and clanging through the open window.

10 The Seeker

The noise inside the belfry grabbed Father Leo's heart, stopped it, restarted it again.

... and Jesus is a fish trapped inside a bell...

Poisson was wrapping a descending bell rope around a bloody hand. The priest quickly scanned the room. No Marie. Where was Marie?

The rope around Poisson's hand jerked up with the swing of the bell, pulling him off the floor.

'What have you done with her?' Father Leo screamed.

... and the bell is a fish...

Poisson rode the rope back down to the floor, unwrapped his hand, let the rope fly back up into the thunder.

'Marie! Where is Marie?' Father Leo shouted again.

Poisson grabbed the other rope as it was descending and coiling on the floor and quickly wrapped it around his other hand. When the rope shot back up, he sailed into the air with it.

... and I am a fish...

Landing back on the floor, Poisson pulled the descending rope as hard as he could, laughing. The beam above them groaned. The sound enveloped the priest, made his stomach fly up towards the roof, his groin drop through the floor.

'What have you done with Marie?'

... and the world is a fish...

Poisson grabbed the slack rope as it was coiling on the floor and, this time, wrapped it around his neck. 'Marie?' he shouted. 'You want Marie?' When the rope started to rise again he grabbed it above his head with both hands and shot towards the ceiling.

'That's how it's done!' Poisson shouted, flying upwards.

Same as his sister, Father Leo thought. The last time he'd visited the sister, she was crouched in her usual corner of that long room with the brown linoleum floor and caged windows, looking down into her lap, whispering, whispering. But as soon as the attendant had tapped her on the shoulder, told her he was there, she'd looked up at him, hiked up her skirt, spread her knees (why didn't they make them wear underwear in that place?), and pointed at the dark patch of hair between her legs. 'You know how it's done?' she'd whispered. The attendant had calmly pulled the skirt back down.

... and God is a fish...

'All of you have no idea how it's done,' Poisson shouted, on his way down. 'You're nothing but greed.' He landed on the floor and swiftly unwrapped the rope from around his neck. There was a red line across the skin.

He will have to be protected from himself.

'You talk of love,' Poisson shouted. 'But you know nothing.' He reached out, grabbed at the rope he'd just used – still descending, coiling – lifted an arm's length worth and wound it around his neck again. Almost as soon as he'd done it, the rope slowed, stopped falling, began to rise back up towards the bells.

'You think you know how it's done, but you know nothing.'

'It's going to be alright,' Father Leo shouted. 'If you just tell me –'

'You don't know love!' Poisson screamed and stretched his arms out to either side. 'This is how it's done!'

No –

Father Leo lunged at the rope above Poisson's head with both hands just as it snapped taut.

... and Poisson is a fish...

11 The Lover

Stephanie Mertz shouted into the microphone, over the din of
the bells. 'We are responsible for what we imagine! If we
imagine we are clocks, then we will become clocks, separate
from the world, imposing our own order on everything! If we
imagine we are bodies – sensing bodies – then how can we
ignore the setting sun, the rising moon? Living is an act of
imagination! How can we ignore the supreme pleasure of a
lover's touch?'

Stephanie lowered the microphone and dramatically looked
from face to face in front of her. Ten seconds went by – the
crazy ringing of the bells made it seem like minutes – then she
lifted the microphone to her lips and shouted, 'And if we are
brave enough to feel our own bodies, it will become impossible
to ignore the pain from the poison all around us!'

Clapping, cheers.

Guy stood at the edge of the circle, scanned the crowd for
Liesl. Every so often he would recognise someone, give them a
little smile, but most of the people in the Place were from
somewhere else. Activists; crazies; drifters who'd heard
someone mention that Contexture would be performing in
Villon at a party in Brussels or Cannes or Bonn or Barcelona;
photographers; journalists; drunks; thieves.

The Place had become a pickpocket's paradise.

Stephanie began talking about a garden of earthly delights. It
was pretty much the same talk she'd given him over the phone.
'Sensuality is the arrow that will sink into the heart of the
machine and kill it! If you recover your senses, how can you not
then find the world that has been created for capital, for profit –
this badly made, bad tasting, consumer world – intolerable! Don't

258

let anyone tell you what's good for you! Start from fundamentals – your own senses! Interpret the world for yourself!'

'Right now,' Stephanie continued, 'we can move from the dead world we've created with our lack of imagination to a live one.' She pointed up at the belfry. 'Listen to that. Really listen. As if you were only a pair of ears.'

Some people looked up at the belfry; others looked around, smirking; still others looked down at their shoes, eyes closed, and concentrated.

Guy closed his eyes, listened. The vibration of the bells washed over him. Liesl was out there somewhere. He opened his eyes, scanned the crowd again.

'You think Marie's gone mad?' someone said over Guy's shoulder.

He turned. Madame Eseuil. She stood next to Dehanschutter, arms crossed over her chest. She leaned in close, nodded towards the belfry. 'That woman says "ears, ears, ears" but it's all bells, bells, bells to me. What do you think is going on up there?'

'I have no idea.'

'*This* is your big revolution, Guy?' Dehanschutter said. 'Talking about ears and bodies?'

Madame Eseuil ignored Dehanschutter. 'Poisson must have finally driven Marie completely over the edge.'

Guy turned back to the centre of the Place. Stephanie was saying, 'There is no beginning, no end! The garden is right here!' His cue. Heart racing, he made his way to Stephanie's side, having only talked the troupe through the trick once.

'Go Guy!' someone yelled over the noise of the bells. Laughter. He looked out into the sea of faces, saw only a sea of faces.

The dancers assembled themselves into a puzzle of body

parts that looked like a huge headless, armless, legless animal. The skeletal lines of their costumes made an intricate pattern of stripes along the curved folds of the cumbersome beast. How they managed to get all their heads tucked into the folds of each other like that Guy could not imagine.

The animal began to move, undulate, across the cobbles towards him, nudging against his leg. Because there was no script – almost everything Contexture did was improvisation – he froze for a second. What to do?

You have to prepare for the unknown, petit.

He tipped his head down and Chiqui's old top hat slid off his head, tumbled end over end down his arm, into his waiting hand. He plunged a hand into the hat, pulled out a bouquet of flowers and stuffed it into one of the seams between the bodies. Claps, cheers. The flowers slipped out of sight, deeper into the animal.

The animal split in half, both striped beasts sprouting legs – four apiece – rising up to walk. The new creatures walked in opposite directions, circumambulating the perimeter of the crowd, crashing – inevitably – like silent film stars – into each other. The two bodies fell, crumbled into individual dancers. The dancers curled into balls, rolled across the cobbles, some bumping into each other, some rolling alone.

Guy donned the top hat again and walked into the centre of the circle the dancers had made. A long thin snake rose from his right front pocket. As it rose into the air, the dancers rolled and rolled around him, coiling at his feet in thick layers. He grabbed the tail of the snake as it floated past his face, swung it once, twice, three times, around his head. In the middle of the fourth circuit it burst into a flurry of flower petals, scattering over the heads of the audience.

Cheers, whistles.

The dancers rose to their feet, freezing into angular poses. A few remained on the ground, began snaking across the cobbles towards a group of seven skeletons that had formed a tunnel – hands and feet planted flat on the ground, backs arched. The ones snaking across the cobbles undulated through the tunnel of bodies while the ones who had been holding angular poses ran over to the tunnel, draped themselves across the arched backs. Soon, there were so many dancers wrapped over the tunnel it was impossible to see the dancers wiggling through it.

The dancers began to shake, vibrating, and the ends of the tunnel moved towards each other, bodies rising, the tunnel halving, until there was a column of bodies three metres high.

Stephanie wriggled out of the top, completely naked.

The audience hooted, clapped. A Roman candle whined across the sky, trailing smoke, and exploded with a flaccid pop, unable to compete with the noise from the belfry.

Fucking Didier!

Stephanie was passed hand to hand around the column, so that she spiralled slowly around it like a snake, facing the crowd. It took minutes – long bell-thundering minutes – for her to get to the ground. More cheers and whistles broke out when Stephanie finally reached the cobbles, head first, and began to undulate slowly towards Guy.

Scratches across her breasts and stomach from sliding over stone, Stephanie entwined herself around Guy's leg, while another dancer – male, this time – emerged naked from the top of the column; writhing like a butterfly fresh from its cocoon.

It was almost time.

But Stephanie was at least four metres from her mark. Had she forgotten where she was supposed to be?

Another Roman candle sailed overhead, popped innocuously into oblivion.

If a rocket hits the framework –

More bodies began rising naked up out of the column until the column dwindled down to four skeletons who remained costumed, standing shoulder to shoulder, while the naked ones – Stephanie included – folded into each other, separated, folded again, creating the shape of a whale, a walking elephant, a turtle, and what looked like a dragon (a series of elbows as the scaly back).

He had no idea what was going on. Had they completely forgotten what he'd told them?

He approached the beast and the dancers slid off one another, revealing Stephanie on top of one of the male dancers in a lover's embrace.

They were exactly where they were supposed to be.

Guy pulled Chiqui's wand from inside his jacket, walked around the couple, waving it slowly above them while the bells rang and rang.

The couple began to rise, teetering ever so slightly. Their faces looked strained, but confident. There was nothing to do but keep waving the wand, coaxing them up, up, a metre above his head, a metre and a half. When they reached the safe zenith, about two metres above the crowd, the bells suddenly stopped, leaving the dancers floating suspended, mid-air, in a wondrous silence.

No one spoke.

Guy lowered the wand and stared at the illusion of the couple slowly turning above him. There it was – what Chiqui had been showing him every single day they'd been together. Right up to the end, lying in the hospital bed, barely able to lift her long hands – those once-beautiful, skilful hands – she had still been trying to help him to see: 'I am really dying, *petit*.' And when he hadn't been able to answer her, to acknowledge what she'd said, she had answered for him: 'Just because everything's an illusion, *petit*, doesn't mean it's not real.' Then, painfully, through the death mask, she had given him that enigmatic half-smile.

Illusion is just another illusion.

Stunned by the simplicity of it, he let the wand slide through his fingers to the ground. He scanned the faces of the crowd. All eyes were lifted up, looking at the turning couple. There was a television crew at the top of the church steps, filming it all. And there was Liesl, standing next to the cameraman, looking right at him. He took off his hat and opened his arms to her. She blew him a kiss.

The naked couple turned and turned.

VII

And the Fish Is a Fish

Philippe Souzain rode up rue d'Arcy, dodging the people drifting back to their cars. The boxes of doll heads Guy had given him bumped up and down in the basket hanging from his handlebars. The crowd was still thick, and he accidentally clipped a man wearing a blue cape. The man ran after him, shouting obscenities, but the boy easily left the caped man far behind.

Beyond the old town wall, cars were parked along the right side of the factory road, all the way to the edge of the quarry fence. Philippe was glad to see there were still a few fish scattered in the road. Most were crushed, though. Stragglers from the kermesse and rally sat on the hoods of some of the parked cars, smoking, drinking, waving their bottles at Philippe as he passed.

'Saint Woelfred!'

'Fuck the dumps!'

'Hey! Little Einstein!'

This last was from Marc Didier, sitting on the hood of his Citroën with a skinny woman in a red vinyl dress, wearing a blonde wig. The woman took a huge swig from a beer bottle, then nuzzled Marc's cheek, smudging his face with red lipstick. Philippe slowed, stopped next to Marc's car.

'Did you see the levitation?' Philippe had been close, near the TV cameras.

'Spectacular!' Marc said, taking the bottle from the woman next to him, lifting it in a salute towards Villon. 'We made the news, Einstein. Villon has achieved its fifteen minutes of fame.' The woman growled softly into Marc's ear and Marc laughed, touched his head to hers. 'I would introduce you, young Souzain, but I have no idea who she is. We danced behind Woelfred together. And – as luck would have it – she doesn't speak a word of French.' He pointed at the boxes in Philippe's basket. 'Now those look familiar. I wonder where you got them.'

'I'm taking something to Guy's house for him,' Philippe lied. He didn't want to tell Marc what he was going to do with the heads. Marc worked at the factory.

'Well, you look busy, my little friend,' Marc said, 'so I won't take up any more of your time.' He raised his bottle to Philippe and took a drink.

Philippe pedalled past the last of the parked cars, stopped just before he reached the factory gate. Someone had cleaned the road of fish in front of the gate, tossed them into the grey-dusted grass growing at the foot of the quarry fence. Philippe leaned his bike against the fence and looked down into the lake. Even though the sky was grey, the water in the lake was blue.

It's that colour blue because it's so deep, Casimir had told him. They've been digging there for over one hundred years. You'd think they would have reached China by now. And then

265

Casimir had leaned close to Philippe's face and whispered, a faint trace of alcohol on his breath, *Can you imagine what monsters have been carved up out of that stone?*

Philippe lifted the boxes out of the bike basket, looked left, right, then crossed the road. He leaned over the guardrail, stared down at the crushed white stone rumbling on top of the moving black conveyor belt below, then looked up and down the road again – just to make sure no one was watching.

As he was tipping the first box of doll heads into space he spotted a lone barge – loaded with cement bags – stopped in front of the canal bridge. The pilot was reaching his hand out to a woman standing with a small child on the concrete apron under the bridge.

Marie.

Twenty-five doll heads rained down onto the conveyor belt and bounced off the limestone with a firm plastic thwack that ricocheted off the factory wall. But Philippe didn't hear, he'd already turned away, was running across the road, hurrying back to his bike.

He flew towards the canal bridge, keeping an eye on the barge. The woman and child had climbed on board and the barge was moving underneath the bridge. When Philippe reached the bridge the barge had already chugged through to the other side. He skidded the bike to a stop at the top, out of breath, and looked over the rail.

Marie and Emile were standing on the stern, holding hands. Her black eyes stared up at him. Philippe, as if in a trance, slowly lifted his hand, and Marie, just as slowly, lifted her free hand to wave back. And they stared at each other, hands raised, as the barge churned the water to foam, heading south.

April 10th, 1987
Aden, Yemen

Dear biologiste-who-wants-to-live-in-caves,
Faded, cracked buildings; barren mountains beyond. A strange
feeling in the air. There was a battle here in Aden last year.
Thousands of people killed. I heard two English types talking out
in the hotel hallway yesterday: politics I can't begin to fathom. I
am outside the confines of any world I've ever known.

I am lost, yes, but it's a different kind of lost from the one that so
overwhelmed me in Cairo. I'm not sure how to describe it. In a
bizarre way, it feels exciting. I've had a strange, heightened
awareness since I landed here. Maybe because of the recent violence,
but I think it's more than that. There's excitement because I'm no
longer afraid of losing myself.

What's there to lose?

Peel back the layers and you get more layers. It's all a
labyrinth. Like looking for the real Rimbaud. The only thing to do
is finally let it all go.

I need to tell you this before I leave Aden, though: I met a
man in Cairo who was heading back to Germany with nothing to
show for two years' work in the Saudi oil fields but drunkard's
lies. He'd lost all his money gambling. I felt sorry for him and
told him about Casimir's little nest egg. Now, sitting here in my
hotel room, looking down at the people passing below my
window, I feel foolish. What do I care now if Casimir wants to
sell the lost Rimbaud poems to the highest bidder?

You might want to warn him.

Meanwhile, I saw naked dancers floating over Villon's
Grand Place on the cover of Le Monde *yesterday. It looks like*
the rally you were covering caused quite a stir. I hope it all

worked out for you, for Villon.

I'll be taking a ferry to Ethiopia soon. On to Harar, where Rimbaud lived on and off for eleven years, inside a walled Muslim city. Am I still looking for Rimbaud? For myself in Rimbaud? I think, at this point, I just want to see Harar. As itself.

And Rimbaud? Maybe, in the end, he finally understood a truth that I'm only just beginning to fathom: that Rimbaud – in whatever shape or form – was an illusion.

Raoul

Acknowledgements

This book came to light with the help of many people. As Chiqui would say: nothing exists as a separate thing.

First off, I would like to thank Louis Owens, wherever he is now, for giving me good, practical advice when I was on the verge of hanging up my fiction shoes. I would also like to thank Halina Duraj for telling me a story about heat shock proteins; Alejandro Escudé, Kirsten Lunstrum, and Jennifer Mason for several conversations that made their way into the novel; Pam Houston, for letting me know what worked and what didn't during the initial stages; Ravi Dykema, who said, 'Stop in the middle of the day and feel your arms and legs'; and Diane Butler, whose example from a long ago improv class helped keep the novel as grounded and 'embodied' as was possible.

A debt of immense gratitude and thanks goes out to Karen Fowler, who was there at the beginning, encouraging me along with questions that gave me a larger picture of the project, and who stuck by the novel during the 'wilderness years' with much needed sympathy and humour.

Thanks also to my parents, sisters, and larger extended family, for encouragement and support. In a world where most value is equated with money, it's rare that a family acknowledges the artists in their midst as worthwhile (but, then, maybe we have to – there's an awful lot of us).

Thanks also to everyone at Parthian for taking the book on and moving it through the publishing stages so quickly.

A final huge thanks to Michaela Kahn, my wife, also there from the beginning, who listened patiently to my long, empty-